THE GEORGIAN RAKE

Alice Chetwynd Ley

THE GEORGIAN
RAKE

Published by Sapere Books.

20 Windermere Drive, Leeds, England, LS17 7UZ,
United Kingdom

saperebooks.com

ISBN: 978-1-912546-81-7

To Ken

Chapter I: A Marriage is Promoted

The picture dominated the room. It hung above the mantelshelf, and attracted the eye from the first moment of entering the door. It showed a young woman with very deep blue eyes in a pointed face; the mouth was full and red, with a whimsical twist to one corner which promised a roguish sweetness. Fair curls fell softly on to a white neck rising out of a fichu of fine lace, and the blue of the gown matched those deep eyes.

The man who stood before the fire glanced up at the picture, and his look momentarily softened. The sound of a step outside hardened it again. He faced round slowly as the door opened.

A younger man entered, magnificent in a velvet coat and breeches of tawny brown, with red heels to his square-toed, buckled shoes, and a foam of lace at his throat. His carriage was assured, almost arrogant.

"I believe you wished to see me, sir?"

It was a pleasant, drawling voice, self-possessed and cool.

"Ay." In contrast, the older man seemed uncertain, a little on the defensive. "Sit down, Charles. You'll take something?"

Charles Barsett nodded, and seated himself to one side of the fireplace with the air of one who is at home in his surroundings. His host pulled the bell-rope hanging beside the chimney piece, and bespoke a bottle of canary of the manservant who answered its summons.

"My aunt is well, I trust?" asked Charles, politely.

"Oh, ay, Fanny is well enough," replied the other, uneasily. "A touch of the megrims now and then — you know how it is — but well enough, ay, to be sure."

The younger man nodded slowly, a mocking light in his dark blue eyes.

"And my — er — esteemed cousin?"

Lord Barsett bridled. "Damme, Charles, I never can understand why you must mention your cousin Roger in that demmed offensive tone! He has been a good enough friend to you, b'God, and if only you had the half of his virtues, I might die happy tomorrow!"

"Then let us be thankful that I have not," retorted Charles, with a smile.

Lord Barsett choked, but was spared a reply by the entrance of the servant bearing a tray holding a decanter of wine and two glasses. The man set the tray down upon a side table and, at a nod from his lordship, withdrew silently.

The elder of the two gentlemen crossed to the table and poured the wine, handing a glass to his guest.

"Your continued health, Father," said Charles, raising his glass in salutation.

"Much you care!" retorted Lord Barsett, but he raised his glass in return, and drank.

Charles shrugged lightly, twirling the stem of the glass idly in his fingers.

"Now I wonder," he said softly, "just what it is that you want of me? Forgive me, my dear sir, but you are not much in the habit of seeking my company."

"And you, may I point out, are not much in the habit of giving me the opportunity!" retorted his father, in some heat. "I hear of your being seen everywhere — gambling dens, prize fights, and in the company of rake-hells such as that

Dashwood fellow —but you are not often to be met with in St. James's Square!"

"I am aware that you are well informed of my movements, particularly of the shall we say — more spectacular variety. I do take part in quite a number of respectable activities, my dear sir, little though you may be disposed to believe it. Why, only yesterday evening, I was at a ball — a most tediously respectable ball in the house of an unexceptionable hostess; no less a person than my Lady Twyford."

He put up an elegant hand to smother a yawn at the recollection.

"Lady Twyford!" exclaimed his father, quickly. "'Tis strange —" He broke off. His son regarded him curiously.

"Now, what should be strange about my Lady Twyford, I wonder?" he mused, as if to himself.

"Oh, naught!" returned Lord Barsett, hastily.

His son turned a quizzical eye in his direction for a moment, shrugged elaborately, and continued to sip his wine.

Lord Barsett cleared his throat uneasily.

"The fact is, I thought we might have a little talk, my boy. I — I am made uneasy by these constant rumours concerning you that run round the Town."

"So?" Charles raised one eyebrow in a manner bordering on the diabolical.

"That fellow Sir Francis Dashwood, who is such a crony of yours — damme, the things one hears of him! It's even said that he goes in for devil worship at that place of his on the Thames — what's the name of it? I tell you I won't have our name bandied about in any such connection! A few wild oats I might perhaps understand — Lud knows I've no wish to be thought a Puritan! But even you must see that it's high time you settled down, Charles."

"There's no harm in Mad Francis," replied his son, soothingly. "He's but a jester: his antics amuse me."

"Amuse you!" stuttered his lordship. "I suppose you will tell me next that it also amuses you to have our name dragged in the dust, to be the centre of one scandal after another! Egad, I can't imagine whom you take after! Not, I fancy, myself! And certainly not your — mother."

He glanced up at the picture.

"That is the real reason of our quarrel, is it not?" asked Charles, softly; and now the drawl was less pronounced. "You have never forgiven me for being the cause of her death."

The room was suddenly silent. Lord Barsett stood motionless before the fireplace, still staring up at the portrait of his wife. His son watched him, an inscrutable expression in the dark blue eyes, so like those of the picture. At last the older man came out of his reverie, and spoke in a low, passionate tone, as if to himself.

"When they brought you to me, I told them to take you away again. At that moment I felt that I never wanted to set eyes on you. You were bought at too dear a price —too dear a price — "

His voice broke, and he clasped his hands together as though the past had come to life, and he felt afresh the sharp agony of close on thirty years ago.

The silence lengthened. Charles Barsett sipped his wine, staring thoughtfully at the glowing logs in the hearth.

"No matter." His tone hardened, and became calmer. "Charles, don't you think it high time you were wed?"

Charles raised a quizzical eyebrow.

"No, my boy, let us be serious for a moment, pray. You are close on nine and twenty."

"So?"

"We must have an heir. At your age, I had already taken care of the succession. What have you to say?"

For answer, Charles surveyed his empty glass.

"Why, sir, I say that I think perhaps I will partake of another glass of this excellent canary. Is there much more of this in your cellar?"

"Another two dozen left of that year — damme, don't try to turn the subject! Oh, yes, by all means take another glass if you will — but first tell me when you mean to marry, and whom."

"When? That I cannot say at present. Whom? Well, now, whom do you suggest?"

Lord Barsett gasped. "Can you be serious? No, b'Gad, I should know better than to ask! But surely you have some notions of your own on the subject?"

Charles gently shook his head. "Acquit me."

"Damme, what runs in your veins? Water? By all accounts, you are hot enough in some quarters — notably around Covent Garden! You cannot choose a wife as you would choose a horse!"

"I cannot but agree with you," replied Charles, solemnly. "One needs to exercise great care in the choosing of a horse."

His father made a despairing gesture. "This is just what makes it so impossible to talk to you, Charles — you will take nothing seriously, no, not even your marriage!"

"My hypothetical marriage, sir," corrected his son, gently. "So far, you have failed to provide me with any candidates for my approval."

Lord Barsett gave him a long look.

"That sounds as though you mean to consider the notion?"

"I hope I know my duty," said Charles, mockingly. "We must have an heir, as you so justly point out. Well, father, whom shall I wed?"

Once more Lord Barsett considered this enigmatic son of his.

"Can it really be that you have no one in mind? There are a score of pretty young women to be met with every day of the week; and I have it on good authority that you are sufficiently impressionable."

Charles laughed shortly. "Faith, you know more of me than I do of myself, it seems! Very true, there are young women in plenty, each one an exact replica of the last — charming, accomplished, schooled for the Marriage Mart — and dull: b'God, how dull!"

His father looked at him curiously. "What would you have? Genteel females are all turned out more or less to a pattern — it's only to be expected. Of course, your mother was different —"

He broke off, and looked up at the portrait with a reminiscent smile touching the corners of his mouth. It faded as his glance returned to the man at his side.

"You cannot hope to find another such," he said. "And I doubt if you deserve that you should. But there is a girl —"

"Ah!" said Charles, meaningly.

"Very well," answered his father, on the defensive. "We seem to be agreed that a wife you must have, and you insist you have no partiality for any one particular female."

He hesitated for a moment, and examined his son's expression critically, but could read nothing there. The deep blue eyes were hooded; the lean face with its patrician nose and firm mouth which had an ironical twist at one corner, gave no indication of what was passing in its owner's mind.

He's a stranger to me, thought Lord Barsett, angrily. My own son, and a complete stranger, damn him!

Aloud, he said abruptly, "What think you of the Twyford chit — whatsername? — Isabella, ain't it? Well, what do you say?"

"Isabella Twyford," repeated Charles, thoughtfully. "Now, let me think... is she the red-headed one?"

"No, no!" replied his father, a shade testily. "Dammit, you were at a ball in the house yesterday, by your own account — you must surely remember the chit!"

Charles sat up suddenly, an expression of alarm on his face.

"Never say that she is the pudding-faced female who has been dogging my footsteps for the past two months!"

Lord Barsett stared. "I don't know what you're talking about. There's nothing wrong with this girl's looks — far from it. I can only suppose you must have been in your cups last night. It's a great deal too bad of you, or you must be aware that Twyford was a particular friend of mine until we both married; when he went to live in the country — somewhere in Berkshire, I think, or it might be Oxfordshire — anyway, it don't signify. Since then, we'd lost touch with each other, until he set up a house in Town not two months since, to bring this girl of his out into the Polite World. A taking little thing, she is, too, not unlike your mother — though of course, she can't hold a candle to her! But the chit's pretty, with taking manners — conversed with me for close on half an hour, and never once looked as though she thought me a dull old codger!"

"Perhaps she means to set her cap in your direction," put in Charles, with a grin.

"Pah!" snorted his father.

"She might do worse," went on Charles, banteringly. "A wealthy widower — better an old man's darling, you know —"

"Pah!"

"Your conversation becomes monotonous," reproached his son. "Where is that sparkling wit that once held us spellbound?"

"I wish you will stop gammoning, and come to the point," said Lord Barsett, testily. "Will you or will you not have the Twyford girl? She's a good match, y'know — old name, and a fortune in her own right, I understand, let alone what will come to her from Twyford; not that *that* signifies — you are well-breeched enough on your own account — still, a handsome dower ain't to be sneezed at!

"And also a taking little thing, into the bargain!"

"So you say, but I can't at this moment recollect her features. However, by all the evidence, you are no mean judge. As to whether I'll take her — doesn't something depend upon the lady herself?"

"Oh, as to that —!" Lord Barsett shrugged. "You'll have her father's goodwill, I'll engage for that."

Charles cocked an eyebrow. "Young ladies have been known to have a mind of their own in these affairs."

"When it comes to marriage no dutiful daughter has a mind of her own: and Twyford's girl will know her duty, I'll be bound," replied his father.

"She will? You disappoint me."

"Disappoint you? Devil take you, Charles, I wish I understood what you would be at! Do you mean that you hope the girl will refuse you?"

"Do I?" Charles paused to consider this. "It's an interesting question, and I am unable to answer it. But in any event, that wasn't my meaning. I intended to say that I am not enchanted by the notion of taking a dutiful daughter to wife."

"Then you're a bigger fool than I took you for!" retorted Lord Barsett, forcefully. "May I ask what kind of female would have the power to enchant you, as you put it? No, don't answer me! I fancy I know only too well!"

Lines of amusement crinkled the corners of Charles's eyes.

"I doubt it," he said, and rose lazily to his feet. "But you'll pardon me, I feel sure, sir — I have an engagement in an hour's time, and cannot stay longer."

"But you haven't given me your answer!" protested his father.

"Haven't I? How very remiss of me! Very well, then, I consent to try my luck with the beautiful and talented Miss Twyford."

"You choose your adjectives well for a man who can't even remember what the female looks like!" grunted Lord Barsett; but relief had crept into his voice. "When do you mean to make your offer?"

"Let me see." Charles drew a small notebook covered in red leather from an inner pocket, and consulted it, a light frown on his forehead. "Tomorrow — no, it cannot be tomorrow, I see I am to buy a horse. The next day, then — alas, engaged also! Do you know, sir —" putting the book away, and surveying his father ruefully — "I fear we cannot undertake to attempt the matter until next week?"

"Pah!"

"For once, I agree with you. It certainly is disgraceful that a man should be so set about with engagements that he cannot count upon a day to himself in order to get him a wife. And I dare say, you know, sir, that something of the same difficulty may in the future crop up in connection with the provision of an heir. I am so seldom at home —"

"Off with you!" stormed his lordship. "Don't let me set eyes on you again until you have settled all with Isabella Twyford!

Mayhap she will be able to knock some sense into your thick skull, for I tell you I despair of it!"

"Perhaps: I shouldn't count on it," warned Charles, gravely. "My respects to my Aunt Fanny — and, of course, to my revered cousin. Your servant, sir."

He bowed with an extravagant flourish of his lace handkerchief, and left the muttering Lord Barsett alone in the room.

As he passed into the hall, his face changed for an instant; the mocking mask fell away, and something very like regret came in its place. The former expression returned, however, as a servant walked deferentially towards him, bearing a tricorne hat and a pair of elegant gloves of York tan. Charles accepted the articles, and was continuing on his way through the hall, when the door which gave on to the street opened, and a gentleman entered.

He paused on seeing Charles Barsett, and greeted him with a note of eager welcome in his voice. The response he obtained seemed cool in comparison. No one watching these two now could have guessed that once they had lived as brothers, and that their affection for each other had been a byword among those who knew the family intimately. Shortly after the death of his wife, Lord Barsett had taken his widowed sister Frances into his house as its mistress: at that time, it had seemed an ideal arrangement for everyone concerned. Fanny had married a man of good family who was an inveterate gambler; after losing everything he possessed at the gaming tables, he had seen nothing better to do than to blow out his brains, leaving his wife and son to the charity of their friends. Lord Barsett had contributed generously to his only sister's upkeep; but Fanny's tastes were expensive, and there can be no doubt that she and her baby son had felt the pinch before their arrival in

St. James's Square. From Lord Barsett's point of view, nothing could have been more convenient. He had no intention of marrying again, and the advent of Fanny and her child would provide Charles at once with a substitute mother and a brother. This relieved my lord from the necessity of giving another thought to the child whose coming into the world had robbed his father of his most cherished possession.

Women vary, however, in the degree of maternal feeling they possess. In Fanny it was not sufficiently strong to embrace a nephew as a son, even though he should happen to be a helpless mite of a few months old. For her own son, Roger, she had a blind devotion which she soon taught her brother to share. There was no doubt that Roger was a taking child, too; his amiability and eagerness to please were remarked upon by everyone. Only Charles's own nurse showed a preference for the heir to the house; and it was said that she was prejudiced by her great affection for his dead mother, whose own nurse she had been.

The two cousins stood facing each other now, the one cool and sardonic, the other warm and friendly. Roger Thurlston had all his father's good looks; a pair of fine grey eyes set in a handsome countenance, and a tall, erect figure. People said that it was a shame that such a personable young man should have nothing but what a fond uncle might choose to bestow on him; and what, they asked, was to become of Mr. Thurlston when his uncle died? The bulk of Lord Barsett's fortune and property must come to his son Charles, and it was not to be supposed that *he* would do much for his cousin. Rumour had it that there was no love lost in that quarter, although no one knew quite when it was that the affection of boyhood had cooled, nor what had been the cause. It was said in some quarters that the wildness of the one had caused the other to speak out in an unguarded fashion, and thus incur enmity.

"Won't you stay, Charles?" pleaded Roger, with a smile. "Lord knows how long it is since we had a chat together."

"A million regrets," drawled his cousin, "but I am already late for an appointment. I fear I must forego the pleasure of your company on this occasion."

Roger protested with evident regret, but Charles was not to be moved, and, after taking leave in an offhand manner, left the house.

He proceeded on his way on foot, and had turned into Piccadilly, when the slowing down of a carriage made him turn his head. The window of the carriage was lowered, and a plump, white face crowned by a gipsy straw hat appeared in the aperture.

"Well, I declare, and if it isn't Mr. Barsett — and on foot!" exclaimed the owner of the unfortunate face, in a quick, gushing tone that set Charles Barsett's teeth on edge. "Can I have the pleasure of driving you anywhere, sir? I am out *solely* to take the air, you know, and am not in the least hurry in the world — I do so *love* driving around the Town, I declare you may ask me to take you *anywhere*, and I shall not regard it as the *least* little trouble at all! I shan't take no for an answer, and so I warn you!"

She paused momentarily for breath. Charles bowed, cursing inwardly. It was Miss Dunster, a young lady of fortune from the West country, who had recently arrived in Town, so Aunt Fanny unkindly said, for the purpose of finding a victim in fresh fields. Certainly she had made a most determined pursuit of all the eligible bachelors during the course of her stay in London, but even the most hardened fortune-hunters seemed reluctant to take on the plump, gushing female. For some reason, her fancy had recently lighted upon Charles: this was odd, because the rumours concerning him were usually sufficient to frighten off young ladies from the country just as thoroughly as they attracted most Town-bred females. "I believe I need not put you to so much trouble, Miss — er —"

For the life of him, he could not remember her name. She smiled in what was intended for an arch manner. It failed signally.

"There, you naughty man, I do declare you've forgotten my name! But never mind, I am *very* forgiving, as you shall find. I am Georgina Dunster — now, don't you dare forget again!"

She wagged an admonitory finger which somewhat resembled a white slug, and broke once again into her devastating smile.

"I beg you will step into the carriage directly. Daker —"

She turned her head to give the order to the coachman to dismount and let down the steps; but Charles stopped her hurriedly with a gesture.

"No. I protest, Miss Dunster, I am vastly obliged to you, but I positively must walk. Doctor's orders, you know."

Her mouth fell open in an unlovely fashion.

"Doctor's orders —?"

Charles nodded shamelessly. "My rheumaticks, alas! Must keep on the move."

He sighed, and shook his head with a melancholy gesture.

"*Anno Domini*, my dear young lady," he said, with a passable imitation of his father's manner. "It catches us all in time."

She stared. "I — I see — but surely you can't be much above —"

"I'll wish you good day," said Charles hastily, before she could finish. He bowed, and was gone with an alacrity which ill bore out his story.

Let us hope that will discourage the female a bit, he thought grimly. Brr! What a fate to overtake a man! But I wonder if — looks apart — the fair Isabella will be any better, after all?

Chapter II: The Mysterious Abbey

"It's a linch-pin's broke, Miss Mandy."

Amanda Twyford wrinkled her tip-tilted nose in disgust.

"How tiresome! Is nothing to be done, Jem?"

The old coachman shook his head; but before he could make any other answer, Miss Brown broke in upon him.

"Tiresome! I should imagine that to be an understatement. It is nothing short of disastrous, when we are already delayed upon our journey by some two hours or more! It was all very well to call in upon Mrs. Matchett on our way, but we ought not to have allowed her to persuade us to stay to a meal."

"But I was hungry," protested Amanda.

The governess frowned disapprovingly. "A young lady of breeding is never hungry," she pronounced. "Or, if she is, she should endeavour to conceal the fact."

"Stuff!" replied Amanda, lightly, with a toss of her honey-coloured curls. "You know very well, Brownie, that if I am hungry, I don't care who should be aware of it; and it's a poor thing if I may not tell my own aunt."

"What we want," said the coachman in a practical manner, ignoring this interchange, "is some tools — better still, a blacksmith."

"And where are we going to find one?" asked Miss Brown, scathingly. "There will be nothing but a cottage or two until we reach the village of Maidenhead — if that should be within our power!"

"Tom could mayhap ride ahead, and bring back help," said Jem, musingly. "But it's a tidy way —"

Amanda had been strolling up and down the road for the last few minutes, and she now broke in eagerly with a suggestion.

"There's a huddle of buildings at the bottom of this lane," she said, pointing to a winding track on the left-hand side of the road not fifty yards from the spot where the broken-down coach was standing. "It will most likely be a farm, but we could try there for help."

Jem walked over to the hedge where she was standing, and peered in the direction she indicated. The lane ran through sloping meadows down to the bank of the River Thames; a brisk ten minutes walk would take them to the buildings which could be seen from the road. He nodded approvingly.

"A good notion, Miss Mandy. I'll just step down there — I'll not be long away, and young Tom can see to the horses."

"I'll go with you," announced his young mistress.

"In all that mud?" asked the governess, incredulously. "You must have run mad! I positively forbid it."

Amanda turned a pair of clear blue eyes upon the governess, and a cajoling note crept into her voice.

"Dear Brownie, pray don't do that! I should like a short walk of all things at this moment, but I should so dislike to disobey you!"

The governess sighed, and capitulated. There was a strong will here, that could be led but not driven; and, officially, her jurisdiction over Miss Amanda Twyford had now ceased. The girl was in her charge only until she had been safely delivered to her parents in London. Moreover, there was no real reason for supposing that she would come to any harm in old Jem's care. He was an established servant of the family, who adored his young mistress, and had set her upon her first pony at the tender age of seven. She could come to no harm beyond a muddied petticoat; and that, thought Miss Brown with a wry smile, was no unusual hazard with Amanda.

"Oh, very well, if you are set upon it," she conceded. "But have a care to her Jem, and do not let her out of your sight."

Jem promised absently, more taken up with the business of getting his coach back upon the road than with his young mistress's whims and fancies. Without more ado, the two of them set off at once down the lane, Amanda raising the skirt of her dark green travelling dress to display a glimpse of white-stockinged ankle which brought a blush to the watching Miss Brown's cheek. A bend in the lane soon hid them from her sight.

It was not very long before they reached the building which Amanda had pointed out; it was, as she had surmised, a farm. The gate was set open, and a black and white collie dog came bounding out at them, barking fiercely.

"Down, boy!" said Amanda vigorously, as two muddy paws landed on her skirt. The dog wagged its tail, and jumped up once more for good measure, thus completing the ruin of her gown. Regardless of this, she laughed, and patted the animal's head.

At that moment, a burly, red-faced man clad in a suit of fustian and wearing a pair of very muddy high boots, strode across the mire of the yard to inquire their business. Jem explained their predicament. The man eyed Amanda curiously as he answered in his slow country burr.

"There be a blacksmith over at Med'nam; ye can get there by way of the ford."

Jem peered inquiringly over towards the river. The farm was set a little way back, but the track continued down to the river bank. There was no sign of a jetty on either side that he could see.

"Ye'll need to walk a distance beside the river in that direction," said the farmer, indicating with a jerk of his thumb the way they must follow. "Ye'll find a boat tied up along 'o the bank there. Ferryman lives in a cottage hard by. Smithy's at the top o' the lane, when ye're across."

They thanked him, and he went about his business again, whistling to his dog to follow.

"You'd best go back now, Miss," said Jem.

Amanda shook her head. "I'm already as dirty as may be," she answered. "It can't signify if I accompany you to the other side of the river on your errand."

Knowing well from past experience that it was useless to argue with his young mistress when her mind was made up, Jem did not waste his breath in making any reply, but proceeded to lead the way along the narrow, muddy track which ran beside the river. They followed this path for quite a distance before they finally caught sight of a boat tied up to the bank a few yards ahead of them.

Amanda glanced across to the other side of the river. There was a small wooden jetty, and a lane which was bounded on its one side by a high wall. She surmised that there must be a riverside residence on the other side of the wall; if so, the house was open to approach from the river bank, for there was no fence or wall erected there, only a thick belt of trees.

Curiosity impelled her to look more closely. It was still early in May, and the foliage was not yet well advanced; through the tall elms and dipping willows, she caught a glimpse of masonry. She stopped in her tracks, peering intently, then darting to and fro on the path in order to obtain a better view. There could be no doubt of it; what she had espied was a ruined stone tower, and some crumbling pillars, thickly covered in ivy. An excited exclamation escaped her.

"Jem!" Her voice quivered with eagerness. "Do you see what I see?"

"I see you 'opping about like a tarnation frog," grumbled the coachman.

"Come along, do, Miss Mandy!"

"No, but Jem — truly I've discovered something most exciting! Only come over here, and look closely through those trees!"

He obeyed, and followed her pointing finger with his eyes. After a moment, he turned to her questioningly.

"Some kind of old ruin, b'aint it, Miss?"

He sounded only mildly interested; nothing short of a linchpin could arouse him to enthusiasm at that moment.

"Beneath yon ruin'd abbey's moss-grown piles, Oft let me sit at twilight hour of eve'," quoted Amanda, ecstatically. "Oh, Jem, only fancy! Isn't it splendidly Gothic?"

"I wouldn't know, Miss; learnin' b'aint much in my line. But if you want to get on the road to Lunnon tonight —"

"Just imagine, Jem," breathed his mistress, ignoring this warning, "if it should really be some ruined Abbey, where once monks dwelt —"

"Popery, Miss Mandy," said the practical Jem. "Don't hold with it. Let's get on, now, do!"

But Amanda remained rooted to the spot, showing no disposition to continue towards the boat, where already the ferryman, having observed their approach, was waiting. There was a sparkle of excitement in her blue eyes, and purpose in the firm set of her chin.

"I would like to have a closer view of that ruin, Jem," she whispered, in awestruck tones. "And it would be quite a simple thing to do! If we were to be landed on the opposite bank at a point beyond that wall, we have only to walk through those trees at the river's edge! What do you say?"

He shook his head firmly. "For one thing, it's trespass; for another, we can't spare the time."

He made so bold as to take her arm and attempt to urge her onwards; but Amanda shook him off gently, abstractedly.

"Surely no one would think it trespass to look at an old ruin?" she said, incredulously. "There can be no harm! I tell you what, Jem, if you do not like the notion, why do you not ask the boatman to land me on the opposite bank while you continue on your way up the lane to the blacksmith's? I can then take a peep, and await you on your return. I dare say you will not be gone above ten minutes."

"Oh, no!" replied the coachman, decidedly. "D'ye think I dare face your governess if I lent myself to any such pranks? She said most partic'lar not to let you out of my sight!"

Amanda stamped her foot in vexation.

"It is for you to do as I say!" she began; then broke off at sight of his hurt expression.

"Dearest Jem, do not be a spoil-sport! I can come to no harm, for indeed you will not be long away! Only think what fun it would be to explore a ruin that one never knew existed before!"

He looked at her pleading face, and his expression softened.

"Ye're a right madcap," he pronounced, "and a fine day it will be when ye gets a husband to curb your wildness! Still, ye're nobbut a child, when all's said, though I'll wager ye can take care of yourself like any lad! Very well, then, I'll let ye do as ye wish, but not a word to yon governess, mind, or my life won't be worth a moment's purchase!"

Amanda promised readily enough, delighted at having won her way, and they came to the boat.

The ferryman was a man of slow wits and few words. When Jem explained to him what was wanted, he favoured Amanda with a long, unbelieving stare, then shook his head.

"Best not," he advised, gruffly.

Jem questioned him sharply, somewhat alarmed at his manner, but there was nothing to be obtained from him other than a repetition of the same words.

"Ye hear what he says, Miss; reckon you'd better stay along o' me."

"Fustian!" whispered back Amanda. "Very likely he's a natural, poor soul. It's no use to take any account of what he says. Be sure and pay him well, Jem."

Seeing that she meant to persist in her plan, Jem said no more, but ordered the man to put in to the bank alongside the willows. Once there, Jem leapt out to steady the boat for Amanda to alight; but with a lithe movement, she was on the bank in an instant. The coachman climbed back into the boat, a worried frown on his face.

"I'll be here again in a trice," he said, in a low tone. "Do ye keep out of mischief meanwhile."

She nodded, and stood a moment to watch the boat putting in to the jetty; then she turned and walked purposefully through the thick belt of screening trees in the direction of the ruin.

A light mist was coming up from the river, and the Spring light was already beginning to fail. Everything seemed very quiet all at once, quiet and somehow almost eerie. The grass was damp beneath her feet as she paused for a moment, checked by a slight feeling of apprehension. She pulled her cloak more firmly about her, and continued on her way. There were no fences even here, past the first belt of trees; she had feared that perhaps there might be. Not a soul was in sight as yet. There was nothing to hinder her from taking a peep at the Abbey, if Abbey it indeed was; and where could be the harm? All the same, her footsteps lagged a little as she continued towards her objective.

Eventually, she came out of the trees, and saw the building clearly before her across an expanse of lawn. She had been mistaken, she saw at a glance; it was not a complete ruin. She stood stock still, and surveyed it nervously.

Before her was a low, rambling three-storied house, stained red. Built on to one end of it was the tower which had first attracted her notice, and underneath were the ivy-entwined cloisters which had made such a strong appeal to her romantic spirit. Her eyes roved farther, and took in a low, grey building which had the look of a domestic chapel, and which was some little distance removed from the house. Scattered about the extensive grounds were statues, too far away from her present vantage point to be recognisable.

She gazed anxiously at the house, prepared for instant flight; but it wore a curiously uninhabited air. The close-curtained windows returned a blank stare to her scrutiny; no smoke issued from the chimneys, there was no single sign of life in the outbuildings or gardens. She glanced again at the tower and the dim cloisters. An irresistible urge suddenly overcame her to set foot in them. Acting on impulse, she moved quickly forward, her feet swishing through the damp grass. She stepped beneath the cold, grey arches on to the moss-grown stone floor.

Her blood tingled with excitement. She would walk here for a moment, explore the ruined tower, tread in the footsteps of those who had once slowly paced here in silent meditation. Consciously, she summoned up a mood of mystery and foreboding. What stories could these stones tell, she wondered, of those who were long since dead? They had walked these cloisters before her in the distant past, and now only tombs remained to speak of their existence, she thought, enjoying the shiver of apprehension that ran down her spine; unless, perchance, their spirits continued to walk in this secluded spot…

At that very point in her reflections, a step sounded on the stone floor behind her.

She turned quickly. Her heart was pounding and her legs felt curiously weak.

"What are you doing here?"

The voice was harsh, but a gentleman's, and decidedly of this earth. Amanda let out her pent-up breath in a heartfelt sigh of relief. The man standing accusingly before her was attired in a greatcoat and riding boots: she judged him to be somewhere in his late twenties. He looked stern and arrogant, and did not remove his tricorne hat when he addressed her. She noticed this with trepidation. Such a breach of manners must indicate an uncommon degree of annoyance. Perhaps he was the owner of the house? She began a stumbling apology.

"I — I beg your pardon, sir — of course, I had no right — but seeing the ruined tower from the opposite bank, I thought —"

"Indeed you had no right."

The ice in his voice seemed to cut through Amanda's blood. She winced inwardly.

"I am glad that you have sufficient wit to realise it," he continued in biting accents. "Perhaps you will oblige me by removing yourself from this place instantly."

"Of — of course." Amanda swallowed nervously. "But if you would only let me explain, sir —"

"Your explanations, my good young woman, could only be tedious. I prefer your absence to your conversation. Good day."

This was not to be borne. Amanda's consciousness of being in the wrong faded abruptly before such cavalier treatment.

"I am *not* your good woman!" she retorted, incensed. "If you would only permit me to explain, I was about to inform you that I believed the place to be a ruin — had I realised that it was inhabited —"

She stopped suddenly, seeing only too well the weakness of her defence. He raised one eyebrow in what she thought of as a supercilious manner, and examined her muddy skirts and shoes with a cold detachment that brought the hot blood to her cheeks.

"You must, however, have seen your mistake as soon as you stepped out of the trees. I am right in supposing that you came from the river bank?"

She nodded, momentarily humiliated: the movement caused the hood of her cloak to fall back from her head, thus revealing her honey-coloured curls. He glanced at them, and his lip curled sarcastically.

"This is no place for curious schoolgirls. If I find you here again, I shall be obliged to take sterner measures than warning you off. And now — go."

"Very well."

Amanda drew herself up to her full height, and turned to step out of the cloisters on to the lawn. Then her dignity cracked suddenly. She turned her head impulsively towards him.

"But I think you are vastly uncivil, sir and I am *not* a schoolgirl!"

"That is apparent," he said, and laughed softly.

It was too much. With difficulty Amanda resisted a long since forgotten impulse to put out her tongue. She turned and fled.

She did not pause for breath until she had once more gained the river bank. There was as yet no sign of Jem. In the present stormy state of her feelings, she was glad of this. A short wait would cool her red cheeks and steady her breathing. Her thoughts raged within her. Schoolgirl, indeed! That had stung, as well it might to one not yet quite eighteen, and fresh from the schoolroom. His tone, so peremptory, so — so arrogant! Of course a still, small voice whispered, she had been in the wrong — but to refuse to listen to a civil explanation, to treat her as a mere, vulgar, prying slip of a schoolgirl! Justice insisted that in a sense he had been right, she had indeed been prying; but injured vanity would not heed. She had been treated abominably — the man was a monster!

Presently, her rage cooled sufficiently for her to realise that the boat was approaching the spot where she stood. In another moment, Jem had jumped out to help her safely aboard. There was another man in the boat now, a brawny, bearded giant whom she had no difficulty in identifying as the blacksmith. He clutched a bag to his wide chest, and she guessed that he carried the tools of his trade. He gave her a queer look as she seated herself in the boat, a look that put her in mind of the one bestowed on her by the ferryman when Jem had explained her intention of exploring the ruin across the river.

It was not until they were walking back towards the farm that Jem made any reference to her exploit.

"Did yon place please ye, Miss?" he asked.

She shrugged. "Well enough."

He nodded towards the blacksmith, who was walking a little apart from them.

"Burly Joe over yonder seemed uncommon put about to learn that I'd left my mistress there," he said, with a chuckle. "Seemed to fancy there might be 'obgoblins, or some such; but more 'e wouldn't say."

Amanda glanced sharply at the man, and beckoned to him to draw nearer. He approached, tugging at his forelock.

"What is the name of that place across the river where we were just now?" she asked.

The man seemed reluctant to answer. "Med'nam Abbey, ma'am," he said, at last.

"Then it is an abbey!" exclaimed Amanda. "Or perhaps I should say that it once was. What is the name of the owner?"

Once again, there was a slight hesitation.

"Mr. Duffield did own it," rumbled the man, reluctantly. "But now it belongs to a gennelman from Lunnon way — dunno the name for sure, ma'am."

"What is all this talk of hobgoblins?" continued Amanda.

The fellow glanced half-fearfully over his shoulder, and seemed more unwilling than ever to reply.

"Come," said Amanda, encouragingly. "I'm sure you're not afraid, a big fellow like you!"

This remark seemed to put the blacksmith on his mettle.

"There be queer tales in the village, ma'am," he said, shame-facedly. "No servants live in the 'ouse, only an old man an' 'is missus, who keeps theirselves to theirselves. There be coaches come sometimes wi' crests on the panels, too, but they never stays long an' no one ever sees their owners in the village. An' there be some who say —" his voice dropped almost to a whisper — "that they do 'ave seen ghosties a-flittin' up an' down the lawn from t'other side o' the river. An' if ye stand 'neath the wall of a night — if so be ye should be so bold —

ye'll mayhap hear shrieks an' laughin' — fair curdles yer blood, it do!"

He shivered as he finished speaking, and quickened his pace with another backward glance. Amanda, her curiosity now thoroughly aroused, would have liked to question him further, but she saw that he wanted to have done with the subject, and, moreover, doubted if he could add anything to what he had already said.

"Sounds a bag o' moonshine to me," stated Jem, in a downright way; and he proceeded to lead the man on to talk of coaches and horseflesh, subjects on which he seemed infinitely happier to converse.

Amanda remained apart, lost in a reverie which remained unbroken by the governess's horrified reception of her when at last they reached the road. Miss Brown's remonstrances, as so often, fell on deaf ears; and with very few words on Amanda's part, the time passed until the men had contrived a repair of the coach. The blacksmith was dismissed with a fat fee, and the vehicle resumed the journey to London.

Chapter III: Interlude at the Castle Inn

"You are uncommon silent, Miss Amanda," said the governess at last, astonished. In general, the girl's tongue ran on at great rate, but now she had been answering Miss Brown's remarks in monosyllables for the last half-hour.

Amanda started guiltily.

"Am I, Brownie? I was — just thinking."

"This is a change indeed," replied Miss Brown, with a twinkle. "May I be permitted to know the subject of these deep deliberations?"

Prevarication had never come easily to Amanda, but she recognised the need for it now.

"I was wondering," she said slowly, "how I shall find life in London. Bella talks endlessly of the diversions to be met with — balls and masques, gay company, splendid attire and the like — but somehow I'm not altogether certain that I shall feel as she does. Lately, it seems that our notions are not always alike."

"That is not surprising," replied Miss Brown. "Miss Isabella has shown signs of arriving at discretion this last twelve-month, but you, I fear, are still a sad hoyden! You have been accustomed to a deal of freedom in the country, you must realise, and cannot expect to go on in the same way in Town. Far be it from me to appear to be in any way criticising your excellent parents, but if there has been a fault, it has been on the side of indulgence. You cannot fail to be aware that I have several times represented to your dear Mama —"

"Yes, oh, yes, I know!" cut in Amanda. "But, dearest Brownie, pray do not moralise! You must realise by now that I am quite beyond hope of reform!"

The governess glanced at the girl at her side, and her hard, capable expression softened. To be sure, Miss Amanda was not a Beauty like her sister; she lacked the classic perfection of feature which the older girl possessed. But there was a vitality and warmth in her expression, a roguishness in her smile, that went straight to the heart of the beholder: while that profile, thought Miss Brown, with its tip-tilted nose and firm little chin, put one in mind of a cheeky London sparrow searching for crumbs.

"We would not have you changed," she said, on impulse. "You are possessed of that most human of all virtues — a warm heart."

Amanda looked her surprise. It was unlike Brownie to give way to sentiment. Then she remembered that this was to be their last journey together, and her expression sobered.

"Dearest Brownie, I shall miss you so!" she exclaimed, impetuously. "I know I have been a wretch to you at times, but indeed and indeed, I do love you!"

Miss Brown drew a clean handkerchief from her pocket, and blew her nose vigorously.

"There, there, we must not give way to our feelings!" she said, in a brisk tone. "After all, I am to go only as far as Richmond, and to your own young cousins, so we shall see and hear of each other from time to time. You are a young lady now, and must take your place in the world. You no longer have need of a governess."

"I suppose not," admitted Amanda, a little sadly. "But, Brownie, do you not sometimes wish that we need never have changes — that we might always keep people just as they are at this moment — that they didn't have to leave us, or grow old? I do, often!"

Miss Brown was moved: but she showed it in characteristic fashion by squaring her shoulders, and recommending Miss Amanda not to indulge in morbid thoughts. In this direction she was aided by the arrival of the coach at Salt Hill, where it was necessary to change horses.

By now it was quite dark, and the Castle Inn was a blaze of light. Ostlers ran to and fro in the yard, for this was a busy posting-house. Jaded horses were being led away to the stables and fresh, prancing animals brought out to be set to the waiting coaches. One or two travellers had alighted to seek refreshment within doors on this sharp Spring evening, while the business of changing horses was afoot. Amanda turned eagerly to Miss Brown as their own animals were being unharnessed.

"Do let us go within, Brownie! I would dearly like a cup of coffee or chocolate!"

"There will scarce be time," demurred the governess. "We are already late, and must cross Hounslow Heath, which, as you are no doubt aware, is a notorious haunt of highwaymen. It will be better to do so as early in the evening as possible, when there will be other travellers abroad."

"Pooh!" Amanda wrinkled her nose. "The men are armed, are they not?"

"If by armed you refer to the old blunderbuss which has probably not been fired these ten years, and is, in any event, kept underneath the box — yes, then I suppose you may say that they are," replied the governess, dryly.

"Oh, come, Brownie, it may never happen!" said Amanda cheerfully. "'Pon rep, I would dearly love to see the highwayman who would dare hold you up! He would indeed be a bold man!"

Miss Brown smiled and allowed herself to be persuaded. With a word of explanation to Jem, they made their way to the door of the inn.

It opened straight into the public coffee room. Miss Brown looked disparagingly about her as she entered. The room was a pleasant, low-ceilinged apartment, set about with oak beams. A bright log fire burned on the hearth, and before it stood a high-backed wooden settle. There were a few people sitting on a bench over against the far wall, and a gentleman was leaning negligently against one of the beams, reading a newspaper. Amanda noticed out of the corner of her eye that he was dressed for riding, in buckskin breeches, high boots, and an olive green coat. His travelling cloak and hat were flung carelessly on a chair beside him. He had a decided air of fashion. This much she took in quickly, without appearing to pay any particular attention, while she followed Miss Brown, who steered her purposefully in the direction of the settle before the fire.

"We may as well be warm, child," said the governess, seating herself and drawing off her gloves. She spread out her fingers to the welcome blaze. "It is a chilly night."

A pretty serving wench presently came by, and Miss Brown gave their order in a clear, decisive voice that carried across the room. The gentleman with the newspaper momentarily looked up, and Amanda observed that he was youngish, and decidedly handsome.

After an interval, the maid returned, bearing the refreshment they had bespoken, and placed a tray upon the small table which was set close to Miss Brown. While the governess busied herself with the cups, Amanda looked about her. Her eyes followed the maid idly. The girl had almost reached the door which gave on to a passage communicating with the kitchen quarters and the tap room, when a man entered the coffee room from that direction. He had a fine, swashbuckling air about him that evidently owed something to liquor, for his gait was unsteady, and his wig a trifle askew.

He bore down upon the serving-wench, and circled her slim waist with one arm. She evidently did not welcome this gallantry, for she squeaked in protest. He tightened his grasp with a laugh. All at once, with a force unbelievable in one so slight, she pushed him off so that he staggered, and almost fell. With an audible curse, he made a grab for her; but she eluded his grasp easily, and ran from the room.

Amanda could not repress a smile at this scene; it was unfortunate that the man should have happened to glance in her direction at that same moment, and observe her amusement.

He tugged at his crumpled cravat with an unsteady hand, and started waveringly across the room towards her. She hastily turned away, accepted a cup from Miss Brown's hands, and began to sip her coffee. Nothing daunted, the fellow seated himself beside her upon the settle, and favoured her with a long, insolent stare which seemed to burn into the back of her neck. Her face she kept studiously turned away.

"S'fine evenin'," he offered, in slurred tones.

Amanda ignored this, and continued to sip her coffee and converse with her governess. The man edged a little nearer to her. She turned then, and gave him a frigid stare which must have deterred a sober man. He registered no effect.

"D'ye go to Lunnon?" he asked, with a bold leer.

Amanda felt just the least bit dismayed, and turned a look of appeal on Miss Brown.

"I believe," said the latter, in loud, clear tones, "that it will be necessary to summon the landlord."

At that moment, a shadow fell across the settle. Looking up, Amanda saw that it was the gentleman whom she had noticed reading the newspaper when they had first entered the room. He addressed himself to their tormentor.

"I believe these ladies wish to be private."

His tone was quiet, but carried authority. The man looked up.

"Wassat to you?" he asked aggressively.

"Perhaps I could better explain myself outside."

Again he spoke quietly, but there was menace in the tone, and his hand rested lightly on the hilt of his sword.

How the matter would have ended, Amanda was fated not to know; for, somewhat to her disappointment, the landlord came over to them at that moment, having been hastily summoned by the maid. With a jerk of his thumb, he indicated that the man should leave his inn at once. Evidently the fellow recognised this authority, and was not prepared to argue the matter; for he rose unsteadily to his feet, mumbled something inaudible, and took a wavering course for the door.

Amanda turned to thank the stranger for his intervention, but the landlord's profuse and prolonged apology drowned her opening words. The stranger bowed, and withdrew instantly to the other side of the room, where Amanda noticed he picked up his hat and cloak, and presently left the inn.

They also left, after paying their score, escorted to their coach by a still apologetic landlord.

"This will have been an object lesson to you, Miss Amanda," warned the governess, as the coach rattled over the cobblestones of the yard on to the road for London. "You will perhaps now see how unwise it is to venture into an inn unless escorted by a gentleman."

"I suppose so," conceded her charge, "although it was not so very dreadful, Brownie, after all. Did you not admire our deliverer?"

"A very proper gentleman," approved Miss Brown. "He did not force his company upon us, but withdrew instantly when the landlord arrived."

"Very." Amanda's dimple appeared. "But do you think that perhaps he would have retired quite so promptly — had I been unchaperoned?"

"You are a minx," replied the governess, severely.

"Oh, Brownie!" Amanda dissolved into laughter. "I was only roasting you!"

"Of that I am quite aware. Do not imagine that I have spent ten years in your company without understanding you a little."

"I wish I understood myself," replied Amanda, thoughtfully.

"Which of us does?" asked Miss Brown. "But I do beg of you, Miss Amanda, to put a guard upon your tongue and your actions while you are in Town. Your impetuosity may lead you into sore trouble one of these days, and must frequently be giving a false impression of you to strangers. A young lady of fashion —"

"That I will never be!" declared her charge, passionately.

"Who knows? Miss Isabella is changed —"

"Ye-es; perhaps she is, a little. But I think it is mostly play-acting. Underneath, she is still the same Bella who used to get up to such mad starts!"

"Mm." The governess pursed her lips consideringly. "No doubt we shall soon see her wed."

"Wed — Bella?"

"Why, yes. You must surely realise that your Mama had that in mind when she brought your sister to Town."

"Poor Mama!" said Amanda. "If that was her only object, then she is wasting her time."

The governess raised her brows.

"Oh, you must know, Brownie," said Amanda, impatiently, "that Bella means to marry John Webster! He quite dotes on her — anyone may see it — and I know she is fond of him; though, of course, you cannot expect her to own it!"

"Fond, yes, but whether your sister feels that degree of attachment for Mr. Webster which leads to marriage is quite another matter. I do not think that she would have been so eager to go to London had such been the case."

"Oh, I expect she means to have her fling first," replied Amanda, with a shrug. "You know how it is with Bella, Brownie. She is never so happy as when she is surrounded by admirers! But I am certain that John is really the one for her, and she will settle down happily with him, after being the Toast of the Town for a season!"

"However that may be, I do not imagine that your Mama views Mr. Webster's claims with favour," said Miss Brown, thoughtfully.

Amanda stared. "Why ever should you say so? Why, John's father and Papa have been neighbours for close on twenty years, and always on the best of terms! We have known John since we were in leading-strings!"

"Nevertheless, I fancy that your Mama looks higher than a country squire for a son-in-law," explained the governess.

Amanda was silent for a moment, thinking this over.

"Then she is a great goose!" she said, at last.

"Child! Remember, you speak of your mother!"

"Even the best of mothers can be a goose sometimes!" replied the irrepressible girl. "But it makes no odds: Bella will have her own way in the end, that I promise you!"

Miss Brown shook her head dubiously, but had nothing more to say on that subject, and as she forbore from starting any other, the conversation languished.

Amanda, deep in thought, stared from the window at the pools of light made on the dark road by the lamps of the coach. They were crossing the heath; shadows of trees and bushes sprang up out of the gloom, briefly illumined by the rays of light. As she watched this shadow play, something of the mood which she had summoned up at the Abbey returned to her. Behind the clip-clop of the horses' hoofs lay a quiet that was as thick and impenetrable as the night. Their coach was a tiny, lighted world in all that vast expanse of darkness. Outside it lay mystery and silence.

Suddenly that silence was shattered by a pistol shot.

There was a pounding of fresh hoofs on the road, and a sickening lurch as the coach drew abruptly to a halt. Through the momentary stillness rang out a hoarse cry: "Stand and deliver!"

Chapter IV: Amanda is Resourceful

The two occupants of the coach exchanged startled glances. Only Miss Brown's arm went out and tightened about Amanda's waist: for this troublesome young woman, the governess was prepared to give her life, if need be.

"Let down the winder!" grated a harsh voice.

Amanda's pale lips set firmly, and she made no effort to obey.

"Do as I say, or I'll knock it in!"

Once again the two ladies exchanged a brief glance. Then Miss Brown leaned over and lowered the window with a hand which trembled only slightly.

"That's better!" said the hateful voice, with a throaty chuckle. "No 'arm'll come to ye if y'do as I say. Make a 'eap o' all yer val'ables, an' pass 'em through. I'll give yer two minutes. After that —"

He left the sentence unfinished, but at that moment he moved into the light of one of the lamps, and the two in the coach saw the black outline of the horse pistol which he held in his right hand, levelled at the open window.

"Jem!"

Amanda raised her voice in a desperate appeal.

"Ain't no manner o' use callin' Jem," chuckled the masked figure. "'E's been taken care of. Best get on wi' it."

"If you've done Jem a mischief," said Amanda, vehemently, "I'll — I'll —"

"What'll ye do?"

The figure moved nearer to the window, and raised the pistol menacingly.

"Get on wi' it — I'm warnin' ye for the last time, I ain't a patient man."

He thrust his left hand through the open window as he spoke, palm extended almost under Amanda's nose. Frightened as she now was, the thought of harm having come to old Jem made her blood boil: the temptation proved too much. She bent over the hand, and sank her teeth into it until they reached the bone.

There followed a startled howl of anguish, and the pistol dropped with a clatter into the road. For a moment the man spun round in agony, nursing his injured hand and emitting loud and violent curses.

While the first highwayman had approached the occupants of the coach, his companion had held the coachman and stable-lad at bay with a pair of unflinching pistols. It had all occurred too suddenly for them to have time to make any defensive move; the blunderbuss of which Miss Brown had spoken was inaccessible, and they were otherwise unarmed. Now, however, the unexpected outcry made by the first highwayman caused his confederate to relax his vigilance for a second, and turn his head in the direction of the noise.

The moment's respite was enough for the groom, a young, active lad. He made a sudden wild leap from the box, landing on top of the second highwayman, and knocking the pistols from his hold. One of the weapons discharged harmlessly into the ditch, but the noise startled the horses. They reared and plunged; Jem was wholly occupied in preventing them from bolting, and unable to lend his companion any aid.

At the sound of the scuffle, the first highwayman recovered his wits, and stooped quickly to retrieve the weapon he had dropped. He turned to help his confederate, but this worthy was lying prostrate on the ground, temporarily winded by having received the full weight of the stable-lad on his stomach.

The groom, unhurt and fresh as ever, launched himself fearlessly upon the other man, and proceeded to give a good account of himself by knocking the pistol once more from his opponent's grasp, and planting him a facer.

Amanda let loose a cheer, and clenched her fists as she watched Tom's gallant battle with his heavier opponent. Things might have gone badly with the boy, however, for she noticed that the other man was beginning to struggle to his feet, and Tom could be no match for the two of them; but, at that moment, the sound of a horse approaching at the gallop made everyone turn in the direction of the noise. The moon, appearing briefly from behind a belt of thick cloud, revealed to all the figure of a horseman traveling at breakneck speed, his cloak streaming out behind him as he rode.

With a last desperate heave, the groom's opponent flung the lad against the side of the coach, and took to his heels. The second man followed, before Tom could recover sufficiently to prevent it. In a moment they had mounted the horses which had been tethered to the bushes at the side of the road, and were galloping off across country as though the devil were at their heels.

By this time, Jem had the horses under control, and could venture to leave the box for a moment to see how his companion fared. He found Amanda bending over the boy in the road. Tom was sitting up and rubbing his head ruefully.

"You all right, lad?" asked Jem, anxiously.

The groom nodded. "They'm got away, though," he answered dejectedly.

"That was not your fault!" said Amanda, warmly. "You were splendid, Tom! My father shall know of this, you may be sure!"

"Thank you, Miss." The groom's eyes glowed at the praise. "But I fear all would have been lost without yonder horseman," he added.

Amanda turned. The rider was now close upon them; in another moment he had drawn level with the coach and, dismounting hastily, came towards the group standing in the road.

"Can I be of any assistance?" he asked, a trifle breathlessly. "I trust no one is hurt? I saw that you were waylaid, and made what speed I could."

As he stepped into the light cast by the lamps, Amanda recognised him for the gentleman who had so recently come to their aid in the Castle Inn.

The groom rose from the ground, and coachman Jem touched his cap.

"All's well, praise be, y'r honour," he answered. "Though but for you coming up in the nick o' time, dear knows what might have happened! What did you do, Miss Mandy, to make yon rogue squeak?" he asked, turning to his mistress.

"I bit his hand," she returned, with satisfaction.

"You what?"

The gentleman regarded her with incredulous amusement. Jem and the groom broke into a simultaneous guffaw of laughter.

"I am very glad of it," said Amanda, decidedly. "I only wish I'd been able to serve his other hand in a like manner!"

A chuckle escaped the stranger at these words.

"I make no doubt of it," he said, gravely. "Well, there is little occasion to inquire if you are hurt, madam. What of the other lady who is travelling with you? I trust she may not be overset by this unfortunate experience."

His words brought Miss Brown's head to the open door, and she was heard to say that she did tolerably well.

"But we owe you a double debt of gratitude, sir," she continued. "For, unless I mistake, you are that same gentleman who rendered us a service in the Castle Inn, not an hour since? Please to accept our most heartfelt thanks for your timely intervention in both instances."

Amanda echoed these sentiments, but the gentleman waved aside their expressions of gratitude.

"Pray say no more, I beg: it is fortunate indeed that I chanced to be riding in this direction, as I count myself happy in being able to serve you. Perhaps you will permit me to present myself? I am Roger Thurlston, nephew to my Lord Barsett."

The bow that accompanied this announcement was a triumph of politeness; Amanda, oblivious of the dusty road, sank instantly into a curtsy.

"I am Amanda Twyford, and this is my governess, Miss Brown. We are happy to make your acquaintance, sir, though the circumstances of our meeting might, perhaps, have been better chosen."

"Truly," he said, with a smile that had great charm. "But I am not unacquainted with your name: are you by any chance a connection of my Lord Twyford, who is a great friend of my uncle's?"

Amanda exclaimed in delight, "Why, yes! I am his younger daughter! To be sure, I remember now to have heard something of the friendship between your uncle and my father — it was in their young days, was it not?" She turned eagerly to the governess. "How very odd this, Brownie, to be sure!"

Miss Brown assented quietly. Her features had relaxed a little upon hearing the name of their deliverer: to be sure, one could not quarrel with any gentleman who had twice in one evening come to their rescue, but it was so well to know just who the young man was.

He was smiling. "It is indeed odd, as you say, Miss Twyford. But I am surprised to learn that my lord has two daughters. I have already had the pleasure of meeting your sister, and thought her to be an only child."

"Oh, yes, I quite see how that is," said Amanda quickly. "You see, I was so foolish as to catch the chicken pox just as Mama had planned to leave for Town, so it was necessary for me to remain in the country until I was quite recovered. And I am now, am I not, Brownie? Not even one little spot remains," she added, ingenuously.

Miss Brown gave an admonitory cough. However great a debt one owed to a stranger, it was scarcely necessary — or expedient — to burden him with the more intimate details of one's history. Amanda took her meaning, and threw her a challenging glance.

Mr. Thurlston noticed this by-play with some amusement.

"Well, I must not detain you here any longer," he said, with another bow. "So long as you have come to no harm you will be wishing to continue your journey."

He put out his hand to assist Amanda to mount into the vehicle. She stepped up lightly, seating herself beside the governess. He was about to turn away, having seen her settled, but a thought seemed to strike him all at once, and he paused.

"Since you are journeying to London, I wonder if you would honour me by accepting my escort? I, too, am bound for Town, and I should deem it a pleasure — nay, a privilege —"

Miss Brown and Amanda exchanged glances; the governess nodded lightly, and Amanda accepted the offer with alacrity.

Mr. Thurlston closed the door of the coach; Jem and Tom had already returned to their stations on the box, and Amanda, leaning from the window, now gave the order to start. Mr. Thurlston remounted his horse, and stationing himself close to the window of the coach, kept pace as the vehicle moved off along the dusty road which glimmered white in the light of the now unclouded moon. The hoofs of the horses beat out a rhythmical pattern of sound in the quiet of the night.

Amanda presently turned a sparkling look upon her governess.

"Do you know what, Brownie? I think we have had a most splendid adventure!"

Miss Brown did not positively sniff, because it was unlady-like to do so; nevertheless, she came as near to it as a gentlewoman might with propriety.

"If you call it a splendid adventure to have your life threatened by highwaymen, I suppose you may say that we have," she answered, dryly.

"To be sure, that was an unpleasant moment," admitted her charge; "but it was soon over, and only think how romantic it is to be saved from an unpleasant situation for the second time by such a handsome gentleman! You will not deny that he's handsome, I hope, Brownie?"

"He's a very well-looking gentleman, certainly," allowed the governess, grudgingly.

"Pray, Brownie, temper your enthusiasm with a little moderation!" mocked the girl.

"I am neither so young nor so impressionable as you," Miss Brown reminded her. "And I beg that you will curb your tendency towards the romantic. It is true that this gentleman has rendered us a signal service — though unwittingly, in the last instance, at any rate — but there is no need on that account to assume that he is the embodiment of all the virtues. I should allow yourself a longer acquaintance before you make a final pronouncement on his character. There is grave danger in yielding to hastily formed opinions."

"Oh, Brownie!" sighed Amanda, wearily. "Not for anything would I be possessed of your cautious disposition!"

"I pray Heaven," replied the governess, in a serious tone, "that you may never have occasion to be. We would not have you changed, Miss Amanda."

The girl made no reply, but leaned back in her corner, sunk in reverie. The rhythm of the hoofs, the gentle swaying of the coach, the peace of the night after the excitement that had so far attended their journey, all combined to lull her into a state bordering on sleep.

The vehicle rolled onwards, through the village of Hammersmith with its bustling inn where the Bath coaches changed horses, out through open country on the bumpy road to Kensington. Gradually her head drooped forward.

There was a sudden jolt as the coach found a pothole in the road. The jerk brought her wide awake, and conscious for the first time of the drumming of rain on the roof of the coach. She looked about her: water was streaming down the window, and by the light of the lamps she could see great puddles standing in the road.

"Our poor Mr. Thurlston!" she exclaimed in dismay. "He will be quite drowned!"

The governess assented, and clucked her tongue.

"I think we must ask him inside," continued Amanda. "What do you say, Brownie?"

The governess hesitated for only a second.

"If you desire it. He has, after all, been of inestimable service, and the weather is very severe."

"He may tie his horse to the back of the coach," went on Amanda, and rapped loudly on the window for Jem to stop.

The change was soon effected, and the unfortunate Mr. Thurlston, having divested himself of his dripping cloak and hat, seated himself in the opposite corner to Amanda. She glanced approvingly at the impeccable cut of his clothes. He had a decided air of fashion, without betraying anything of the dandy.

The conversation turned at first, naturally enough, upon the weather. Such a subject is at all times inclined to be soporific. Taking into account the fact that Miss Brown had travelled a long way and endured a good many trials with fortitude that day, it is scarcely surprising that she presently began to nod. Amanda noticed this with pleasure, for she had a question burning on her lips that could not be put to Mr. Thurlston in the hearing of the governess.

She waited until she was certain that Miss Brown slept, then leaned forward in a conspiratorial way.

"Are you by any chance at all acquainted with the village of Medmenham, sir?" she began, in a low tone.

He shot her a keen glance, and confessed that he knew it a little.

"Then have you managed to come at a solution of the mystery of the Abbey?" she whispered, eagerly.

"The Abbey?" Consternation sounded in his voice, muted as it was. "What do you know of that?"

"Little enough," she confessed, ruefully. "I was hoping that you might tell me more."

He bowed, but made no reply. Miss Brown stirred slightly, Amanda watched, her heart in her mouth, until the governess's head sank once more on to her chest.

"Pray do not be so provoking!" she whispered at last. "I was there quite by chance this afternoon, and was warned off the grounds by a horrid person! And then the village blacksmith told a tale of hobgoblins that intrigued me vastly! Do please tell me more, if you know anything to the purpose!"

He hesitated for what seemed to her a long time.

"I fear," he said at last, "that I am unable to satisfy your interest. But you spoke of a horrid person —?"

"I believe it was very likely the owner. He was cold and — and forbidding — and vastly insulting into the bargain!"

"Can you describe his looks?"

Amanda considered for a moment.

"He was of about your age, I should say. Tall, with a stern face and sneering mouth."

He shook his head.

"It was not the owner; he does not answer such a description. That much I may tell you. Moreover, I fancy I know who it may have been. But — if I might presume to venture a word of advice, Miss Amanda — I feel that I ought to warn you that Medmenham Abbey is not considered a suitable subject for conversation in Town. I trust you will forgive my mention of this, and would not venture to advise you, but that I know you are lately from the country, and therefore have been shielded from the gossip that runs round constantly in London. An unguarded word on this head may give a wrong impression — I was bound in duty to warn you. Pray do not hold it against me, I beg."

Amanda readily agreed to overlook any seeming interference, and was about to try him further; but, at that moment, the coach struck a deep pothole, and Miss Brown awoke with a start. She looked sharply at the other two travellers, but Mr. Thurlston had, with commendable promptitude, started a trifling conversation to which there could be no possible objection.

The governess sighed, her mind at rest. Not so Amanda's, however. She was consumed by a positive fire of curiosity, and more determined than ever that at some time she would solve the mystery of the Abbey.

Chapter V: Isabella Twyford Receives Two Offers of Marriage

My Lady Twyford was sitting up in bed sipping at her morning chocolate when her husband entered the room. She motioned to him with one white hand to take a seat by the side of the great four-poster. He obeyed, frowning.

"This business concerning Bella —" he began.

"Charles Barsett has spoken to you?" she asked, eagerly.

He nodded; the frown did not leave his face.

"I encountered him at the Cocoa Tree yesterday evening. He's a demmed queer customer, Margaret! — 'Believe you and my father to desire a marriage between your daughter and myself,' he said. 'May I have the honour of waiting upon you tomorrow?' Not another word, I give you my oath! I was taken aback, and stammered out I know not what; and then the demmed fellow turned away with a bow, for all the world as though he was buying a horse from my stable, instead of asking my daughter's hand in marriage!"

His wife nodded. "It's well enough," she said sagely. "So long as he offers it's no matter as to the manner of it! 'Pon rep, we may congratulate ourselves, my lord! It will be a match that will set the Town by the ears!"

"Mm." My lord pursed his lips, and his frown deepened.

"Why, Isabella has scarce begun on her season in Town!" exclaimed his lady, ecstatically. "And already she is promised! I only hope we may be as fortunate with Amanda!"

"Amanda?" He looked up, startled, and shook his head. "I hope we shall keep her with us yet a while. She's but a child."

His wife looked amused. "She will be eighteen next month, do not forget. At her age I was already a bride."

"Will she?" He stared. "Egad, so she will! I cannot believe it! Little Mandy —"

He relapsed into silence. Pictures formed in his mind which took him back across the years. Amanda, a whirl of arms and legs, her honey-coloured curls tossing in the breeze as she ran down the drive to meet him coming home from a journey; her clear, childish voice crying "Papa! You're home at last!". Amanda, white-faced but indomitable, only eight years old, confessing that it had been herself, and not John Webster, who had climbed into the apple-loft against all orders, and frightened the housekeeper. Odd how sharply such pictures of past events etched themselves on the mind — not always of the most important events at that. He sighed.

"I trust we're making the right decision," he said, slowly. "Concerning Bella, I mean."

It was his wife's turn to stare. "'Pon rep, I cannot think what you mean!"

He hesitated. "It is just that — Barsett is a very old friend, there couldn't be a better fellow! But this son of his —"

"Yes?"

My Lady Twyford placed her cup and saucer upon the bedside table, and turned an inquiring look upon her spouse.

"His reputation —" began my lord.

"Fiddle-dee-dee!" answered his wife, with a toss of her head in its beribboned night-cap. "I hope you do not expect me to censure a man in this day and age for being somewhat of a rake!"

"'Tis not only that." His voice was troubled. "He keeps company with that odd fish, Dashwood. There are rumours running round the clubs concerning a society which Dashwood has founded, and which meets somewhere along the Thames, Marlow way, I believe."

"Pah!" she shrugged her shoulders lightly. "The latest *on dit!* Do I not know them? Pray what is supposed to be so very dreadful about this — society?"

She infused a deal of scorn into her voice. My lord looked a trifle sheepish.

"No one really knows, but all kinds of conjectures are made. Orgies, say some, but others say —" His voice sank a tone — "black magic."

She laughed musically.

"Orgies! Half the clubs in Town have orgies, I daresay! Oh, yes, I know that such things are not supposed to come to female ears, but believe me, women are not near so stupid as they pretend to be! And if there is one thing more laughable than orgies it is black magic!"

My lord's look of chagrin deepened, and he shuffled his feet awkwardly.

"You may laugh," he said, with a touch of defiance. "But do you care to think of our girl tied for life to a man who indulges in such pleasures? Better a wholesome country lad, say I!"

She stopped laughing, and regarded him sharply.

"No doubt you have someone in mind?"

"You know well enough that I mean John Webster, our neighbour's son. A fine young man, and known to us from the cradle! Moreover, I'll lay any odds that Bella's fond of him."

"You must be aware, my lord," answered Lady Twyford, with a touch of asperity, "that I went to the trouble of bringing Isabella to Town in order to avoid such a match. What, shall she wed a country squire's son when she may have the pick of the Town beaux, and a handsome fortune into the bargain? Not to speak of the title some day!"

"That don't signify!" he answered impatiently. "The Websters are an old family, well-connected, and young John has an adequate competence. Besides, Bella has more than enough for both! Let the girl be happy, and to the devil with your ambitions!"

"I fear you must reckon with Isabella's ambition, too. She thinks better of her claims than to be content to become a mere Mrs. Webster. Oh, yes, there was perhaps some girl and boy nonsense between them, but that is quite over, I assure you. As for Charles Barsett, a wife will give his interests a new direction. I don't despair of your finding him as dull as any husband breathing, when they've been wed a twelvemonth."

"I only hope you may be right," he replied seriously.

"Of course I'm right!" was the confident reply. "I know what is best for my own daughter."

The subject of this discussion was at that very moment giving audience to the country squire's son. John Webster contrived to look singularly ill at ease, in spite of the fact that he was a tall, handsome young man, clad in a suit of puce satin laced with gold which became him extremely. His dark brown eyes avoided the hazel ones of Miss Isabella as he took the seat which she indicated, and he showed no disposition to break the silence which fell uneasily between them.

"It is a lovely day," offered Isabella, tentatively.

He agreed, and continued to study the pattern of the carpet with apparent interest.

"Of course, it cannot be expected that the weather should be settled at this time of the year," she continued, with spurious animation.

"No," he said absently.

Isabella racked her brains furiously for something further to say, but without success. She was a tall, slim, elegant young woman, with hair of a brighter gold than her sister's, and with a classical beauty of feature which Amanda lacked. She was dressed in a blue and white striped gown of deceptive simplicity, and wore the tiniest of lace erections on her gold curls. The whole produced a pastoral effect that was at once simple and charming. Mr. Webster raised his eyes briefly, and was quite overcome.

"Do you suppose it will rain later?" asked Isabella, in desperation.

At that he made an impatient gesture, and stood up abruptly.

"Bella, this is too ridiculous!" he burst out. "All the years we have known each other, and the first time we encounter each other in a fortnight you must speak to me of the weather!"

Isabella looked slightly ruffled. "Well, you do not help me overmuch," she said, accusingly.

"I know," he answered, with a smile of surprising sweetness. "You see, I was nerving myself to speak my errand."

"Your errand?" repeated the lady, nervously.

He nodded, and came impetuously over toward her, taking both her hands in his before she could resist.

"Yes, Bella, and I think you know what it is. We have been too long acquainted to require the idle pretences of polite society. You must know, my dearest Bella, in what esteem I have held you these past three years. Put an end to my misery by telling me that you will do me the honour to become my wife."

She affected a start, and drew her hands hastily from his. He looked surprised.

"Bella, surely you are not going to be missish?" he protested. "My feelings must have been plain, and I have always thought that I could count on a return of my regard."

"Indeed?"

The single word was charged with scorn. A man more versed in the ways of women might have taken warning, but forthright John Webster plunged on, unheeding, to his downfall.

"You cannot have forgotten the Hunt Ball last year?" he asked incredulously.

She tossed her head, and the morning sun, striking through a window, glinted on her golden curls.

"To be sure, that *is* an occasion in the country," she replied, indifferently. "But I have attended at so many vastly superior balls since then here in Town —"

"Isabella —" he exclaimed indignantly. "How can you pretend to misunderstand me! I will not believe that you meant nothing by what passed between us on that occasion?"

An angry spot of colour showed on her cheeks.

"It is very ungentlemanlike of you to be reminding me of — of a foolish indiscretion!"

"Indiscretion? Is that what you call it?"

He fixed her with a cool, steady regard of his brown eyes. Her glance dropped away from his, but she shrugged her shoulders, affecting a light tone.

"To be sure. I may perhaps have been a trifle giddy and thoughtless, but I was young, and unused to the ways of the world —"

"Young!" he broke in heatedly. "What nonsense is this? You knew very well what you were about! Egad, it is not so many months back!"

"How dare you!" flashed Isabella. Then, with an effort at calmness — "This is a stupid fuss to be making over one little kiss, after all!"

A look of pain came into the brown eyes. He tried to study her face, but she kept it half turned from him.

"Was it indeed no more to you, Bella, than just a light kiss? Do not tease me, I beg of you, but answer truly!"

She steeled herself against the pleading in his tone, and shook her head. His hands, which had been raised almost in supplication, dropped to his sides. He regarded her for a long moment in silence.

"It was much more to me than that," he said in a low tone. "I thought of it as our betrothal."

"Then you took too much upon yourself!" retorted Isabella, stung to anger by a complexity of emotions.

"So I perceive." He answered her in a flat, expressionless tone, and turned to go. "If I have importuned you, I ask your pardon."

"There is no need of asking pardon!" exclaimed Isabella, the tears starting behind her eyelids. "It is all a stupid mistake! If you must know, I am about to become affianced to Lord Barsett's son —"

He started, and turned pale.

"Charles Barsett! You will wed a man of his reputation!"

The words were forced from him by his emotion. He regretted them as soon as they were uttered.

"I don't know what you mean," she said coldly. "Lord Barsett is a friend of Papa's. It is all arranged."

He bowed.

"I see. It only remains for me to wish you happy, and to relieve you of my presence."

"I hope we may still be friends," said Isabella, extending her hand to him.

He took it, held it for a moment while his grave, unhappy eyes looked into hers; then stooped to kiss it.

"No," he answered seriously, straightening himself and releasing the hand. "There can never be so little as friendship between us, Bella. Since you are to wed another, there must be an end to our association."

She could not readily find an answer. While she was still at a loss, he bowed and abruptly left the room.

On his way down the passage to the hall he almost bumped into Amanda.

She was dressed for walking, and in one hand carried a straw hat which she dangled negligently by its ribbon. She hailed him with uninhibited delight. He murmured some incoherent greeting, and hurried past on his way to the door which gave on to the street.

She stared after him for a moment, puzzled. It was no way to greet a childhood acquaintance after an absence of several months. Frowning a little, she pushed open the door of her sister's apartment.

"Bella!"

She closed the door quickly, and went over to her sister. Isabella lay in a crumpled heap on the sofa, sobbing bitterly. She raised her tear-stained face for a moment, then flung her arms about her sister's neck.

"Oh, Mandy!"

"There, my love!" Amanda soothed.

They clung together wordlessly for a little while. Then Isabella withdrew from her sister's embrace, and dabbed feverishly at her eyes. Amanda saw that the worst of the storm was over, and judged that she might now satisfy her curiosity as to its cause.

"What does it all mean, Bella?" she asked. "I passed John on his way out just now, and he went by with scarce a greeting, and here I find you in tears! Can it possibly be that you two have quarrelled?"

"Ye-es," replied Isabella, shakily. "That is to say, no! Well, not precisely."

"Take your time, my love," suggested Amanda, generously.

"Oh, Mandy!"

Isabella looked as though she was about to succumb to another bout of weeping. Amanda decided quickly that she must be prevented: if something was seriously wrong, as appeared from the evidence, then the sooner it was confided the better. There was no sense to be got out of Bella while she was in this state.

"Come, dearest, it's of no use to say 'Oh, Mandy'! Only tell me what is the matter, and then I may try if I can help you!"

Isabella shook her head despondently. "No one can help me!"

"Fustian!" said her sister energetically. "Just you try me, that's all!"

Isabella swallowed, and blew her nose daintily.

"You don't understand, dearest. There's — nothing wrong, really. Only — only…" Her lip trembled, and she finished with a gulp — "John has just made me an offer!"

Amanda stared for a moment, then burst out laughing.

"Is that all? You goose! Then why do you cry?"

"Because — because he says — we may no longer be friends —"

"No longer be friends —?" Amanda wrinkled her brows in perplexity. "Whatever can you mean? Isabella —" as a thought suddenly occurred to her — "you surely cannot mean that you have *refused* him?"

A tinge of red appeared in Isabella's cheeks, and she avoided her sister's glance.

"You have!" exclaimed Amanda incredulously. "I can see from your face that you have! But why, Bella, in Heaven's name?"

Isabella's eyes roved round the room as if in search of help. "There has not been time to tell you since you arrived," she said haltingly, "though I imagined that perhaps Mama might have dropped a hint to you. The fact is that — Papa has arranged a marriage for me with the son of an old friend of his."

Amanda's red lips parted in amazement. She stared wordlessly at her sister for some minutes.

"It cannot be so very surprising, after all!" said Isabella defensively. "You must have realised that Mama intended to make a match for me in Town if she could!"

Amanda sat down suddenly upon a low stool covered in red damask that was close at hand. She was recalling what the governess had said to her on the journey to London.

"Mama, yes," she answered slowly. "I know well that she is ambitious for you. But — Papa would never force you against your will —"

"Who said that he does?" asked her sister, with a touch of defiance.

"You cannot mean —" once again Amanda looked at the other in amazement —"that *you* are willing for this match?"

Isabella raised her head. The traces of tears were still on her cheeks, and her lips trembled ever so slightly, but her expression was determined.

"Why should I not be? He is heir to my Lord Barsett, and quite the most eligible beau in Town!"

"That is no good reason," retorted Amanda roundly, "for marrying anyone!"

"It is not only that — he has an air, and every female in Town is quite wild for him, I assure you!"

Amanda eyed her sister with disfavour.

"I tell you what it is, Bella; I don't think London has improved you!" she said candidly. "You were in love with John right enough not two months ago — you know that you were!"

Isabella had the grace to look a little shame-faced, but she shook her head.

"Perhaps I thought I was, but that was before I had really had much opportunity of meeting many gentlemen."

"Fiddle-dee-dee!" retorted her sister impatiently. "There were five and twenty in the county from whom you might choose, and choose you did!"

"Oh, in the country things are so vastly different!" said Isabella loftily. "One must do what one can — it would never do to seem to be on the shelf, you know —"

"I find you quite horrid!" said Amanda scornfully. "Do you mean to tell me that you have been toying with poor John's affections all this time, only so that you might have an admirer in train? If that is so, Isabella Twyford, you're not the girl I took you for!"

For a moment it looked as though Isabella would flare up in answer to this outspoken criticism; then her expression changed, her lip quivered, and she said pleadingly, "Pray do not let us quarrel, Mandy! I have lost one friend already!"

"Oh, very well, you obstinate goose!" replied Amanda affectionately. "But do not let Mama choose your husband for you, Bella!"

"Perhaps when you see him for yourself you may better understand his attraction for me."

"And when will that be?"

"He is to call upon Papa this afternoon to make a formal offer for my hand," replied Isabella.

"'Pon rep, two offers in one day!" said her sister, in awestruck tones. "You must be quite the most sought-after young woman in Town, my dear!"

Her tone was light, and Isabella laughed in relief. To quarrel with Amanda was no new thing, but seldom had she heard so much real censure in her younger sister's voice as when they had spoken of John Webster.

"Let us forget the whole sorry affair," she said hurriedly. "We have our dresses to choose for the Masque, and there is little enough of the morning left to us. I think I shall go as Proserpine, in white, with trailing bands of flowers — what of you?"

Amanda wrinkled her brow. "Diana, I think," she decided. "And then I may have a bow and arrow, and shoot at anyone who annoys me!"

Isabella looked suitably alarmed, and they set off on their errand.

It was some hours later that Charles Barsett was announced to my Lord Twyford. He presented himself arrayed in a suit of blue satin, the open coat revealing a waistcoat elaborately embroidered in silver. A diamond pin sparkled in the snowy lace at his throat, and a sapphire ring glowed deeply on his right hand.

He had not been closeted alone with his lordship for long when a footman was despatched to summon Miss Isabella. She was sitting with Lady Twyford and Amanda in an upper room, expecting at any moment to be summoned, and suitably nervous. Her mother threw her an encouraging look as she rose to follow the servant.

"Pray remember what I told you, Isabella."

She nodded, not trusting herself to speak. Her face had paled slightly.

"I'll go down with you," said Amanda, ranging herself at her sister's side.

"Amanda, no! You cannot!" warned her mother.

"Don't worry, Mama, I mean to accompany her only to the foot of the stairs."

Lady Twyford clucked disapprovingly, but Amanda passed an arm about her sister's waist, and led her from the room.

They walked slowly down the winding staircase. At the foot, Isabella hesitated, and turned towards her sister appealingly.

"You must go in, dearest," whispered Amanda, her blue eyes serious. "But do not hesitate to send him about his business if you should find that you have changed your mind!"

Isabella shook her head wordlessly, and moved reluctantly from Amanda's sheltering arm. She straightened herself, and, head held high, passed into the room where her father and her suitor were awaiting her.

Amanda stood motionless in the hall, a prey to uneasy feelings. Isabella must do what she wanted, of course; but did she truly know what she wanted? She was an acknowledged beauty, and had been made much of on that account: perhaps it might have gone a little to her head. And then there was Mama, with her ambitious schemes, and her forceful manner; it was difficult to withstand her wishes unless one felt very strongly.

She can only decide for herself, thought Amanda, unhappily. Pray Heaven she may choose aright! She can never find anyone more worthy of regard than John — but does he perhaps seem a little dull when compared with these fine Town gentlemen? She sighed heavily.

She must have been standing there for some time, lost in thought, when suddenly the door opened, and her father came out into the hall, accompanied by a stranger. She looked up, and caught her breath in surprise as her eyes rested upon the lean, cynical face with its deep blue eyes and sneering mouth.

There could be no doubt at all about it: this was the gentleman she had encountered at Medmenham Abbey.

Chapter VI: Dinner in St. James's Square

Amanda continued to stare at him, lips parted in surprise, until her father noticed her standing there. He paused in the middle of some remark which he was making to his guest, and steered Charles Barsett in Amanda's direction.

"This is my younger daughter, Amanda; this is Mr. Barsett, Mandy. He has this moment become affianced to your sister."

Charles Barsett made a magnificent leg; but Amanda was too overcome to move. So this was the man who was to wed Isabella!

He straightened himself, raised one eyebrow slightly in surprise at her lack of response, and the corner of his mouth twisted in a cynical smile.

"Amanda, child!" chided her father gently.

She recovered herself, recollecting her lack of manners, and sank into a curtsy.

"I must wish you joy, sir," she said with a straight face.

"Must you?" he murmured. "Then I must thank you, little sister-to-be."

It was too much! He was mocking at her! Amanda searched his expression with angry eyes, but could discover no hint of recognition there. All seemed perfectly proper: so, at any rate, her father seemed to think, for he smiled indulgently, and led his guest away across the hall in the direction of the door to the house.

A knock sounded before they could reach it. The porter opened the door to reveal, standing upon the step, Amanda's deliverer of two days' since, Mr. Thurlston.

Charles Barsett paused in his stride at sight of him. The watching Amanda saw a guard come over his face.

"Give you good-day, cousin," he drawled.

"Charles! I did not look to find you here —"

He broke off, seeing Amanda, who had come forward towards the door.

"Miss Twyford! I but called to see how you did after your recent ordeal; the sight of you is sufficient reassurance, however."

"It is very kind of you, sir," began Amanda quickly. "But pray, have the goodness to enter. Papa, I would make known to you the gentleman who rescued us from the highwaymen on our journey here — you remember, I told you of it."

Roger Thurlston had stepped over the threshold at her invitation, and now exchanged bows with my Lord Twyford.

"My dear sir," said my lord, "I should like to express my gratitude for your service to my daughter. If you will pardon me for one moment, while I see Mr. Barsett to his carriage — but I collect that you are related?"

The cousins eyed each other warily for a second: then Charles Barsett bowed ironically.

"I have that honour," he said, and the drawl was more pronounced.

He is insufferable, thought Amanda. He sneers even at his own cousin! How can Bella hope ever to be happy with such a man?

She bent all the brilliance of her smile upon Roger Thurlston.

"Shall I take Mr. Thurlston to Mama?" she asked her father.

"Do so, my dear, I know that she will wish to add her thanks to mine. I shall join you presently."

"Pray do not put yourself to the trouble of accompanying me to my carriage, my lord. I believe I may do very well alone," said Charles Barsett, with his sardonic smile.

Lord Twyford protested, but was politely overborne, and, after due farewells had been taken, the door closed upon Isabella's future husband. The others made their way to the drawing-room where Lady Twyford had been left sitting alone.

Here they were joined in a few moments by Isabella. Her colour was heightened, and her manner more than usually animated. Amanda threw her a troubled glance, then proceeded to forget her for the duration of Mr. Thurlston's visit.

He did not stay long. When he had departed, everyone pronounced him to be very agreeable. After that, the conversation was all of Isabella's engagement.

"Barsett has invited us to dine in St. James's Square tomorrow," said Lord Twyford. "It is short notice, I know, but I promised for us all."

His wife nodded absently.

"Isabella, my love, what will you wear? There is the blue —"

My lord held up his hands in horror.

"Egad, if you are to talk of dress, I'm off!"

Amanda, too, listened impatiently while her mother contrasted the merits of Isabella's various gowns. She was longing to have her sister to herself for a while. Her opportunity did not come until my lady went herself to speak to Isabella's maid concerning the all-important subject.

"Bella, there is something you must know!" she exclaimed urgently, as soon as the door had closed behind her parent. "That man — the gentleman to whom you are engaged — he is the one I saw at that place I told you of!"

Isabella appeared not to digest this information at first.

"Surely you can't have forgotten!" exclaimed Amanda impatiently. "I told you the whole story that same night, when I arrived. What I'm saying is that the horrid creature whom I encountered at the mysterious Abbey is none other than your Mr. Barsett!"

"How can you be sure?" asked Isabella dubiously.

"I could never forget that horrid, sneering face! And, moreover, the voice is the same, though he was more pleasant today than upon that occasion. There is no doubt at all in my mind."

Isabella turned this over in silence for a few minutes.

"I can't see that it signifies," she said at last.

Amanda stared.

"Not signify that you are to wed a man who has some connection with a place of ill-repute?" she asked in horror.

"You do not know that. There may be some other explanation of his presence there. After all, you were there, too, yet have no connection with it."

"But I told you that he warned me it was no place for me. Why should he do so if he knew nothing of it?" Isabella sighed.

"I cannot say. In any event, what have you to go on but rumours concerning this Abbey — rumours, moreover, that amount to little more than the gossip of villagers? You refine too much upon what you heard from the blacksmith, Mandy. I daresay it is all a hum."

Amanda started to her feet.

"I see that you will not believe me, but had you been there you must have felt something — a — an emanation of evil, if you like — I cannot better describe it!"

Her sister burst out laughing.

"Oh, Mandy, Mandy! Your sense of the dramatic plays you false! You should take to the stage, my love, where your talents would be better employed."

Amanda set her small, white teeth.

"Very well, laugh," she retorted. "But if I could prove to you that your affianced was mixed up in something discreditable, would you still wed him, Bella?"

"That depends."

Isabella's face sobered, and she was silent for a moment or two.

"Amanda," she continued, in a gentle tone, "I have already heard certain things concerning — Mr. Barsett. You do not know so much of the world as I, and perhaps they would not be greatly to your liking. But, believe me, it is no uncommon thing for a man of fashion to be — to be somewhat of a rake. Mama has explained it all to me. Such things, she says, usually right themselves after marriage."

"Pooh!" exclaimed Amanda scornfully. "What kind of ninny do you take me for, pray? I do not need that Mama should explain such matters to me — *that* I perfectly comprehend! But it is not of that I speak: there is something more in this — something evil —"

Isabella smiled wearily, and shook her head.

"Rumour and imagination, love, of that I feel convinced! Let us leave the subject, I beg you, for I find it tedious."

Amanda glanced at her sister, and saw with surprise that her face was tired and drawn. Compunction seized her. Bella did not appear to have much joy of her engagement; it would be unkind to tease her any more on the subject at present. But decision hardened within her. She was determined to know for certain the truth of these rumours she had heard, and if Charles Barsett should prove to be what she thought him she would move heaven and earth to save Bella from his clutches. She fancied that there was one person, at least, who might help her by telling more of what he knew concerning the Abbey. She determined to seek him out as soon as possible, and then remembered that she would in all probability meet him in St. James's Square on the morrow. With that for the moment she had to be content.

Charles Barsett had for some years maintained a bachelor establishment in Albemarle Street. The arrangement suited everyone perfectly, Charles perhaps most of all, but it did put certain difficulties in the way of his entertaining his betrothed. On this account, my Lord Barsett had decided to invite the Twyford family to dine in St. James's Square. Even in fashionable London, dinner was an early meal, and so the party arrived in daylight. Hours of anxious consultation had resulted in the choice of a dull green silk for Isabella, open at the front to reveal a petticoat of oyster satin embroidered with sprays of yellow flowers. The green of the dress enhanced the lights in her hazel eyes, and her golden curls shone as though polished with silk.

Her mother gave her a complacent look as the party were shown into the drawing-room. No one could look handsomer than Isabella when the dear child was in looks; Amanda, in her simple white gown with its tiny embroidered sprays of blue flowers, was nothing to her. And yet — Lady Twyford anxiously scanned the faces of her two daughters — that dimple which lurked at the corner of Amanda's wide, generous mouth, the twinkle in her light blue eyes, these spoke of a happiness which seemed conspicuously wanting in Isabella's countenance. Bah! The child was nervous, my lady told herself, a thing perfectly natural and proper in her new situation as an affianced bride.

The sight of the picture arrested them on the threshold. They all stood still for a moment, gazing up at it.

"My wife," explained Lord Barsett, shortly. "She did not survive Charles's birth."

"You are very like your mother," remarked Lady Twyford to Charles.

He bowed slightly, but before he could make any reply, Amanda said quickly, "Do you think so, Mama? I am not of your opinion. The lady in the picture has a sweet face."

Lady Twyford frowned ominously, and a lazy smile twisted Charles's mouth. "And I have not?"

"If you had, sir, you would scarce thank me for saying so," replied Amanda, with a quizzical look.

My Lord Barsett, who had been studying her attentively since her first remark, broke into a guffaw of laughter, in which the other gentlemen joined. Only Lady Twyford did not smile, but caught Amanda's eye with a warning glance.

"Miss Amanda has your measure, Charles," remarked Roger Thurlston, still chuckling.

Charles Barsett regarded her gravely for a moment.

"Egad, I hope not!" he said, in mock horror.

Amanda realised that she would presently be brought to book by her Mama for her outspokenness, and recklessly plunged in deeper.

"Indeed, no," she replied, with a serious air. "I judge Mr. Barsett to be a deep character, who is not to be known on a short acquaintance."

Once more the gentlemen chuckled indulgently at this sally, and a smile of pure delight appeared momentarily on Charles's face.

"You do me too much honour, madam," he said, with an extravagant bow.

"She is a sad rattle-pate, I fear!" exclaimed Lady Twyford, thinking that her younger daughter had been allowed enough licence. "Amanda, dearest, you are not in the schoolroom now, recollect!"

Amanda was silent for a moment, not, as her mother hoped, because she had felt the justice of the reproof. She was feeling a little chagrined at her lack of success in goading Mr. Barsett. Grudgingly, she was obliged to admit to herself that, fiend though he was, the man undoubtedly possessed a sense of humour — in Amanda's view, one of the most necessary of the virtues.

Mrs. Thurlston now gave a skilful turn to the conversation. She was a thin, elegant woman with a faint air about her of long-suffering. Amanda disliked her on sight, and wondered how it was that such a pleasant gentleman as Mr. Thurlston came to have such a very disagreeable mother and cousin. Mr. Thurlston himself was very attentive to her, and she soon began to enjoy herself. If this was a sample of life in Town, then perhaps she could, to a certain extent, understand Bella's enthusiasm for it. There was something vastly agreeable in having a gentleman at one's side dancing attendance on one, and all the while making airy, amusing conversation. She laughed a great deal, her blue eyes sparkled with animation, and her cheeks were becomingly tinged with colour.

From the other side of the great dining table, with its glitter of silver and gleam of glass, Charles Barsett considered her with an ironic glance. Then he turned to the quiet, subdued girl at his side, the girl he was soon to marry.

"We now have an opportunity, Isabella," he drawled, "of becoming better acquainted."

She started a little at his use of her name. He looked amused.

"You would perhaps prefer that I do not call you by your Christian name?" he asked ironically. "You find it a trifle ah — intimate?"

"I —" Isabella choked, and could not for a moment continue. "Of — of course, you must use it if you wish — it is just that — it seems so strange —"

He waited until the end of her stumbling explanation, not attempting to help her out.

"Many things," he reminded her, with a twisted smile, "will seem strange from now on."

She blushed, and looked down at her plate.

"I — I suppose so," she answered, in a voice a little above a whisper.

His smile widened, and he considered her out of half-closed eyes, as she remained motionless, head bent, cheeks flushed. The shapely hand that held her knife quivered slightly.

A dutiful, obedient daughter, he thought, remembering his father's words; yes, she is that. Poor fool, why doesn't she fight back, give me a run for my money? That might be sport — but this is an imperfect world, Charles, my boy. You must not look for more than duty and obedience in a wife. And she is handsome — she will do very well.

Across the table, Amanda had noticed her sister's discomfiture, and turned impetuously to her neighbour.

"I wonder what your odious cousin has said to make Isabella look so wretched? 'Pon rep, he is a monster!"

The enormity of making such a comment to a member of Mr. Barsett's own family suddenly smote her, and she put her hand quickly over her lips in a gesture of dismay.

"Oh! I beg your pardon! What have I said?"

"Don't put yourself about," he answered reassuringly. "We have all at times given vent to unguarded expressions of opinion, and yours is a frank and open nature. Truth to tell, I feel a little as you do." He glanced surreptitiously at Isabella. "Your sister is discomposed. Charles must have been clumsy."

"I believe it was deliberate!" declared Amanda emphatically. Then, with a change of tone, "But I must not offend you again."

He shook his head, smiling. She leaned a little nearer, and said in a low, urgent tone, "Mr. Thurlston. There is something I must confide to you."

He encouraged her with a look, but made no other reply.

"You may remember that I told you I had met a gentleman in the grounds of — of that place that shall be nameless? Well, I am convinced that it was none other than your cousin!"

She glanced at him sharply to see how he took this information.

"Quietly," he admonished her, in a low voice. "We draw attention to ourselves."

She looked up and met her mother's eyes upon her in a warning glance. No one other than Mr. Thurlston could possibly have heard the words she had spoken; evidently her manner had been at fault.

"See if you cannot smile a little," he suggested, in the same subdued tone. "Make believe that we are conducting a trifling conversation. Yes, that's better."

Amanda, quick to benefit from instruction, was endeavouring to follow out his directions.

"You are not surprised at what I tell you," she accused.

"No. That is because I already know of my cousin's connection with the Abbey."

"What is the place? What goes on there?" asked Amanda eagerly. "Is it — something shameful?"

He forgot his caution for a moment, and gave her a grave look.

"I may not tell you what I know. Please forgive me, and forbear to question me further on that subject."

"But I cannot!" burst out Amanda, in deep disappointment. "Who is to tell me, if not you? You surely can't be so unkind!".

"Why not ask my cousin?" he suggested, with a mocking lift of his eyebrows which momentarily gave him a fleeting resemblance to Charles Barsett.

"'Pon rep, I've a mind to do it!"

He looked at her curiously.

"Would you dare? Ah, I see I have said the wrong thing. I might have known that one of your spirit — but, seriously, Miss Amanda, I don't advise such a step."

"Do you not?" she replied, with a tilt of her determined chin. "And why not, pray?"

"I have already told you. It is not a fit subject —"

"La, sir! Is your cousin then such a model of propriety?"

"Quite the reverse — though he is the best of fellows, of course. But you would not wish to be doing anything improper, I know."

"Then you know me very little," said Amanda with a defiant laugh. "I have had my fill of propriety during my years under a governess, and am now ready to fling my bonnet over the windmill!"

"You will think better of it," he said, smiling at her.

She shook her head, but said no more. She was quite determined to solve this stupid mystery, and did not greatly care how she came at a solution. As for Charles Barsett, she thought nothing of lowering herself in his eyes. She told herself that she would dearly love to shock him, if such a thing were possible.

Dinner over, the ladies rose to leave the gentlemen over their wine for a space. Mrs. Thurlston led the way back into the drawing-room, and, seating herself beside Lady Twyford, began a conversation.

"So very charming a girl, your eldest daughter, if I may say so. Charles is fortunate indeed."

"There is good fortune on both sides, I believe," replied my lady, complacently.

"To be sure, oh, yes. Charles, of course, has been somewhat of a disappointment to his father, but I daresay all that is past, now that he is to wed. And dear Isabella must be a steadying influence upon any man, I am sure. It is strange, is it not, how different blood relations can be? My own son, Roger, has never given us a moment's uneasiness."

Lady Twyford made some polite reply, and signalled with her eyes to Amanda to come over to the sofa where she and Mrs. Thurlston were sitting. She wanted to have a few moments' conversation with Isabella, who was standing by the spinet, idly turning over some music, an air of dejection on her lovely face. Amanda, always quick to take a hint, obeyed, and after Lady Twyford had drawn her younger daughter into conversation with Mrs. Thurlston, she rose and went over to the elder girl.

"Isabella!" she said sharply, in a low tone that could not carry to the others. "Whatever is amiss with you?"

"I don't know what you mean, Mama," replied Isabella, in a dull voice.

"This mooning air of yours, and the lack of your usual spirits. This is no way, silly girl, to hold a man. Why, Mr. Barsett looked positively bored at dinner."

"I cannot help it," said Isabella, a shade truculently. "I do not happen to feel in spirits today."

"Then you had better look to your interest, and pull yourself together. A man wants something more from his betrothed than blushes and a straight face! You can be animated enough when you choose — why, I remember only a few short months ago, at the Hunt Ball —"

"Pray, Mama, do not speak of that." Lady Twyford looked in amazement at the pain in her daughter's voice. What could ail the child? Nerves, she supposed.

"Well, well," she said soothingly. "It is one thing, to be sure, to flirt with an agreeable young man, and quite another to know how best to conduct oneself with one's affianced! But you need have no fears, my child; Mr. Barsett has been about the world a little, and will do nothing to embarrass you — you may safely be a little less guarded, more animated, more yourself. It will not do to make him tired of you quite so soon."

"You think he — feels anything at all for me, Mama?"

The words were painfully drawn out of her. Her mother looked at her pale face in alarm.

"To be sure he does! Or, at least, that must depend upon you. Gentlemen are only too ready to fall in love, but we must give them some small encouragement — as much as is proper, of course. He cannot fail to admire you, lovely as you are — though perhaps I should not say so! See to it that he finds you gay and charming as well, and his conquest is complete. No more of these dull looks and missish airs, I charge you strictly, mind."

"Very well, Mama, I'll — I'll try," whispered Isabella dutifully and at that moment the gentlemen came into the room.

Music was proposed, and Isabella prevailed upon to sit down at the instrument. Charles Barsett moved to her side, in order to turn the pages of the music for her; Lady Twyford noticed with approval that her daughter gave him a coy look that must, reflected the lady, have been vastly fetching. Indeed, there was now a welcome change in Isabella's manner. She chatted and laughed a great deal, in the intervals between one piece of music and another, and glanced roguishly out of her bewitching hazel eyes at Charles. Two spots of colour tinged the cheeks that had been pale before, and when she talked her hands fluttered restlessly.

Amanda noticed this with a frown, and watched Charles Barsett's reaction to it, but there was no reading anything into his habitual expression of bored cynicism. Presently she was invited to take her sister's place at the spinet. By what she afterwards saw was an unlucky chance, she broke into the opening chords of 'Barbara Allen'. It was an old family favourite, and had been sung in the past on many an evening when John Webster and his parents had been dining with the Twyfords. Amanda's clear, childish treble underlined the pathos of the simple words.

"All in the merry month of May When green buds they were swellin', Young Jemmy Grove on his death-bed lay For love of Barbara Allen."

As she sang the final verse, her glance strayed across the room to her sister. To her dismay, she saw that Isabella's eyes were misty, and realised that she was not far from tears.

"Oh, do let us have something gay!" cried Amanda, crashing a last chord in undue haste. "I know what — Mr. Thurlston and his cousin shall dance us a reel!"

There was a general laugh at this. Charles Barsett sauntered over towards her.

"A splendid notion," he approved, in his lazy drawl. "But Roger and myself are ill-sorted partners. Perchance you and I, Miss Amanda, might cut a better caper."

"You think so?" she replied, smiling archly.

She was thankful to focus the attention of the room upon herself for a while: it might give Isabella a chance to recover.

"I am nearly sure of it," he answered, with his twisted smile.

"Oh, no, sir," protested Amanda, giving him a meaning look. "I am not yet sufficiently versed in the art of the dance to do you credit. After all, I am only a schoolgirl."

There was a pregnant pause. Out of the corner of her eye Amanda observed that Isabella had recovered, and was watching her sister in amazement.

"But no!" protested Charles Barsett gently. "What can make you say such a thing?"

"Someone told me so once," said Amanda, looking him straight between the eyes. "A curious schoolgirl — that was the expression, if I remember rightly."

"Indeed?" He raised his quizzing glass, and studied her attentively. "It was — ungallant of — the person concerned."

"He was an ungallant person," stated Amanda, forthrightly.

At this point, Lady Twyford considered that it was high time to put an end to this extraordinary conversation.

"La, child!" she exclaimed impatiently. "How you do run on! Really, she says the oddest things, my Lord," she apologised, turning to Lord Barsett, who sat beside her.

"I knew someone else, once," he answered, reminiscently, "who said — and did — the oddest things. It did not prevent her from being the most charming woman on earth."

And he looked up at the portrait over the mantelshelf. All present followed his gaze.

"Thank you, my lord," said Amanda, softly.

Chapter VII: The Conspiracy

Amanda awoke early the next morning. She leapt out of bed, and drew the curtains hastily back from the window. Bright spring sunshine flooded into the room; across the rooftops the fresh green of the budding trees in the park caught her gaze. On a sudden impulse, she decided to go riding; Isabella had told her that everyone went riding, driving or walking in the park when the weather was fine. However, she supposed that she would scarcely encounter many people there at this hour. It was close on seven o'clock, an unfashionable time of day in Town.

Quickly donning a smart brown riding habit and a tricorne hat trimmed with yellow plumes, she made her way quietly to the stables. Here she encountered Tom, busy polishing the harness. She asked him to saddle her mare.

"Will you be wantin' me to go with you, Miss?" he asked, as he set about the task.

She shook her head. "It's only a step away, Tom, and I daresay you have enough to do."

Tom looked troubled. "Reckon as 'ow 'er ladyship wouldn't like for you to go off on your own, beggin' your pardon, Miss."

"Nonsense," said Amanda, briskly. "Anyway, my lady cannot mind, for she will not know; she is not yet astir and I shall be back directly for breakfast."

The groom did not presume to argue the matter further, and leading out the horse, assisted his mistress to mount.

A short trot brought her to the park. She had judged aright: at that hour it was deserted. She found an open stretch of ground and urged the mare to a gallop. She and the horse moved in one rhythm, the air seeming to rush towards them, her curls blowing back from her face. She reined in at last, exhilarated and panting slightly, with flushed cheeks. She leaned over and patted the animal's neck.

"Good girl, Sukey! That was prodigious."

It was then that she noticed a figure strolling aimlessly in her direction. A second glance told her that it was John Webster. She hailed him with delight, and rode forward to meet him. He put out a hand to assist her to alight, but she came lightly down without his aid, and stood beside him on the grass.

"Of all people, you are the very one I most wished to see!" she exclaimed animatedly.

He looked at her with lacklustre eyes.

"I'm glad to see you, too, Mandy. I — I'm sorry — about the other day."

"You mean when you charged past me in our house with scarce a word?" she asked, with a little teasing smile.

"It was abominable of me to be so rude! But —"

"I know!" she broke in gently, seeing that he was uncertain how to finish. "Bella told me all."

"All?" His tone was something between anxious and eager.

Amanda studied him with compassion in her blue eyes.

"Well, at any rate, she told me that you'd offered for her, and that she had refused you," she replied gently.

"So now you know why I was blue-devilled," he said shortly.

There was a pause of several minutes. He stared out unhappily over the fresh green of the sunlit grass.

"I suppose," he said at last, awkwardly, "I suppose she has — accepted that other fellow?"

Amanda nodded sympathetically.

"But I don't believe she has much joy of the contract, John, give you my word! You should have seen the miserable countenance she put on yesterday evening when we were all dining at my Lord Barsett's! And later, when I sang 'Barbara Allen', she was close to tears."

This seeming betrayal of her sister was calculated to put some heart into John. Amanda felt very strongly that, in accepting Mr. Barsett, Isabella had chosen against the dictates of her own feelings and under the compulsion of her mother's persuasion. There could be no doubt in Amanda's mind that her sister truly loved John Webster, and therefore no good reason for discouraging his suit of Bella. Her efforts appeared to have small success, however, for he shook his head dismally.

"She may perhaps feel some sentimental attachment to what is past," he said, in a bitter tone, "but she made it quite clear that nothing would prevent her from marrying Barsett. Your mother has fired her with ambition, and I can offer nothing to compete with his possessions."

"Then what do you mean to do?"

He stared at her, and shrugged hopelessly.

"What is there to do? I thought that perhaps I might make the Grand Tour. I have never travelled beyond spending a week or two in France; and at least I shall be far away when the marriage takes place. I shall perhaps have accustomed myself to the notion by the time I return — if, indeed, I ever return."

The last words had a tragic ring. Amanda did not seem to be impressed.

"I see," she said, bitingly. "So you mean to run away, John Webster! Have you forgotten the apple-loft?"

He shot a startled glance at her, and then grinned.

"Egad, no! What a hoyden you were in those days, Mandy."

"Perhaps we were all a little different then, but I did not think to find you so much changed. You were prepared to take a whacking on that occasion, so that I might not get into trouble, I remember."

He shrugged, and the grin widened.

"What's one whacking more or less? But you saved me by owning up, stupid creature!"

"It was no good, John; I shouldn't have slept at nights with that on my conscience. But why is it that you have grown so very poor-spirited now?"

"Poor —! Egad, that's coming it too strong, Mandy!"

"It is not," she answered, emphatically. "What else do you call it, to run away and leave Bella to marry a man whom she does not care for, and who is, moreover — I know not what, but some kind of fiend!"

"His reputation is a wild one, to be sure," he said, consideringly. "But that may alter — marriage often settles a man —"

"You sound for all the world like Mama!" she exclaimed in disgust.

"It may very well be true," he said, soberly.

"His reputation is not all the trouble." She looked about her, and sank her voice a little. "John, do you happen to have heard speak of Medmenham Abbey?"

"Of what Abbey?"

She repeated the name in a voice of foreboding. He looked puzzled at her manner, as well he might, and shook his head.

"No, should I have done? What is all the mystery?"

"That is what I would dearly love to know!" said Amanda, and forthwith told her story.

John listened in silence. Towards the end, his expression grew a shade impatient.

"Sounds all a hum to me," he pronounced, when she had done.

"'Pon rep, I don't know what is amiss with everybody!" exclaimed Amanda, in disgust. "No one, not even you, who say that you love Bella — positively no one will take my story seriously."

"You can't expect that they should," he answered, judicially. "What charges have you to make against the man but the fact that you met him in a place about which there is a deal of local gossip? You've lived in the country, Mandy — you know well just how much reliance can be placed upon the idle chit-chat of villagers!"

"There's no smoke without fire," insisted Amanda, pursing her lips. "And that blacksmith was prodigiously afraid, I give you my word! A big, burly man, too, not a weakling."

"But they're superstitious, aren't they, country folk?" asked John dubiously. "And legends gather about these ancient buildings —"

"Oh, very well," said she, in a huff. "If you are determined to believe Mr. Barsett to be an angel of light and goodness, and a fit husband for Bella, pray don't let me stop you!"

"Don't be absurd. I was only trying to —"

"To be reasonable!" finished Amanda for him, in high dudgeon. "It's being reasonable that's lost you Bella, let me inform you."

"What do you mean?"

"Well," said Amanda, now so annoyed that she did not spare his feelings, "it was only reasonable to suppose, from the way that Bella had always behaved towards you, that she was in love with you. So I suppose you took it for granted that she would accept you when you made your offer?"

"Well, yes, perhaps I did," he admitted reluctantly. "But —"

"Do not tell me. I can see it all clearly. You made your offer in such a way that she must have seen you took her acceptance for granted. Am I not right?"

He stared at her for a moment in silence.

"Perhaps I may have done," he said, at last. "But I assure you, Mandy —"

"John Webster, you're a fool! You know nothing about the way to handle females!"

"I never did set up to be a womaniser!" he retorted, with some heat.

"Don't be so superior about it. It is not a matter for pride."

"I care nothing for the affection of a female who needs to be flattered into an acceptance of my hand. Had she truly loved me, Bella would have accepted me, however clumsy my wooing."

"You —you — ninny!"

They had been hurling the last few interchanges at each other's heads with scarcely a pause for breath. They stopped now, glaring angrily.

Suddenly Amanda laughed musically.

"Do not let us quarrel, John."

He grinned sheepishly, and at once put out his hand. She placed hers within it, and his grip tightened.

"Egad, you're a regular fire-eater! And I don't like Barsett as a husband for Bella any more than you do. But, after all, one must try to be fair —"

"That is the advantage of being a female," replied Amanda, with a dimple. "One is not haunted by this notion of fair play. I do not mean to let my sister wed this man — and I shall not scruple to go to any lengths to prevent the match."

"The ruthless sex," he answered with a laugh. "But what do you mean to do?"

"I have a plan," she said, with a tinge of excitement in her voice. "It came to me in the night. You would not allow me to finish telling you, John, but this business concerning the Abbey is not only villagers' gossip as you suggest, for Mr. Thurlston has admitted to me that there have been rumours concerning it in Town. But try as I will I cannot persuade him to tell me more. I think this is very likely because it's something not considered fit for the ears of a female — and that is why I want you to help me."

"You want me to question Thurlston?" he asked, frowning. "Somewhat difficult to ask him to discuss his own cousin's shortcomings, isn't it?"

"If only your notions were not so proper! I don't know how we are to go on unless you can lose some of them."

"Still, it isn't at all the thing, you must admit," persisted John.

"Oh, you can surely work the conversation round to the subject," exclaimed Amanda impatiently. "And if not, perhaps you can manage to learn something at the clubs — you do belong to some of these clubs, do you not?"

He nodded. "Your father put me up for the Cocoa Tree and White's when I first arrived in Town, but I don't patronise them much of late."

"Well, that must be remedied," said Amanda, forcefully. "Henceforward, you must go there every day, and keep your ears open. And we must both watch Charles Barsett. Do you suppose you can contrive an invitation to his house? I may scarcely go there."

He stared at this suggestion. "Why should I desire an invitation to the fellow's house? Lord knows, he is the last from whom I should seek friendship."

Amanda wrinkled her nose at him.

"Stupid! Why, to spy upon him, of course!"

He looked at her in horror. "Spy upon him?"

"Do not tell me that it isn't at all the thing," she warned him, "or I shall do you a mischief! There may be something to be discovered there — some letter left lying about, a scrap of conversation you may manage to overhear —"

"Good God, Amanda! Can you suppose that I could possibly —"

"If you do not, I shall. Can you not see that all's fair in love and war?"

He made no answer to this, but kicked at a stone lying on the grass.

"Do you want Bella to marry this man?" insisted his tormentor.

"You know I do not. But if she has chosen him —"

"To expose his character to her would soon put an end to that," replied Amanda, confidently. "There is no love between them. It is purely a marriage of convenience."

"Are you sure? He must admire her — who could not?"

She looked at him pityingly. "Poor John! You are head over ears, aren't you? Perhaps that is the trouble."

"What do you mean?"

"Nothing, only that Bella is used to admiration. Perhaps a little indifference might be more stimulating to her."

"I've already told you —"

"Yes, I know," she interrupted him, "you are not a — how did you put it? — a womaniser. It's a pity — but we must not allow ourselves to argue again," she put in hastily, as she saw that he was about to speak. "We must concentrate upon the purpose in hand. Do you agree to my plan?"

He hesitated. "I don't like it, Mandy."

"Very well." She elevated her chin. "I must do the best I can on my own account."

"No!" He seized her hand, alarmed. "You mustn't embroil yourself in such an affair. Oh, very well, I'll do what I can; but don't expect me to spy upon Barsett, mind, for I won't undertake it."

"No matter," said Amanda, prepared to make concessions so long as she had gained her point. "There may be some other way, just so long as you can bring me the gossip from the clubs. We must meet here again — what say you to Thursday, at this hour? That will give you three days in which to find out something."

He agreed reluctantly.

"And cheer up," she said, as a parting shot. "You are the one Bella loves, of that I am certain, and who should know her better than I?"

"I only hope you may be right," he replied, as he assisted her to mount.

"Of course I'm right. Goodbye, John, don't forget — Thursday, here. I have great hopes of you."

She waved airily and was gone. He watched until she was out of sight, then shrugged moodily, and took his way home, deep in thought.

It was to be a frustrating day for Amanda, in spite of this promising start to it. When she returned home, she found her mother and sister had already risen, and were inquiring for her. Her airy explanation of having gone riding in the park on impulse brought down trouble on her head for venturing out unattended.

"I positively forbid you to go riding without your sister — or else a groom in attendance," snapped Lady Twyford, who had slept ill, and was consequently not in the best of humours.

"But, Mama, that is absurd," flashed Amanda. "Why, in the country I was used to ride for miles without an escort."

"That is no way to address me, Miss," my lady reminded her acidly. "Foolish child, have I not told you that what will do very well in the country is not permissible here in Town? 'Pon rep, if you are ever to get a husband you must mend your ways, and cease to behave like a schoolgirl!"

This unfortunate remark precipitated an outburst in which Amanda was understood to say (though not altogether coherently) that she had better things to think of than getting a husband, and that any gentleman whom she chose to honour with her hand must make the best of her as she was. She then retired to her bedchamber, where she stamped her feet several times, ripped the plumes off a bonnet which she had always disliked, and then felt a great deal better. She returned to the morning-room a very angel of placidity, made an affectionate apology to her Mama which was graciously received, and the incident was shelved.

But ill-luck seemed to dog her footsteps for the rest of the day. Mr. Thurlston paid a morning call, but Isabella and Lady Twyford did not leave her alone with him, so she had no chance of trying him further to see if he would tell her anything more on the subject which at present occupied her thoughts to the exclusion of all others. Apart from this little rub, the visit passed off pleasantly enough, for he was an amusing companion. She found herself laughing in spite of her preoccupation, and felt a tinge of regret when he finally rose to go.

Her next disappointment lay in the failure of her attempts to have a heart-to-heart talk with Isabella. After leaving John earlier in the day, she had determined to do this: Bella must be made to undertake some serious soul-searching in regard to her engagement. Perversely, Bella refused to co-operate. Her manner was gay and carefree to the point of abandon, and she laughed to scorn all Amanda's suggestions that underneath this sparkling façade lay a broken heart. Once again she recommended her younger sister to curb her sense of the dramatic. It was almost too much for Amanda, after her mother's earlier remarks.

She rallied, however, and had high hopes that the evening might bring them into company with Mr. Barsett. She had not entirely forgotten Roger Thurlston's jesting suggestion that she might tax his cousin with her questions: as Mr. Thurlston had afterwards realised with dismay, she was quite capable of doing this, if no other way presented itself. As it happened, she was not given the opportunity, for it turned out that Charles Barsett had a prior engagement for that evening, and was not to see his betrothed until the next day, when he was to attend the whole family to the Opera.

Amanda sought her bed that night in no very restful frame of mind. She was a great planner, and liked to put her plans into execution immediately. All this inaction chafed her, and it was only the hope that perhaps John Webster had been more fortunate than herself in uncovering information that finally soothed her to sleep.

The following day brought Mr. Thurlston calling again, a circumstance which caused Lady Twyford to make certain remarks to her younger daughter.

"We are seeing a vast deal of Mr. Thurlston, Amanda."

"Are we, Mama? Yes, perhaps so. Don't you think him very agreeable, however?"

Lady Twyford glanced sharply at her, but was disarmed by the ingenuous expression of her face.

"Very," she answered dryly. "But I feel that I must warn you, child, that his expectations cannot be great. He will have nothing but what my Lord Barsett chooses to settle upon him, and rumour has it that his cousin is not —" she hesitated — "is not predisposed in his favour."

"Warn me?" Amanda's blue eyes grew round in surprise. "What, pray, can I possibly have to say to Mr. Thurlston's expectations, Mama?"

"Nothing, child, nothing," said her mother, hastily drawing her embroidery frame towards her. "Your eyesight is keener than mine: would you say that this blue is the same shade as the one I have used in that cluster of flowers?"

Amanda dutifully inspected the silk, and decided against it, but was quite aware of her mother's subterfuge. So Mama was considering Mr. Thurlston in the light of a possible suitor, was she? Amanda allowed her thoughts to play round the notion, and discovered that she did not dislike it. He was handsome, agreeable, everything that a gentleman should be; he was, perhaps, just a trifle old — full ten years her senior. Still, she had the notion that, if and when she married, she would prefer her husband to be some years older than herself. She was not unaware of a certain impulsiveness in her character, which her strong common sense warned her would be the better for a restraining hand. Younger men were, in general, themselves too impulsive to supply this need. But she had as yet no serious thought of marriage, which she tended to look upon as a necessary evil which must, at some time in the future, overtake her. Until that time, she wanted only to amuse herself; besides, there was this business concerning Bella to occupy her attention.

It filled her thoughts for the rest of the day, and only when she was seated with her family and Charles Barsett in a box at the Opera did she allow herself to be momentarily diverted. The scene was such a splendid one; never had she viewed so much finery at one gathering. The array of costly silk and brocades in all the colours of the rainbow; the nodding plumes of the women, and the jewels which glittered in the blaze of candlelight left her quite awestruck.

Charles Barsett glanced at her speaking countenance, and a little smile which for once contained nothing of mockery curved the corners of his mouth. He sat next to Isabella, as was to be expected; on his left hand was my Lord Twyford. Amanda was seated at her father's other side. The lights dimmed even as she was gazing her fill at the splendour of the audience, and she transferred her attention to the stage as the first chords of music sounded from the orchestra, and the curtain began slowly to rise.

The piece was Dr. Arne's 'Ataxerxes', with Charlotte Brent singing the part of Mandane. Her high, flexible soprano voice wove its way effortlessly through the intricacies of the music. Amanda, listening now intently, forgot her plans, her fears for Bella, her distrust of Charles Barsett: all gave way before the flood of melody which engulfed her spirit.

She came to at last with a start, to realise that the lights were blazing in the theatre, and a swelling murmur of conversation rising from the audience. A discreet knock sounded on the door of their box, and a footman entered. He bowed, and proffered a folded paper to Charles Barsett. Charles took it, with a slight lift of the eyebrows.

"You will forgive me, Isabella — my lord —?" He excused himself to his neighbours, and, opening the paper, scanned the message it contained in one brief glance. Then he rose, thrusting the paper carelessly into a pocket in the skirts of his handsome rose satin coat, spoke a few brief words in an undertone to the servant, and returned to his seat between Isabella and her father.

Amanda watched the incident with quickening interest. It might be nothing to the purpose, but she was determined to have that paper. But how to obtain it? Could she perhaps persuade her father to change places with her? If so, it might be possible to pick Mr. Barsett's pocket. To be sure, she had never attempted anything of the kind before, but it must be simple enough, surely, as hundreds of rascals made their living at it in the streets of London.

"Papa." She touched his arm. "Papa, I cannot see well as I should like. I wonder if you would mind changing places with me?"

Before her father could make any reply, Charles Barsett had risen to his feet.

"Pray sit here, Miss Amanda. I must apologise for not having seen to it that you were seated to better advantage."

She had the grace to blush even before her mother broke in.

"What nonsense is this, Amanda? I am sure we can all see perfectly! There is no difference, you must realise, whether you are here, or in your father's place. I wish you will have a little more conduct, Miss!"

But Charles Barsett was insistent, in his urbane way, upon changing places with her, and Amanda made the exchange with a feeling of having one more item to add to the score of resentment against him. She had succeeded in making herself appear ill-mannered without either achieving her design, or coming any nearer to doing so.

She clenched her white, even teeth behind the cover of her fan. The remainder of the performance failed to charm her, her mind was preoccupied with plans for gaining possession of the note. None of these appeared satisfactory even to her optimistic eye.

As so often happens, her opportunity came at last by chance, not by scheming. At the conclusion of the performance a great mass of people congregated in the entrance hall awaiting the carriages which were to bear them homewards. As the vehicles drew up outside, there was a sudden unmannerly surge forward in the region where Amanda and her party were standing; for a few moments she was tightly pressed against Charles Barsett. Her eye had noted the position of the pocket where he had thrust the note: now her hand went out swiftly, exploring.

Her fingers closed around the paper. She withdrew it, and with a hand that trembled slightly, thrust it into the bodice of her low-cut gown. The whole operation did not take more than a few seconds, and she felt sure that no one could have noticed, shielded as she had been from view of her victim's body.

The pressure eased, and presently my Lord Twyford's carriage was called. Just as the party moved towards it an acquaintance detained Lord Twyford for a moment in conversation. The others went on, and Charles Barsett dutifully stood to hand the ladies into the coach. Amanda came last. He took her hand, and she stooped to enter the vehicle, one foot on the step.

Suddenly a little gust of wind took the paper, which in her haste she had tucked away too insecurely. It fluttered to the ground, opening to reveal a few lines of writing. With an inarticulate little cry, Amanda stooped to retrieve it.

Charles Barsett was before her. The diamond buckle on his shoe glinted as he smartly set one foot on the paper, and bent to pick it up. It seemed to the watching, scarlet-faced girl a long time before he straightened up again. Then he handed her the note with a deep bow. A diabolical smile curved his lips.

"I believe this is yours?" he said.

Chapter VIII: Strange Behaviour of a Rake

"And that was how I gained possession of it!" said Amanda triumphantly. "But, oh, John, it was dreadful when he picked it up and handed it to me! I thought I should die of mortification. He cannot have failed to recognise it, for it had blown open."

John Webster grimaced, and turned the note over in his hands.

"I wouldn't have been in your shoes, not for any sum you could name," he said candidly. "But the fellow can't be so bad, Mandy, after all. At least he didn't denounce you."

"Oh, I grant that his manners are in general perfect," said Amanda, with emphasis. "It is only his principles that are at fault. A small matter, perhaps, but I had rather see my sister wed to an ill-mannered man than to one lacking in morals."

"Egad, I don't quite know how to take that," protested John.

She laughed. "Take it that I consider you the perfect husband for Bella, and we shall both be agreed. John, what can you make of that letter?"

He looked once more at the paper, a deep frown marring his handsome face. Only two lines of writing appeared upon the paper, inscribed in a scholarly hand.

At Hanover Square next Monday at eight. Do not fail me.
Brother Francis.

"It's an ordinary enough note," he said slowly, "apart from the signature. Barsett has no brother, as we are aware."

"Exactly!" Amanda's voice quivered with eagerness. "Then what can the signature mean, John, would you say?"

"It sounds like a jest," he answered doubtfully. "A kind of nickname — the sort of thing we used to do at school. There was one fellow whom we called —"

"Spare me a recital of the nicknames of every boy who ever went to school with you!" exclaimed Amanda impatiently. "It is nothing to the purpose, and only wastes time."

"Oh, very well," he replied huffily. "I fear I have nothing more to add to the discussion."

"Now don't be in a miff," coaxed Amanda, laying a hand on his arm. "If we are to quarrel, I don't know who will help me to save Bella. Besides, I think your suggestion a very sound one."

His face lightened. "Well, I'm deuced glad to hear I can please you in some way," he said, rather in the manner of a small boy. "You seemed so put out at my failure to gather any information at the clubs."

"Well, it was disappointing," confessed Amanda. "I'd counted so much on your hearing what Mr. Thurlston assures me is common gossip. I wish he would not be so reticent," she added with a touch of despair.

"You can't expect him to peach on his own cousin," said John, matter-of-factly. "Even though I've heard that Barsett hasn't behaved any too well towards him in the past."

"I've heard that too," said Amanda. "But so far I can't discover what he's supposed to have done."

"No, well, it's all a thought vague; such things often are. I collect that he's tried to poison my Lord Barsett's mind against his cousin with a view to getting him turned out of the house."

A light frown touched Amanda's brow fleetingly.

"Yet he doesn't seem to have succeeded. Strange — I should have thought him too clever to fail at what must surely be a reasonably simple matter."

"Why simple?"

"Well, after all, he is Lord Barsett's son. He must have some influence with his father."

"Rumour has it that there is very little sympathy between father and son. My Lord Barsett worshipped his wife, according to report, and she died giving birth to the child."

"Yes," said Amanda slowly. "Mrs. Thurlston was recounting the story to Mama the other evening — I overheard some of it. She said that my lord could not bear the sight of the child for a long time afterwards." She paused, a pensive expression on her face. "I did not think of it before, John, but it can be no very pleasant thing to lose one's mother, and have one's father take one in dislike. He must have been a very unhappy little boy."

"Oh, I don't know," said John, a shade uncomfortably. This sudden access of sentimentality on Amanda's part made him embarrassed. "There would be a nurse, you know —and then there was his aunt and cousin."

"She is a detestable woman. I dislike her profoundly. Small wonder that Mr. Barsett should have such an odious disposition."

"Has he?" asked John.

She stared. "Have I not told you so?"

"Yes — oh, to be sure. But —"

"But what?" she asked haughtily. "Do you doubt my word?"

"No," he said hurriedly, "nothing of the kind. But I know you sometimes —" He stopped short.

"I wish you will finish what you are saying," she exclaimed impatiently. "So much is left to conjecture with all these ifs and buts."

He gave a quick laugh. "The truth is, I'm half afraid of you, Mandy. You can be such a fire-eater! What I intended to say was that you are a thought impulsive in your likes and dislikes.

This man found you trespassing, and ordered you off with something less than his usual civility. That is all you know to his discredit.”

Two spots of colour appeared in Amanda’s cheeks. “You can say that? After all that you, too, have heard against him?”

“But that is, after all, only hearsay,” insisted John.

“’Pon rep! Never did I hear the like! Why should so many people say these things if there is no truth in them, pray?”

“Fashionable London is a malicious place,” said John sagely. “I have been here long enough to learn that much. One ill-disposed person begins a rumour, and in no time it is on everyone’s lips.”

“Upon my word, I do not understand you,” exclaimed Amanda, disgust etched in every line of her. “What interest can you possibly have in establishing the fairness of Mr. Barsett’s character, I should like to know? At any rate, you cannot deny that he seeks to force Isabella into a loveless marriage.”

John frowned, and considered this. “That is just what I do deny,” he said at last. “No one but her parents can have the power to force Bella in such a matter, and they would not do so, particularly not your father, with whom the authority must rest finally. You know she is not coerced, Mandy. She herself must desire the marriage.”

“Oh, you are impossible!”

She snatched the letter from his hands, and considered it again. “Do you know what I think, John?”

Her mood had now changed completely; the anger was gone, and a note of excitement had crept into her voice. She did not wait for any reply. “You remember the blacksmith spoke of monks having sometimes been seen on the lawns of the Abbey? He believed them to be spectres, but suppose they were not? Suppose they were human, and this Francis is one of them?"

"I don't quite see — are you suggesting that Barsett is a Papist? That he belongs to some religious order? But no, that does not accord with his behaviour, nor with the tenor of this note. I tell you it is some jest — a nickname —"

"That may be. I cannot account for it any better than you. But I am determined to know who this Brother Francis may be. John, do you think you can discover it for me?"

He gaped at her. "How do you suggest I go about it? There is little enough to go on here, in all conscience."

"There is the place and time of the meeting," she pointed out. "Hanover Square is not, after all, so very large. If you could be there on Monday evening, and observe which house Charles Barsett enters, it should not be too difficult a matter to find out the name of the owner of the place."

He looked uncertain. "I've told you already that I have no fancy to play the spy. Besides, there is one circumstance which puts such a course out of the question."

"And that is —?" asked Amanda with ill-concealed impatience.

"I don't know the fellow by sight. It so happens that I've never yet met him."

Amanda was momentarily taken aback. "But you must have done — you've been in London for close on two months. You were at the ball which Mama gave before I arrived, and Bella tells me that he was present at that —"

"So were nearly a hundred others. Besides, I had no eyes for anyone but Bella."

She sighed. "Well, there is no help for it: I must contrive to go myself."

He started. "Good God, Mandy, you don't know what you're saying! *You* cannot loiter about the streets of London alone."

"You could accompany me," she began eagerly. "I will find some excuse —"

"There must be a simpler way," he cut in abruptly. "No doubt I can find someone to present me to him — though on what pretext I cannot think."

Amanda's eyes glinted. "But I can," she said quickly. "He is engaged to take a dish of tea with us this very afternoon. Why do you not call in upon us then? It can occasion no remark, for as an old friend of the family you must always be welcome."

He shook his head decidedly. "No. I do not wish to encounter Bella — particularly not in his company!"

She thought rapidly for a minute. "Then I will present you myself," she exclaimed at last in triumph. "We will call at his house in Albemarle Street — I cannot manage it today, unfortunately — tomorrow, at eleven."

John pursed his lips, considering this. "Scarcely proper. You should have another female with you."

"Fustian! Are we not almost brother and sister?"

"I suppose one might say so: perhaps that is why Bella —"

"Oh, bother Bella!" exclaimed her impatient sister. "Let us keep to the point for once, I beg! Do you agree to my plan?"

"I suppose so," he answered, reluctantly. "But on what pretext are we to call?"

"Simply that I want to present you to him — as an old friend of the family —"

"Not nearly convincing enough," he demurred. "You are not usually in the way of paying him so much attention, are you?"

For a moment she was at a loss. "No — no, I'm not; that is true enough. But I would dearly love to gain an entry to his house, for there is no saying what I may be able to find there.

If you can only contrive to engage him in conversation while I conduct a search —" She paused at sight of his horror-stricken face.

"I'll be a party to no such hare-brained scheme. Good God, Amanda, you must be off your head!"

She set her small teeth. "Nothing will deter me from preventing a marriage between Bella and that — that monster! For the last time, John Webster, do you mean to help me or not?"

"Oh, of course — to be sure." He tried to soothe her. "But are you quite certain we may not do more harm than good by such means? If we were to be discovered, and Bella should learn from Barsett that I have taken part in such an escapade, she may despise me more than ever. How will that further my cause with her?"

"We shan't be discovered, silly! Do you forget all the affairs of the kind which we've managed successfully in the past?"

"We were children then: this is different."

"Yes, but only because it matters more. That is just why we must not, cannot fail! Now, I have a splendid idea. You find that you are obliged to leave Town suddenly, and do not wish to go without having first met the betrothed of the girl whom you have known since childhood. You wish to carry back some account of him to your parents, very dear friends of our family. You call upon me to take you to Mr. Barsett. How does that sound?"

"Thin," he protested. "Why do I not call upon my Lord Twyford to perform this office for me? And why must I leave Town in such frantic haste, anyway?"

"Really!" exclaimed Amanda in exasperation. "You do nothing but make difficulties. However, I can deal with your first one: my father will be at Tattersall's tomorrow morning to buy a horse. Mama and Bella will be out shopping — so should I, but I intend to have a headache, or some other malaise. You will call upon us, and there will be only myself to aid you."

"I am lost in admiration," he said dryly. "And what of my second objection?"

"Really, I think it is very hard on Bella to expect her to wed a man with so little imagination as yourself. Your father is ill — urgent family matters — an unexpected visitor to your home who hasn't seen you since childhood. I can think of a score of excuses."

He laughed, and catching her unexpectedly by the waist, swung her bodily into the air. "Oh, Mandy, Mandy! You are a terrible child!"

He placed her on her feet again, his hands resting lightly against her sides, and gazed intently into her slightly flushed face. "But you are also a lovely girl," he said, wonderingly. "I never noticed it before."

She looked up at him under her lashes with a coy little smile that yet was as innocent as a child's.

"Am I? Thank you kindly, sir. And now I must be off before Mama and Bella are stirring. Do not forget — tomorrow, between ten and eleven. I will get word to you if there should be any change."

She shook herself lightly free of his grasp, and turned to mount her horse.

"No, one moment, Mandy!"

There was a new note in his voice. She turned towards him, with arched brows. "What is it?"

Her look was clear and ingenuous. His eyes dropped before it.

"Oh, nothing. I'll be there."

He helped her to mount, and stood still for a moment, watching her ride away.

That afternoon, Charles Barsett waited upon his betrothed. Tea and general conversation formed the early part of the visit, but my Lady Twyford soon found an excuse to leave the affianced couple alone. In her view, it could do no harm for the pair to become better acquainted. To be sure, Isabella was acting more in her own interests since her Mama's timely warning, and the engagement would be announced in the newspapers in a day or two; but there's many a slip, reflected my lady, and at present the gentleman appeared disconcertingly heart-whole.

After she had left the two together, a short silence fell between them. Mr. Barsett was the first to break it. "I beg," he said, formally, "that you will inform me, madam, when I may look to find myself the happiest of men."

Her hazel eyes widened, whether with fear or surprise he could not determine.

"I — I do not know what you mean," she stammered.

"Come, it is plain, is it not?" His tone was gentle and forbearing. "I ask you to name our wedding day."

This time there was no mistaking the dismay that overspread her countenance. He watched her gravely.

"I —" Isabella stopped short, then, rallying her forces with an apparent effort, continued, "I had not considered the matter. There is no need for haste, is there, sir?"

"There is no occasion for delay that I know of," he answered smoothly. "Unless, of course, you would prefer a protracted engagement?"

The expression in her eyes put him in mind of a trapped animal.

"It — it will be Amanda's birthday in a few weeks' time," she said hurriedly. "Mama is planning a ball — I would like to defer the — the wedding date until after that event — that is, if it pleases you, sir."

He bowed. "Your wishes are my pleasure. By all means let us postpone the wedding until after your sister's birthday. When is the joyful event?"

"The second week in June — the tenth, to be precise."

"Then perhaps we may fix upon the third or fourth week of next month for our little ceremony?"

"I — I do not know ... I —" Her voice trailed away weakly. She racked her brain furiously for something she could say — some valid excuse she could plead for avoiding the fixing of an exact date; invention failed her.

He watched her struggle in silence through half-closed, lazy eyes. "I perceive that there is yet another difficulty: can it be that there is some other occasion to be celebrated at that time?"

His tone was serious, but there was a mocking light in his eyes. She jumped quickly at the loophole he offered, without giving sufficient thought to her words.

"Yes, yes, you have hit upon it. I have to — that is — I —"

He came gallantly enough to her rescue, a cynical smile marring the generosity of his mouth.

"Let me hazard a guess. Another birthday — your mother's? Your father's? Your own, perhaps?"

She raised her head, and looked him straight between the eyes. For a moment she was the Isabella whom Amanda knew best, and John Webster loved.

She shook her head. "No," she said candidly. "Mama and Papa have but just celebrated theirs, and mine is not until July. I was — seeking an excuse, as you guessed."

"Now we come to it," he said softly. "Tell me, child, is this match to your liking?"

Her eyes widened a little, and one hand went to her throat.

"You can ask that?"

He nodded, all trace of mockery gone from his manner.

"I must know the truth. I would not have you — coerced."

"There is nothing of that kind," she said quickly. "My parents would not be so unfeeling — indeed, they love me dearly."

Her voice choked a little on the last words.

"So I should suppose," he answered quietly, "from my observation of them — in particular, your father. What, then, is the reason of your refusal to fix upon the day?"

She looked away from him, and her words came out in little nervous gushes, while her hands plucked restlessly at the embroidery on her gown.

"It is just that — the thought of being a married woman is — a little frightening — so much responsibility, you know. Mama says that I am giddy, and perhaps it is true, but I do so delight in all the gaiety of the Town. The season is at its height, and it would seem a pity to quit it so soon. A few more months of — of — diversion, before I settle down — I do hope, sir, you can understand —"

She stopped, breathless and confused, unable to meet the steady regard of his deep blue eyes.

"Isabella," he said, in a low tone, "do you love me?"

She started, and turned pale. Whatever she had expected him to say it was not this.

"I am aware that it is not fashionable to speak of love to one's betrothed," he said, with a faint sneer. "You will, I am sure, forgive the lapse."

She raised her head, giving him a brave, proud glance.

"We knew from the first that ours was a marriage of convenience, sir," she replied, in an unexpectedly firm voice. "Neither of us has ever tried to pretend anything to the contrary."

He nodded, and the sneer died out of his look.

"How convenient is it to you, Isabella? Do you hold me in dislike, as your little sister does?"

"Amanda? Does she? I had not observed."

He smiled dryly. "She makes it plain enough. But let us leave her aside for a moment, and speak of ourselves. You have not answered my question."

She shook her head. "No, of course, I do not. But —"

"Ah!" he said softly. "So there is a but?"

She hesitated, and he saw that her hazel eyes were clouded with trouble. "Between dislike and — and love — there are many degrees of feeling," she answered at last. "I — it is difficult to say precisely what are my sentiments towards you, sir."

"Cannot you bring yourself to call me Charles? That in itself might lessen the distance between us."

"I will try to remember," she said, with a sad little smile.

They had been sitting at some distance apart during this conversation. Now he stood up and moved over towards her, taking her hands in his. She looked up into his face, and scarcely recognised it. All trace of mockery had vanished, the eyes were deep and serious, and there was a hint of tenderness in the smile that touched his mouth.

"A marriage of convenience is a mockery, Isabella, but it is possible that ours might be something more. In all my life, I never yet knew any tenderness that was not purchased, save only for that given me freely by one faithful old woman. If I had —" a half-stifled sigh escaped him — "my story might, perchance, have been different. But it is not yet too late; you have the power to change all that, to make me forsake past follies, and live again in the sunshine of your love, my dear."

The last words were spoken on a whisper. Her hands trembled in his. She drew them away, averting her face.

He waited a moment, striving to hide his disappointment. Then he spoke again, gently. "What do you say, Isabella? Can you give me any hope? I am prepared to be patient — I do not expect that you should love me all at once."

"I — I don't know." Her voice trembled. "It may be so — it will take time —"

He nodded. "That is why you wish to postpone our wedding? I understand, my dear, and am content to wait."

She looked up, suddenly made bold by the forbearance of his manner.

"But what of you, sir — Charles? I had thought that this was for you, too, a marriage of convenience. Mama said —"

"I will not insult you by idle pretence," he said quickly. "It is true that I sought your hand without those feelings which should bring a man to seek a wife. But you are lovely, my dear, and also sweet and brave. It should be no difficult matter to love you. Indeed, I find at this moment —" He broke off, his eyes darkening with desire. Suddenly he stooped and gathered her into his arms, while his lips sought hers.

For a moment, Isabella remained passive, but the touch of his lips set her struggling like a wild thing. He released her quickly, cursing himself for a clumsy fool. He had been too impatient, the time was not yet ripe. Then he saw her face, and recoiled in dismay from the stark revulsion written on it.

"You lied to me!" he accused, bitterly. "Such strong aversion as you obviously have for me can never change. I release you from your promise to me."

"No!"

It was a cry of despair. He stared at her, unable to believe his ears.

"You still wish to wed me?" he asked incredulously.

"I have given my word," she answered, clenching her hands until the knuckles showed white. "It is for the best — Mama —"

"Do not commit the error of allowing your mother to choose your husband," he warned her, with compressed lips.

She drew herself up proudly. Her face was pale, but her voice had steadied.

"I myself have chosen," she said quietly. "I know what I am about. As you said yourself, it may work out very well in time."

The cynical smile returned to his mouth, the mocking light to his eyes.

"Doubtless," he said, and bowed ironically. "I must ask you to forgive my — er — romantic flight of fancy."

Chapter IX: A Declaration of War

Charles Barsett partook of an excellent breakfast on the following morning, and was still at his toilet when Amanda and John were announced to him. His valet was just about to assist his master into a coat of red figured velvet with stiff, wide skirts; Mr. Barsett paused before easing himself expertly into the coat, and directed the manservant to show the unexpected visitors into the small withdrawing room. He then shook out his ruffles with a quick flick of his wrists, and sat down at the dressing table. His thoughts were busy as he stared at his reflection in the glass, so much so that he allowed his man to press a patch on to his cheek without making any comment.

The manservant had said that Miss Twyford had called. Isabella? To attend him here, in a bachelor establishment, escorted only by a man — a stranger to him — what the devil was the fellow's name again? Webster, ah, yes, that was it. Who was this Webster? What did they both want with him? And what in the name of all that was wonderful could Isabella be thinking of? Even though they were betrothed, tongues would wag if someone should have noticed her arrival in this fashion. He consoled himself with the thought that it was as yet early in the day for the scandalmongerers to be abroad, and rose to descend the stairs to his visitors.

They both came to their feet as he entered the room. Amanda very properly sank into a curtsy. He recognised her with a quickly controlled start of surprise, and turned an inquiring look in the direction of her companion.

"How do you do, Miss Amanda? I am indeed honoured by this call. I believe I have not the pleasure of your friend's acquaintance."

"Oh, pray forgive me for troubling you at this hour of day, Mr. Barsett," began Amanda, with a fixed bright smile that sat oddly on her usually mobile face. "John —this is John, you know — that is, I should say, may I present Mr. Webster? John, this is Mr. Barsett, who is to — but there, you know all that already —"

She paused for breath, and the gentlemen bowed solemnly to each other, John Webster looking slightly foolish.

"John is a very old friend of ours," continued Amanda, having got her second wind. "He is our neighbour in the country, you know. He finds that he has to leave Town on urgent family matters —" she glanced fleetingly at John, but he refused to meet her eye — "and he does so wish to meet you before he goes. His father will be happy to have an account of Isabella's future husband. You must realise that he has always held her in the very highest esteem."

Charles Barsett bowed again, but said nothing. He was watching her curiously, a sardonic look in his eye. Something lay behind all this mummery, but what? He would give much to know. Perhaps the answer might emerge in the fullness of time, if he were only patient. Miss Amanda Twyford was a disconcertingly forthright young woman, after all.

"Pray be seated." He waved his unexpected guests to chairs. "You'll take some refreshment — a glass of ratafia, mayhap, Miss Amanda?"

She accepted with a gratitude that was touching, could he but have known her detestation of the beverage. Something a little stronger was offered to John Webster, and the order given to a servant.

"And now," began Charles Barsett, urbanely, "what may I have the pleasure of doing for you, Miss Amanda?"

She seemed slightly taken aback. "Oh, why, nothing in the world. That is — our call is purely a social one, sir. As I explained, Mr. Webster so greatly desired to meet you before he left for home."

Charles bowed in John's direction. "It is not, I trust, unpleasant news that summons you from Town, Mr. Webster?"

"What?" said John, with a start. "Oh, no — that is to say — urgent family matters, as Amanda said just now, but nothing of an unpleasant nature, egad, no."

Amanda shot him a withering glance. Surely he could do better than that, the poor ninny?

"That is fortunate," said Charles Barsett dryly.

"Yes, oh, indeed," stuttered John, anxious to redeem himself in Amanda's eyes, which at present looked upon him coldly. "My father is in his customary good health — and my mother — I'm glad to say, and trust they will remain so for many a long year. They would not forgive me if I failed to make myself known to Bella's — that is — Miss Twyford's —"

Here he choked a little, tugged at his cravat, and broke off.

"Quite." Charles eyed him courteously, but searching. "You and your family have been neighbours of my Lord Twyford for many years, I collect?"

"Ever since I can remember," answered John.

"Then you will no doubt be almost better acquainted with my betrothed than I am myself," remarked Charles with a faint smile.

"I — to be sure." John's reply was short and terse.

Amanda wriggled uncomfortably in her chair. She did not like the turn the conversation had taken, having some fears as to its outcome. She was about to break in with a change of subject but was spared her pains by the arrival of the refreshment. This created a slight diversion, and for a while the gentlemen safely debated the rival merits of claret and burgundy. She kept only half an ear on their discourse; she was wondering how to contrive a search of the house. Her problem would have been simpler, she reflected, if she had possessed any notion of what it was she sought: proof of Mr. Barsett's wickedness, yes, but what proof? One thing was certain, however; she would never come at it by sitting here, listening to a rather dull conversation and sipping at a glass of this detestable ratafia. Her quick wits prompted a remedy for both her sufferings. With a skilful, though apparently clumsy movement, she tipped the liquid over her gown and on to the floor.

Her sharp cry of dismay drew the attention of the others, and Charles Barsett started to his feet.

"What's amiss, Mandy?" asked John; then seeing the frantic efforts she was making to dab at the stain on her gown — "What ever can have induced you to be so clumsy?"

Charles Barsett smiled at this remark, which certainly bore out the story of a long acquaintance. He expressed his regret, and offered to ring for the housekeeper.

"Oh, no, there is not the least occasion to trouble her to come down from her room," said Amanda hastily. "If you will have the goodness to direct me, I shall very easily find my way there alone."

But unfortunately for her scheme, Charles Barsett was by far too good a host to permit this, and presently a comfortable looking woman bore the young lady away to repair the damage to her gown as best she might. Once in the housekeeper's room, however, her attention to the stain was perfunctory in the extreme. She seemed anxious to be off again immediately, thought the woman, and wondered very much who this attractive girl with the honey-coloured curls could be. Whoever she was, she evidently was not of the peacock variety, for she did not regard her ruined garments in the least. She declined politely, but firmly, all the woman's offers to conduct her downstairs again, and at least succeeded in leaving the room unattended.

She did not dare to poke about upstairs, however, for fear the housekeeper might emerge again, and descended the staircase as though to return to the drawing-room. Once in the hall, she paused, and looked about her. No one else happened to be about at that particular moment. The drawing-room door was immediately in front of her, and there were several other doors leading off the hall. She chose one at random, and heart beating fast, walked resolutely towards it. Stealthily she turned the knob, and opened it a few inches. If anyone was within, she could always say that she had mistaken the door. But one glance was sufficient to show her that the room was deserted. Considerably heartened by this discovery, she walked in, and softly closed the door behind her.

Then she hesitated, uncertain. What, after all, was she seeking? Her eye lit upon a small escritoire over against one wall, and her heart leapt. Letters, perhaps? Another letter from the mysterious Francis — one which would certainly reveal his identity, or his connection with the Abbey? The very thing! She started forward eagerly.

With one hand on the lid of the desk, she paused, the colour flooding her cheeks as an unwelcome thought occurred to her. Was this, after all, the kind of thing she ought to do? John, she knew, would not approve, and as for Isabella, and Mama —

and Miss Brown! Was it not, perhaps, a trifle mean — underhand?

But if something was not done, and quickly, Bella would wed the wrong man. There was no one but herself to make any attempt to avert such a disaster. Besides, he was a monster — a wolf in sheep's clothing. Were not his methods underhand, too? All's fair, she reminded herself again, in love and war; and sometimes it was necessary to fight an enemy with his own weapons.

She squared her shoulders, and opened the desk. Its contents appeared innocent enough, tidily stacked away in sundry pigeon holes. She ran through them lightly, perfunctorily, yet missing nothing, and replacing everything as she had found it. She came across a stack of invitation cards; here might be something to the purpose! She turned them over quickly, scanning each one. Suddenly her eye caught a name she knew.

"Lord and Lady Twyford request the pleasure of your company at a ball to be given in honour of their daughter, Amanda —"

So Mama had sent out the invitations already! It was the first Amanda had heard of it. She paused in her task, momentarily diverted, staring at the card. How odd of Mama — and not very kind, not to have consulted her first.

Hurriedly she pulled herself together. She must get on; this was nothing to the purpose, and could be taken up at another time when she had more leisure. She finished her scrutiny of the other cards, found nothing helpful, and replaced them. As she did so, her eye fell upon a black, leatherbound volume which was lying in the next pigeon hole. She picked up the book, and opening it, scanned the title page.

Boulton's Complete History of Magick.

Her pulse quickened. Here at last was something — not very much, to be sure, in the way of proof — but still, just a hint of the macabre connection that she had been certain existed. She turned excitedly to the flyleaf. On it was written a name, but not the name she had expected to see. She looked intently at the flowing hand, feeling that she had seen it somewhere before, and quite recently: 'Francis Dashwood'.

It was a moment before she realised the importance of what she had found. Then in a flash it came to her just where it was that she had seen this handwriting before. Here, in all probability, was the true title of 'Brother Francis'.

With trembling fingers, she turned a few pages of the book, and found herself staring at an illustration which made her blood run cold with horror. In a circle of seven guttering candles stood a fearsome warlock in ceremonial robes. In his predatory fingers he held aloft a white wand. From the shadows which closed all about him outside the light of the candles could be dimly discerned the repulsive, twining shapes of serpents with forked tongues, and ghastly twisted demons with staring, evil eyes.

She shuddered, her eyes rooted to the picture by some dreadful compulsion.

"Horrible, is it not? But never fear, the rest of the book is, I assure you, disappointing in comparison."

The drawling voice brought her to her senses. She raised startled eyes, and found herself looking into the cool, amused face of Charles Barsett. She could scarcely have been more dismayed by the appearance of the warlock himself.

The crimson flooded her cheeks.

"I —"

She wanted to beg his pardon, but the words would not come. Whatever could she find to say, she wondered desperately, to excuse her present situation?

"You should have told me that you wished for a book. I would have been happy to have supplied you, Miss Amanda. I fear you must have found my entertainment dull indeed."

"No — I —"

He took the book gently from her nerveless fingers, replaced it, and shut the desk.

"The damage to your gown was effectively repaired, I trust?" he asked, conversationally.

She pressed a cold, trembling hand to her hot cheeks. "Ye-es, I thank you — it was nothing — it does not signify —"

"You were so long away," he explained, in tones of gentle reproach, "that I felt it best to come and see if I could find you."

"Yes — well, I — thought that perhaps you and John would be glad of a little time alone together. A female is sometimes a handicap to male conversation."

"Not at all," he answered gallantly.

"You were talking of wines," went on Amanda, scarcely knowing what she said. "I — I felt that I should only be in the way if I returned —"

"You were mistaken," he said, and his lips curved diabolically. "You must know that I am particularly addicted to the company of — er — curious schoolgirls."

She drew in her breath sharply. She knew that the reproof was not undeserved, but this did nothing to lessen the sting of it. He was revenged indeed.

"So you do remember!" she accused, at once dropping all pretence.

"Yes." He eyed her gravely. "I think perhaps, Miss Amanda, it is time that you and I understood one another. Do you agree?"

She faced him proudly. "I do indeed, sir."

"Then perhaps you would care to sit down?"

She sank carelessly into a chair, her eyes on his face.

"Would it be presumptuous in me to ask," he began, still with that hateful sneer on his lips, "just why it is that I inspire such strong interest in you, Miss Amanda?"

"You deceive yourself," she answered, with some heat, "if you suppose that my interest, as you call it, has any flattering implication!"

He raised one eyebrow. "So you are not, after all, enamoured of me? I am desolated."

She snapped her white teeth together, but made no reply to this taunt. A chuckle escaped him.

"Love such as yours, Miss Amanda, would be, I feel sure, an experience for any man!"

"Do not call me 'Miss Amanda'! I dislike it of all things."

"What shall I call you, then? 'Curious schoolgirl' does not meet with your approval, I already know."

"Do not call me anything at all!" she grated, with flashing eyes.

Once again he raised an eyebrow. "No? But surely that would be most awkward? Even a dog must have a name, you know."

She rose to her feet, her bosom heaving. "If you are to insult me, the sooner we rejoin John the better. He will defend me, I know."

"Very touching," he approved, mockingly. "Injured innocence to the life. But if you were to consider the matter,

Miss — ah — madam — I feel sure you must allow that I am the one who should consider myself insulted."

She had nothing to say to this, and stood silent and motionless.

"You sought me out," he continued smoothly, "on a pretext that I am sure only the wildest flight of imagination could have persuaded you would deceive me. It is quite obvious to me that your good friend, Mr. Webster, has not the faintest desire to make my acquaintance. The visit can only have been made for some purpose of your own. That purpose —" he glanced briefly at the escritoire — "appears to be of questionable morality. There was an odd circumstance the other day, too, which also pointed to a similar conclusion. I should be glad to hear that I was mistaken in my interpretation of your actions. I must confess that the motive for them puzzles me completely."

"You dare talk," stormed Amanda, torn between shame of her behaviour and anger at the cool disdain of his manner, "of questionable morality — you!"

He tilted one eyebrow in the way that she had come to hate.

"Perhaps you would care to explain why I should not?"

"You may well ask! A man of your reputation!"

She tossed back her curls defiantly from her heated cheeks. Her blue eyes flashed fire. His mocking glance held a trace of admiration: she made a striking picture.

"My reputation is the world's to do with as it will," he answered in measured tones which were in great contrast to her own.

"I suppose you to mean that you are maligned! I do not credit it for one moment."

"My dear young lady," he said, wearily, "your beliefs really cannot concern me in the least. What I do feel is my affair is to have some explanation for your — I fear I cannot describe it in any other way — your extraordinary behaviour."

"Oh, you are so cold, so smug, so sure of yourself!" she fumed, exasperated beyond endurance by his manner. "When I do anything wrong, I do it in hot blood, and for what I believe to be a good reason. But you — I know that you would do an evil thing without turning a hair for no reason whatever."

"You do, do you? I wonder — you will, I am sure, forgive my mentioning it — could you possibly manage to moderate your voice? I am not at all hard of hearing, and even well trained servants are sometimes — like schoolgirls — actuated by curiosity."

"You —you —!"

Words failed her, and for a moment she looked as though she meant either to strike him, or else rush headlong from the room. To his surprise, she did neither, but sat down again, and made an evident effort to be calm.

"Of course, it is your purpose to taunt me into storming at you, just so that you may have the satisfaction of making me look foolish," she said, disdainfully. "But I shall not continue to fall into that trap, let me tell you."

"I am glad of it," he answered urbanely, "for now perhaps I can get to the bottom of this affair. Leaving aside my reputation — and my character, if you choose to quibble —" this as he saw that that she was about to protest, and guessed what the tenor of her remarks would be — "Leaving those points aside, I say, why have you chosen to spy upon me?"

She pressed her hands together in her lap. She was determined not to be tempted into anger.

"I'm thinking of Bella."

"Your sister? That does you credit. But I do not quite see —"

"I am convinced that you are not a fit person for her to wed," she stated boldly.

Once again the lifted eyebrow, the satanic smile. She tightened her hands.

"Can any man aspire to deserve any young lady?" he asked mockingly.

"That," said Amanda, emphatically, "is fustian — polite claptrap! I wonder you think to fob me off with such a stupid remark."

"Be careful," he warned, in a more natural manner than she had seen from him as yet. His smile widened, losing its sinister expression. "You are becoming heated again."

"You are enough to provoke a saint!" she countered, but the ferocity had gone from her tone.

"That is true, I fear. I am sorry that you should have such a poor opinion of me. But surely, if your sister and your parents are satisfied —"

"Bella does not know what she wants. And Papa is wholly under Mama's thumb!"

"Now that I have the honour of knowing you better, I am not surprised to hear it. I've heard it said that you are very like your mother."

"You —" she began, almost forgetting her good resolutions, then stopped in time. "I see what you would be at, and you shall not succeed, I promise you."

He threw back his head, and laughed for pure enjoyment. Those who knew him best could have told that such a laugh was rare to him.

"Child, you are refreshing! In future, I give you leave to spy upon me as much as you wish. But do first make your reasons perfectly clear to me, for I find myself in as much confusion as I was at the beginning."

She looked at him uncertainly. He was a very strange man, surely? Perhaps he was just a little mad — not quite accountable for his actions? For there were some quite human, attractive things about him…

Suddenly she remembered the black book, the Abbey, the sinister Brother Francis. Her resolution hardened.

"Bella does not — is not in love with you," she said boldly. "Nor are you with her."

He shrugged. "Sweet innocence, that may seem a dreadful thing to you and, in very truth, it is — but in the fashionable world it is nothing, a mere commonplace. One must learn to accept the ruling of the Monde. You, too, perhaps, one day —"

He broke off, and considered her; the tip-tilted nose, the generous, eager mouth, the candid blue eyes — all bespoke the child, impulsive, warm-hearted and innocent. London would change all that: a few short months, and she would emerge precisely to pattern. He felt a twinge of regret, and sighed.

"Never!" exclaimed Amanda dramatically.

"It is a long word," he warned her.

"When *I* marry," she said defiantly, "it will be because I love someone so much that I cannot live without him."

Once more he studied her thoughtfully.

"Allow me to say that I envy the unknown," he answered, in a serious tone. "He will be a very lucky man."

She coloured, and her eyes dropped away from his. There was silence in the room for several minutes. At last she broke it, almost abruptly.

"It is not only that," she said, "though that is bad enough. You are concerned in something discreditable, I know, though I cannot discover what — something connected with that place where I first met you. If Bella knew the truth, she would never consent to become your wife."

"Have you not told her?" The sneer was back again.

"She will not believe me without proof. That is what I've been trying to obtain — that was my reason for — for what I did."

Now that it was out, and he knew all, she found that she had rid herself of the unpleasant feeling of guilt which had hung about her actions in regard to him. A straight declaration of war was much more to her taste than pretended friendship.

"You but waste your time, child." His tone was not unkind. "Your sister will wed me in spite of all."

"Then you admit that there is something — something dreadful going on at that Abbey place?" she asked quickly.

"I admit nothing. On what, may I ask, are your suspicions founded?"

"On local rumour," she began, doubtfully. She knew that it did not sound very convincing. "And," she added, more hopefully, "on the hints that your cousin, Mr. Thurlston, has let drop."

He started to his feet, his languid manner dropping away from him with astonishing rapidity.

"Roger! What has he said to you?"

She looked surprised. "Not near so much as I should like, but just enough to show me that there is something in what I had already heard."

"Ay," he answered bitterly. "That is ever his way."

She studied him thoughtfully. His deep blue eyes stared beyond her, as though he had forgotten her presence. His mouth was twisted, not with mockery now, but with pain and bitterness.

To her own surprise, she knew a sudden wild impulse to help him; though he seemed to be the very last person who should ever require anyone's help in any way.

"What is this secret?" she asked impulsively. "Whatever it may be, its possession brings you no happiness, I can see. Abandon it, and try to deserve Bella."

No sooner were the words out than she regretted them. What could have possessed her? She did not want him to have Bella, in any event: Bella was for John.

But she need not have feared. Something in what she had said banished the marks of suffering from his face, and brought back the expression which she detested.

"I regret infinitely that I am unable to satisfy your — ah — curiosity," he drawled. "And, talking of curiosity, our friend Mr. Webster must by now be feeling all the pangs of that affliction. If he at all shares your opinion of me, he must surely be picturing you as having suffered a fate worse than death."

"John knows well enough that I can take care of myself," she answered tartly. "Very well, Mr. Barsett, I see that it is to be war between us! I may as well warn you now that I shall not scruple to use every means in my power to prevent your marriage to my sister."

He nodded, unmoved, and rose to his feet.

"So be it," he said. "Your warning is the action of a generous foe. I feel that I must in fairness make some return for it, and so I offer you a like warning. You will have no allies to count upon in your war, my child; they are all ranged on my side."

Chapter X: The First Battle

One outcome of Amanda's exploit in Albemarle Street was that John Webster insisted on posting back to Berkshire that very afternoon.

"We told the fellow that I was going home," he persisted stubbornly, in answer to Amanda's protests. "And, truth to tell, I don't see what else there is for me to do, Mandy. We have meddled enough, and all to no purpose. Bella is the one to decide, and she has made her choice."

"How often must I tell you that she is not happy in it?" asked the girl, a hint of pleading in her tone. If John was to desert her, where should she turn for aid? "She will not discuss her engagement with me, she refuses to fix a date for the wedding, and whenever your name is mentioned she looks like a — like a sick horse!"

"Good God, Mandy!" expostulated the outraged John. "How can you describe Isabella in such terms?"

"Oh, well, I'm only her sister. Besides, it's not so long since you used to call her by far less complimentary names!"

John reddened. "As to that," he said, awkwardly, "we were children then — but it is some years since I was able to think of Bella in any other way than as the most wonderful woman in the world."

"Yes, and that is part of the trouble. But never mind," she added hastily, "we have discussed all this before. The thing is, John, you ought to be here in Town. There is no saying what may come about, and I want you to be at hand to profit by any change in Bella's inclinations."

"What can possibly come about to effect such a change?" he asked despairingly. "Both parties profess their intention of holding to the engagement. There is nothing more to do."

"But do you not realise that I am on the threshold of an important discovery?" asked Amanda, in thrilling tones.

"What discovery? I cannot see it. So far, we only seem to have succeeded in making fools of ourselves, without discovering anything."

"How can you say so? We have found one more link between Charles Barsett and the Abbey."

"What does that avail us? Even supposing your surmise is correct — for this Brother Francis may have nothing to do with the business at the Abbey, you must face that fact — still, even if you are right, and he has, how are you going to prove it?"

"That was where I relied upon you. If you remain in Town you could still bring me the gossip from the clubs."

"Not for long," he replied glumly. "Not if my luck continued as bad, I can tell you."

"Poor John, did you lose heavily?" asked Amanda sympathetically.

"Oh, nothing to signify," he replied hastily. "But one cannot play a good game, you know, if one is trying to listen to every conversation that goes on."

"Well, I must contrive as best I may by myself," she said, in tones of resignation.

"What do you mean to do?" he asked suspiciously.

She shrugged elaborately. "Oh, I shall just wait and see if perhaps I can learn more of this Francis Dashwood. At any rate, we know that he lives in Hanover Square. Then, possibly Bella may stop playing this role she has set for herself, and decide to confide in me, after all. Waiting — it seems that is to be my only way now of hoping to gain the proof I am determined to have."

John was thoughtful during this speech. When she had finished, he said suddenly, "Has it occurred to you, Mandy, that perhaps this Abbey is nothing so very out of the ordinary?"

"What do you mean?"

His eyes avoided her direct gaze, and he shuffled his feet awkwardly. "Well, you see, I daresay you must be aware no, perhaps not — oh, never mind."

Light dawned on Amanda; she tossed back her curls and laughed. "You are trying to say that the place may well be a — a bagnio. Do not fear, John, *you* have not said anything improper — it is I. Stupid fellow, I cannot help but know of the existence of such places."

"Then you should not!" retorted John emphatically. "A gently-nurtured female such as you."

"One may acquire any amount of information concerning the important facts of life from such unexceptionable sources as the Bible and the classics," replied Amanda loftily. "In my view, far more harm is done by ignorance of such matters. However, we are not here to discuss the education of young girls."

He stared in admiration and surprise. "Egad, Mandy, you've a head on your shoulders! No wonder one is apt at times to forget that you're a female."

"I thank you, sir," she replied dryly. "That was a nicely turned compliment. Well, since you are determined to go, I wish you Godspeed, John." She held out her hand. "I suppose you will come to take formal leave of the others?" she added.

He clasped her hand, hesitated a moment, then conveyed it to his lips.

An impish grin spread across her features.

"Is that a peace-offering for your *faux-pas* of a few minutes since?" she asked.

He shook his head. "It is my tribute to a bewitching girl — who is still something of a scamp!" His tone suddenly became serious again. "Mandy, you'll not do anything rash? Somehow, I wonder if I ought to leave you to yourself — Lord knows what scrape you may get into."

"I'll be all right, never fear."

"I shan't be long away, in any event," he promised, unconvinced. "I'll send you a note by way of Tom, your groom. He's a trustworthy lad, isn't he? Then perhaps we could meet as before, in the park, at the same hour. Meantime, take care, Mandy. I simply don't trust you alone, damme if I do."

Amanda slipped back into the house by way of the servants' entrance, hoping by that means to escape observation should Lady Twyford and Isabella have already returned. She need not have troubled, however; they were still from home, as was her father. She heaved a sigh of relief, and went upstairs to remove her outdoor things.

When she came down again, she went to the spinet. Her fingers idly touched the keys, but her mind was not on the music she was playing. She felt that in all her life she had never been so puzzled by anyone as she was by Charles Barsett. He did not attempt to deny or even excuse the reputation which was given him by everyone. It did not seem to concern him in the slightest. Yet she felt convinced that his indifference was a mask which he assumed to conceal his real feelings. Behind it lay, she was prepared to swear, bitterness — possibly even pain.

Then why, she asked herself in wonder, did he continue to commit the acts which earned him such a reputation, if the thought of it filled him with revulsion? Or was there some other reason for his bitterness? Again, he appeared to be bored, languid, cynical, indifferent to the feeling of others; yet showing through this facade were glimpses of quite another kind of man. It was almost as though, she thought with a sudden flash of illumination, he were afraid to be himself — yet which of these two beings was the real Charles Barsett, after all?

Her profound meditations were interrupted by the arrival of a footman with the message that Mr. Thurlston was without, desiring to see the family.

Amanda welcomed this diversion, and told the man to admit the visitor.

When he had been shown into the room, Mr. Thurlston glanced about him inquiringly.

"I am alone," explained Amanda, guessing the meaning of his look. "Mama and Bella should be back at any moment, but I cannot promise for Papa."

"I am sorry," he said. "I would not have intruded had I realised that you were alone."

"Tusk!" she waved the remark aside. "I could easily have denied myself, had I wished."

"True," he answered, with his charming smile. "I am flattered indeed."

"You need not be," she said in a tone of raillery. "I suddenly bethought me that you could be of inestimable service to me."

He bowed. "With all the pleasure in the world, Miss Amanda."

"I have been to see your cousin this morning," she said, coming straight to the point, as was her way.

"Indeed?"

"Do not raise your brows in that fashion; it puts me in mind of him."

"And you do not wish that to happen?" he asked lightly.

"There is no one I would rather forget."

"Poor Charles!"

She frowned, arrested by a sudden thought.

"Why did he leave his father's house while you continued to stay there?" she asked bluntly. "It seems odd."

There was the tiniest of pauses, and a hint of reserve in his manner when he answered her.

"They could never agree, you must realise. As for myself, I am not quite the free agent that my cousin is. I must confess that it would have been agreeable to me to have set up a bachelor establishment, too, but — my uncle never suggested it."

She nodded, seeming not to pay much attention to the latter part of his speech.

"Why didn't they agree? Was it simply incompatibility of temperament?"

"Perhaps so: Charles has more quickness than his father — in that I suppose him to resemble my dead aunt. His habits — those of a young man of fashion and wealth — appeared to disgust my lord. There were frequent unpleasant scenes; it was a relief to everyone when Charles decided to go."

Amanda looked him straight in the eye.

"Do you think him an evil man?"

He started. "Charles? Good God, no! He has been wild, as young men of his set are, and foolish, perhaps. He is his own worst enemy. But evil! That is too strong a word, surely."

"Then what," asked Amanda, suddenly, "is all this affair at Medmenham Abbey?"

He drew back, and glanced hastily at the clock on the mantelshelf.

"I feel that I have stayed long enough for propriety," he said, rising to his feet. "Pray give my respects to your parents and Miss Twyford."

She came to her feet and turned a pleading face upon him.

"Will you not help me, Mr. Thurlston? I must know what goes on at the Abbey, and have proof of your cousin's connection with it. You alone can supply the information I need — you alone can help me to save Bella from an impossible marriage!"

"What do you mean?" he asked, amazed.

"If Mr. Barsett is concerned in evil doings — and I believe that he is — he is no husband for my sister!"

"But the marriage is arranged, is it not? Certainly my uncle supposes so."

"That is not to say that Bella may not cry off if she chooses! No date has been fixed for the wedding as yet."

"That is true," he said, thoughtfully. "But she will scarcely care to make herself the talk of the Town by changing her mind at the eleventh hour. Am I to understand, then, that she is not attracted to my cousin?"

"It is quite impossible to describe to you the complexities of Bella's feelings, sir! You will simply have to take my word for it that she would be ready enough to change her mind, were she given sufficient reason. As for gossip, an heiress of Bella's standing may do as she chooses: the Polite World will not murmur!"

He smiled at her worldly-wise air; it sat very oddly on Amanda.

"Are you then such very wealthy young ladies? So far, rumour has been quiet on that score, at all events."

"Oh, I am nothing compared to Bella! Our maternal grandfather left her a tidy fortune, in addition to what will come to her from Papa. He died before I was born, so, of course, I could not be included in his goodwill! No, I don't think Bella need fear anything from idle tongues; she has only to take herself off into the country, in any event."

"And your parents? How would they feel if there should be a change of plan?"

Amanda considered for a moment.

"I think Mama might be considerably put about — for a time, at least. Papa would never desire anything but our happiness, and would readily give way to Bella's wishes. The crux of the matter is to make Bella desire to put an end to the engagement."

"That will not be easy," he said, frowning. "But it is just possible that I may be able to help you, Miss Amanda. There is vileness enough at Medmenham Abbey for those who are there to see it; but I fancy there is no one whose word your sister would accept, other than yourself. That Charles has been a visitor to the Abbey for some years past, I know for a fact; but it may be that he has given up such diversions with his engagement. You perceive the difficulties?"

"What you mean," she answered, quickly, "is that we should first have to find out if he still frequents the place — and then surprise him there? That you could probably do the first, but that I would have to do the second?"

He nodded: his face was grave.

"It is not an exploit for a timid person. But then, I'm sure that you are not timid. Besides, you might be able to find someone to aid you — there's that groom of yours, who put up such a good fight with the highwayman — could you trust him to hold his tongue?"

"Tom?" She considered for a moment, then broke in, eagerly, "I have an altogether better idea! John — John Webster — he is the very person! He had hoped to wed Bella himself!"

"John Webster?" He was puzzled for a moment. "Oh, yes, I recollect! The young man who is a neighbour of yours in the country." He paused, evidently deep in thought. "Yes, that would be capital," he said, at last. "Capital! But you will have to contain yourself in patience for a time, Miss Amanda. This society which has its headquarters at the Abbey does not meet again for more than a month from now."

She looked at him in dismay.

"Do not be disheartened," he said, in a cheering tone. "It will give us time to make a sound plan. But we shall not have many opportunities of meeting in private like this; how shall we contrive?"

"The Park," answered Amanda, quickly. "In the early morning, before anyone is astir! I meet John there sometimes. I can be there most mornings."

"I will look out for you," he said.

"That is, when I have anything —" He broke off, as the sound of voices floated into the room from the hall. "Your mother," he said, and rose hastily. "I'd best go."

"There is just one thing I must know," she said, hurriedly starting to her feet. "Does the name of Francis Dashwood convey anything to you?"

He nodded, one eye on the door. "Yes. He is the owner of Medmenham Abbey, and the leader of the society which meets there. He's also a close friend of my cousin's. But we must defer our talk till another time — your mother and sister —"

They entered almost as he spoke, and showed some surprise at finding him sitting with Amanda. Lady Twyford's frown spoke volumes, and her younger daughter anticipated a set-down when Mr. Thurlston should have left.

But the reprimand, when it came, had little effect upon her spirits. Events were shaping to a solution of her problem, just when she had almost given up hope of ever discovering what she so ardently desired to know. True, she must be prepared to wait some weeks before she could hope to lay convincing proof before Isabella of Charles Barsett's depravity. Meanwhile, there was something she could do. Mr. Thurlston had seemed to be uncertain as to whether his cousin still took part in the activities of this society he had mentioned. There appeared to her to be a way of finding out quickly, at any rate, although she had been interrupted before she could point this out to him. The note which she had purloined at the Opera had made an appointment between Charles Barsett and the man Dashwood. She knew the time and place; if Mr. Barsett should be there to keep that appointment, then without doubt he was still actively concerned with the body of which this Francis Dashwood was the principal. Why else should he answer a summons of 'Brother Francis'?

She speculated for some time on the possible nature of the society to which Mr. Thurlston had referred, and which gave one of its members such a strange title. What could it be? Imagination supplied a number of answers, but she was completely satisfied by none of these. Reluctantly, she decided that she must simply wait and see — a thing she detested. Meanwhile, thank goodness there was work she could do.

At a quarter to eight on Monday evening, a dark figure loitered under the shadow of the trees in Hanover Square. It was a dull, cloudy night, with a scutter of rain in the air, and a chilly breeze which at times caught at the fringes of the trees, producing a low, moaning sound. The figure moved slowly, keeping only to one side of the Square, and staying well back from the lanterns which hung outside the tall houses. Time passed: the figure kept its lonely vigil.

Presently, there was a second stealthy movement among the shadows, and yet another figure glided into view in the dimly-lit Square. But whereas the first had a hint of indecision in its bearing, this one moved purposefully, with practised skill. A temporary break in the cloud showed him for a ragged son of the London streets, a stunted, pale faced man with a greasy hat pulled well down over his eyes. He looked towards his quarry, lingering all unsuspecting in the gloom of the trees; a mere youth, this, clad in the livery of a gentleman's stable, and no doubt keeping tryst with some unpunctual abigail. There would not be great pickings in that quarter, the man reflected, but it had been a lean evening so far, and a cove must take what offered.

The stunted figure glided nearer to the youth with all the stealth of a snake. Suddenly, he pounced, twining a skinny arm in a stranglehold about his victim's neck. Adroit fingers felt for the expected purse.

Somewhat to the pickpocket's surprise, the youth struggled violently in spite of the cruel hold on his neck. He lashed out with arms and legs, trying in vain to find a target. With his foe at his back, this was difficult enough; and the man's arms seemed as if made of iron. The hold on the boy's neck tightened ruthlessly, and his struggles died away; black specks swam before his eyes, and his senses reeled.

Unnoticed by either during the brief struggle, a sedan chair had at that moment been halted before a house in the Square, and its burden discharged. He was a tall gentleman, clad in coat and breeches of rose satin, and wearing at his side a light dress sword. As he was about to mount the steps of the house outside which he stood, a slight noise made him turn sharply. It came from the direction of the trees. Alert, he stood still, trying to pierce the gloom, one hand resting lightly on the hilt of his sword.

In a moment, his keen eyes had detected the two struggling figures under the tree, one so slight and youthful.

With a speed that belied his former indolent carriage, he crossed the intervening space. His sword glittered in the dim light as he unsheathed it. At the first sound of movement, the pickpocket released his hold on the youth, and made off quickly into the shadows. The boy dropped to the ground like a stone.

The gentleman bent over him, sheathing his sword.

"How now? Are you much hurt, young fellow?"

There was no reply. He bent closer to the recumbent form, his eyes straining through the half light. He gave a start of surprise.

The youth's hat had fallen from his head, and lay on the grass at his side. Over it was spread like a veil a profusion of familiar honey-coloured hair.

Charles Barsett emitted a mild oath, and raised the slender form in his arms.

"Amanda Twyford!" he muttered. "Now, what the devil —?"

Her eyes flickered, and opened wide. They stared in horror as her glance rested on his face, and she started up, pushing him away from her.

"Be easy," he said, in a low, quiet tone. "You are safe. Has yon rogue done you much hurt?"

She shook her head wordlessly. Her face was pale.

"I would have given chase, but my first care was for you. Did he rob you of anything? I fancy I interrupted him in time."

She put her hand into the pocket of the breeches she was wearing; then she blushed.

"No." The word was uttered almost soundlessly.

"Hi, there!" He hailed the chairmen, who had paused in the act of leaving the Square, and were watching curiously from a distance. They came running at his call. "Procure me a hackney."

"Ye'll not be after takin' one o' they god-forsaken, fleabitten carts, y'r honour?" The rich Irish tones caused Amanda to smile, hangdog as she felt at present. "Sure, an' the chair is waitin' —"

A coin spun in the air. The men leapt after it with one accord.

"A hack — and at once," repeated Charles Barsett, authoritatively.

They vanished without further argument. Amanda sat upright. He put out his hands to assist her to rise, which she did somewhat shakily.

"You're sure you are not hurt?" he asked again.

"I'm well enough, I thank you, though a trifle — shaken," she answered, breathlessly.

"The carriage will be here in a minute or two. Lean on my arm meanwhile."

She hesitated, then placed her arm within his. Her head drooped slightly against his shoulder: she found it strong and reliable.

He spoke no more, and presently the clatter of wheels and hoofs announced the arrival of the hackney. He guided her over the grass towards it, and helped her to mount the steps. Amanda's nose wrinkled in disgust as she leaned back against the shabby upholstery; a musty smell pervaded the vehicle, and its floor was strewn with dirty straw. The man eyed her thoughtfully. The pallor of her face gave way to a flood of colour.

"And now," he said sternly, as the vehicle moved forward, "I would like to know the meaning of this masquerade."

She returned no answer, but her colour deepened.

"Spying again?" he asked, with lifted brow.

She nodded, sheepishly.

"Upon my word," he said, dryly, "I am half minded to provide you with a list of my day to day engagements! It might save us both much trouble."

His tone stung her to a reply.

"I warned you that I would never let be until Bella was released from your clutches! If you wish to put an end to my activities, you have only to forego all pretensions to her hand!"

"Is that all? Then perhaps your ingenuity can suggest a way that a man of honour may take to accomplish this so desirable end?"

"A man of honour!" she answered, with biting scorn.

He shrugged lightly. "They say there is honour among thieves."

"There are those who are lower than thieves!" she retorted.

He turned his deep blue eyes upon her. Slowly, his glance raked her from head to foot. She blushed again, for her attire, and moved a little away from him, into the shadow of the coach's dingy interior.

"Tell me," he asked, conversationally, "would you number spies among them?"

Anger flooded her whole being, anger such as she had not known since childhood. She leapt upon him, eyes flashing fire, small white teeth clenched.

"I hate you! You are vile, loathsome, bestial — an outrageous, perfidious — a monster — I hate you, detest you!"

Her clenched fists pummelled at his chest. The diabolical smile came to his lips, and a spark of devilment kindled those deep eyes. Suddenly, he clasped her in a strong embrace, crushing the slim body to him, rendering the small fists useless. His mouth came down upon her soft lips in a relentless kiss. For a long moment, he held her thus; then abruptly released her.

"Do you realise, I wonder," he said softly, "just how completely I hold you in my power? Where do you think I am taking you?"

For a moment, she stared at him in horror. She was still trembling from that rough contact with him, the first embrace she had known from any man. But not for nothing had John Webster called her a fire-eater.

The hackney was bowling along at a fair pace over the cobbled streets; few people were abroad, for it was the hour at which guests had already reached their destinations for the evening's enjoyment, and were not yet ready to return homewards. For a second, she thought of shouting for help, then dismissed the notion. No doubt the coachman had been bribed by this man to ignore any appeals for help, and it was doubtful if anyone else would hear her cries.

There was only one way. She flung wide the far door of the coach with a swift movement, and prepared to leap to the ground.

In an instant, a strong arm encircled her, dragging her back from the open door, and slamming it shut. She was placed firmly back on the seat, the arm still holding her close.

"I see," said Charles Barsett, with amusement in his tone, "that I had underrated you. I shall be obliged to hold you thus until we shall have reached our destination; I trust you will forgive the liberty?"

"I would rather die!" panted Amanda, struggling to free herself.

"Unfortunately, that wouldn't serve either of us," he returned, coolly. "You must, I fear, reconcile yourself to your fate."

Amanda's seething brain calmed miraculously. She could not meet this man on his own ground, by opposing her strength against his, but might not she with advantage employ feminine tactics?

She allowed her head to droop again on to his shoulder, her body to slacken in his grasp.

"I — I fear — I'm going to swoon —" She let the words trail away weakly. He glanced at her in alarm.

"This has gone far enough," he said, quickly releasing his pressure on her waist, "my dear, I but —"

With a quick movement, she whipped his sword from the scabbard, and stood over him, the point inexpertly wavering somewhere in the region of his heart.

"Now," she said, between set teeth. "Stop the hackney at once, or I plunge this into your body!"

His eyes met hers coolly: there was admiration in them.

"As you wish, my child," he answered carelessly. "Perhaps, after all, you do not desire to return home yet. The night is still young."

The sword wavered.

"What do you mean?" she asked, suspiciously.

"Pray keep that weapon steady! You will never hit your mark, you know, if you do not. What do I mean? Why, simply that I ordered the jarvey to take us to your house; and here, if I mistake not, we are."

She peered anxiously from the window, the sword dangling loosely in her grasp. He had spoken the truth. They were that moment drawing up at the entrance to the mews; and here, coming forward stealthily, was Tom, the stable boy, whose clothes she had borrowed.

"Then you tricked me!"

She flung the weapon down. He took it up, and examined it with exaggerated anxiety. "Have a care to that! It is made of finest steel, and a little thing will destroy its balance. Yes, I tricked you: I feel that you richly deserved a sharp lesson."

She looked at him with hatred in her eyes.

"I shall not forget, Mr. Barsett," she said, in level, controlled tones. "Never fear, one day I shall find the way to repay you."

Chapter XI: Amanda has Food for Thought

"How very odd it is," remarked my Lady Twyford, "that John Webster should have returned home without taking leave of us!"

"I told you, Mama," expostulated Amanda, "that he did come to take leave, found you from home, and was unable to stay until you returned. It was on the morning that I had a headache, you may remember, and you and Bella went shopping."

"I still think it odd," insisted her mother. "Pray, what could be the haste?"

Isabella looked up quickly from her needlework. Amanda saw a guilty touch in her glance, but she soon bent her head over her work again.

"Oh, you know how it is," explained Amanda, glibly. "John was ever impulsive. I think he grew tired of the Town and its pleasures, and longed for a breath of pure country air."

"Well, I dare say he will be back soon enough. I don't imagine that he will fail to attend your birthday ball, Amanda."

"That reminds me," said her daughter, in a hurt tone. "Mama, why did you not tell me that you meant to send out the invitations?"

"How do you come to know that they have been sent out?" asked my lady, sharply.

Isabella looked up, interested, and Amanda rated herself inwardly. She must really try to keep a better guard on her tongue; fortunately, this was not so very bad a slip.

"Oh, quite by chance," she answered, airily.

"I suppose John told you," said her mother. "You two have always been very confidential together."

Amanda let it be understood that this was so, without committing herself to a direct lie. She could never make known the real circumstances of her discovery.

"Well, I'm sorry if you should feel slighted because I failed to consult you, miss," said my lady, tartly. "But you have been giving yourself far too many airs since you came to Town, and I was determined that you should not have the opportunity of attempting to decide who should be asked to this ball."

"I had as soon do without one," said Amanda, haughtily, but her lip trembled.

"I knew that, too, and was not to be embroiled in a vulgar argument. You will do as Papa and I think fit."

Amanda looked rebellious, but dared make no reply to this.

"Really, Mama," interposed Isabella, with a trace of indignation, "I cannot think why you should be so unkind of a sudden to poor Mandy! What can she have done to deserve your rancour? And on the subject of her birthday, too, when of all times, she might expect to do as she chooses!"

Lady Twyford had the grace to look a trifle ashamed of herself. The truth was that, of late, she had come to be just a little apprehensive of her younger daughter's will. She would never have admitted to such a thing, however; moreover, she had a very real affection for her children, although at times she tended to treat them as pawns in her game.

"La, Bella, it is very pretty in you to plead for the graceless girl, but you must admit that she has behaved far from well on several occasions. She has been vastly pert and forward with Mr. Barsett; and it was not proper for her to be sitting alone with Mr. Thurlston the other day. Her upbringing has been all that it should be; the fault is in herself."

At mention of Mr. Barsett, Amanda's cheeks flamed scarlet. Her mother attributed this to quite the wrong cause, and was mollified. "Very well, I see that you have sufficient proper feeling to be ashamed of your conduct," she said, patting Amanda's hand consolingly. "Now, only promise me that you will be a good girl at your ball, and we will say no more of past mistakes."

Amanda promised, in a strangled voice; Isabella bent her head lower over her work, to conceal a smile.

"Excellent! We must decide what you are to wear, for the day will soon be upon us. I am nearly certain that it must be white, and silk, I should imagine — but we will consult Madame Celeste on the morrow. Now I wonder — pearls, rubies? Or diamonds?"

She went off into a mild reverie, and Amanda rose to look out of the window, which faced the street. After a moment, she espied a figure crossing from the opposite flagway, and approaching the house purposefully. She recognised it for Mr. Thurlston. Her heart missed a beat.

Presently, the servant announced him. He entered, looking as usual, handsome, poised and debonair. He greeted the ladies politely, and, in response to my lady's invitation, he seated himself at Isabella's side, and began a trifling conversation.

What a splendid conspirator he was, thought Amanda! He did not betray by one word or look that there was any understanding between himself and Lady Twyford's younger daughter. He calmly sat there, chatting equally to all three; and if he could be said to pay more attention to one than another, an onlooker would have placed the preference with Bella, rather than her younger sister. He passed her the scissors whenever she required them — Isabella's passion for embroidery had grown of late — and gave his opinion upon the matching of the silks as though such a decision were of the utmost importance. It was all done very neatly, thought Amanda; so different from stupid John Webster, who in a like situation, had drawn down suspicion upon himself with every phrase he uttered. It crossed her mind that perhaps this might be because John was the more honest of the two: then she remembered the difference in situation of the gentlemen concerned. As the only son of a country squire, John, though not the heir to a great title and fortune, was yet one day to be master of his father's lands and comfortable income; while Mr. Thurlston had nothing but what could be gained only by the exercise of tact, and suppression of his own wishes in deference to those of others.

As time passed, and the appointed period which was the rule for morning calls drew to a close, Amanda chafed a little. She wanted to find a way of gaining a few moments alone with the gentleman, but for once, her ingenuity failed her utterly. She could think of nothing which would succeed in ridding her of both Mama and Isabella at the same time.

She had not looked for help from Mr. Thurlston; as far as she knew, he had nothing urgent to communicate to her, and their agreement had been that only in such a case would he try to see her alone. She was the one who had something to tell. But surely there could be no mistaking the import of a sentence which presently he let fall?

"The Park is so charming at this time of year, is it not? I frequently go there in the early morning, to avoid the crowds."

"That is what I find so vastly disagreeable about London," said Amanda, casually. "Every pleasant green place is filled with a chattering mob of people. It is not so in the country."

"You should try it at seven o'clock tomorrow morning," he said, with a smile. "You would be agreeably surprised."

"I shall most likely be abed," she answered, carelessly, seeming to be only half listening to him.

"She did once go out riding in the early morning," stated my lady. "I did not think it suitable."

He bowed, and changed the subject with alacrity. After a short interval, he rose to go.

"That is a vastly agreeable young man," remarked Lady Twyford, after his departure. "It is a thousand pities that he is, so to speak, penniless."

Isabella sighed: Amanda fancied that she might be thinking of John, but she had no time to dwell on this supposition, for her thoughts were all for the morrow, and for the assignation which had been so neatly made before her mother's face.

Almost she gave up the next morning, supposing herself mistaken, for it was some time before she could find Mr. Thurlston in the Park. Finally, she ran him to earth in a thickly wooded stretch, shielded from view on every side. He greeted her with his usual charming smile, but she sensed that he was ill at ease, and he seemed little disposed to linger.

He had sought her out, he informed her, to tell her that he knew his cousin to have met Sir Francis Dashwood a few days since.

"And so do I know it!" said Amanda, triumphantly. "At least, he didn't meet him, exactly, but he would have done, but for me!"

He asked what she meant, and was told some of the events of that fateful evening. He was given to understand that his cousin Charles had pretended to abduct her, and behaved in a vastly insulting way, but he was spared the full details. This was partly because Amanda did not care to recall them to her own memory; but more from a sense of reserve in dealing with one, who, when all was said, had been known to her but a short time.

"Pretend to abduct you?" he asked thoughtfully, looking into the middle distance.

"Oh, it was all a hum, you know!" said Amanda, hurriedly. "That odious creature actually had the effrontery to say that he considered I needed a sharp lesson!"

"It was unpardonable conduct," he replied, but his mind still did not seem to be on his words.

"Vile!" she agreed, wholeheartedly; then, with her irresistible honesty — "But I dare say my own conduct was not so very admirable, after all!"

"That does not excuse his taking advantage of a defenceless female: but you will be avenged, never fear, one day. I will try to discover when there is to be a meeting at Medmenham, and if he means to be present."

It was a novel idea to Amanda to think of herself as a defenceless female but she let that pass, too taken up with another speculation.

"How do you contrive to find out all these things?" she asked, curiously.

"I have my sources of information," he replied, vaguely, then not for the first time, glanced uneasily about him.

"But I believe we had best not linger here. When some definite knowledge comes to hand, we will meet again, and form a plan for smuggling you into the Abbey. Meanwhile, it will be better not to appear too intimate when we meet in public; we must seem to be two people who have nothing out of the way to say to each other. I'm sure you will agree."

Amanda assented; but somewhere in the back of her mind, a small niggling doubt buzzed about like a restless gnat. She was thoughtful as she rode homewards.

Later that same morning, over breakfast, my lady touched upon the matter of a date for Isabella's wedding.

"It is for you to say, my love, when it shall be," she offered, magnanimously. "That is a bride's privilege, you know!"

Isabella had been expecting this for some time now, and was not unprepared with her answer.

"Mr. Barsett and I have already discussed the point, Mama," she said, carelessly, but with a beating heart. "We were agreed that there is no haste."

"Indeed!" exclaimed my lady, in a tone of surprise. "That seems a very odd decision for a suitor to take."

"Oh, he was for fixing upon a day quite soon," replied Isabella, still airily. "But there is Amanda's birthday ball — and, one way and another, I did not quite see —"

"But you will surely not wish to have too long an engagement, my love. And June is the perfect month for a wedding! We must make a start on ordering your bride-clothes; that can be undertaken at once, while I am about to settle with Madame the details of our gowns for Amanda's ball. We will go this very morning!"

Isabella perforce consented, though without any of the expressions of joy which might have been expected.

"'Pon rep, I find it difficult to understand you!" her mother said, in tones of exasperation. "It has not taken long for the pleasures of the Town to pall as far as you are concerned! When we first arrived, you could think of nothing but balls and masquerades, and what you should wear to attend them! Now it seems all one to you whether you go or stay at home, and never have I seen you betray so little interest in matters of dress! I tell you, Isabella, you are fast becoming a dowd!"

"Nonsense, Mama," ventured Amanda, consuming rolls and butter voraciously, for she had eaten nothing before taking her ride in the Park — "Bella always looks quite the prettiest girl in any room she chooses to enter!"

"Well," admitted Lady Twyford, some-what mollified, "I will agree that your sister is a very handsome female; but she had best have a care, for all that. Good looks do not last for ever. Bella is close on twenty, and the sooner she is wed, the better."

She broke off, observing her younger daughter taking another roll, and spreading it thickly with butter.

"Amanda! Pray do not eat in that abandoned way!"

Suddenly, something seemed to snap in Isabella. She leapt to her feet, throwing down her napkin on the table with disgust.

"I will not be discussed and prosed over as though I were still in the schoolroom!" she exclaimed, in a high, unnatural voice. "I shall wed Mr. Barsett when I choose you hear, Mama? — when I choose!" She burst into tears, and ran from the room. Lady Twyford gazed after her, thunderstruck.

"Well!" she began. "Of all the —"

"Oh, hush, Mama!" interrupted Amanda. "Cannot you see that she is overwrought? I must go to her."

Lady Twyford nodded.

"Of course — nerves, poor child. I well remember before I wed your Papa — try if you may calm her."

Amanda ran lightly upstairs, and pushed open the door of her sister's bedchamber. She found Isabella lying across the great four-poster in an abandonment of grief.

She wisely said nothing for a moment, but gathered the shaking girl into her young arms. After a while, the sobs subsided. Isabella sat up, pushing the hair back from her wet cheeks. Amanda crossed to the washing-stand, and poured some water from a ewer into the basin.

"Bathe your face, my love."

Her sister obeyed, and Amanda watched silently while she repaired the damage to her appearance.

"It won't do, Bella," she said, at last, quietly.

"It must! It must!"

The words were spoken in low, broken tones.

Amanda leaned over, and taking her sister by the shoulders, forced Isabella to look into her eyes.

"Why must it? Tell me that."

"It's all arranged — I could not, for very shame, cry off now — Mama would never forgive me — and I should look so foolish —"

"Better look a fool than behave like one," said Amanda, grimly.

"Oh, you cannot understand! You are too young —"

"I am exactly," said Amanda, counting on her fingers, "one year, eleven months, two days and five hours younger than you."

"In time, yes: I was speaking of experience, of knowledge of the world."

"I have enough knowledge of the world not to wed a man I dislike!"

"I don't dislike him!" retorted Isabella. "That is just what I cannot make you understand! He — in some queer way, he fascinates me — and yet —"

"And yet you don't love him," finished Amanda.

"Oh, why must you talk always of love? What does it signify? The life a woman is to lead after marriage is surely the most important thing to her; as Mr. Barsett's wife, I shall have position, wealth, title — I shall live in Town, and pass my time in a thousand agreeable ways, instead of being buried alive in the country, with no fresh face to see in a round dozen of years! Where did you hear all this talk of love, Mandy? It is — it is vulgar!"

"I heard it from John Webster."

Isabella's face paled slightly. She was silent for a moment, brooding.

"Much he knows of it!" she broke out, at last. "A calf affection — a trifling thing that breaks at the first hint of opposition! If I ever considered love — if I ever allowed myself to do anything so improper — I should imagine it to be a passion that takes one by storm — that carries all before it!"

Amanda nodded. "Yes, I know, Bella: you conjure up the picture of a knight on a white charger, bearing you off in the teeth of all opposition! I am not the only member of the family endowed with a taste for the dramatic, it would seem! Well, I grant you that perhaps John is a little lacking in story-book gallantry, but he loves you truly, for all that! And you should be well matched on that head, for you yourself are grown a very model of propriety these days!"

"Mama is right," said Isabella, forcefully. "You are still a schoolgirl, Mandy."

"Don't dare to call me that!"

"Well you are, you know. But the words certainly seem to have a power of angering you quite out of proportion to their meaning. Why is that?"

"It's because he used them to me when first we met, and — and since."

"He?" Isabella's brows wrinkled in a frown. "Oh, you must mean Mr. Barsett. Yes, I recollect now. But when has he used them since? You have not seen him except in my company, and I cannot recall —"

"Oh, I don't know, precisely!" answered Amanda, hurriedly. This was dangerous ground: she tried a change of subject.

"You did not tell me that he had tried to appoint a day for the wedding."

A faint blush came to Isabella's cheek. She was recalling what had passed at that interview.

"Why do you blush?" asked her sister, deliberately tactless. "Did he make love to you, Bell?"

"Amanda!" exclaimed the outraged Isabella.

"Well, did he?" persisted the shameless girl.

The blush deepened. All at once, Isabella dropped her affectation of shocked modesty, and answered her sister in the old way of their days together in the country.

"It is of all things the most surprising," she said, slowly, "but he did, Mandy. He — he said that perhaps if I could — could learn to care for him, he might renounce those — those wild ways that have given his relatives so much anxiety."

"Lud!"

Amanda emitted a low whistle of surprise. Isabella felt moved to protest at this hoydenish conduct.

"Never mind that now," said Amanda. "What reply did you make?"

"I — oh, I said I would try, but then —" She broke off, confused.

"Yes? Then —?"

"Then he — he kissed me," replied Isabella, looking distressed. "Mandy, it was dreadful! I did not know how to bear it! I am afraid he must have seen how it was, for he apologised for having mentioned the subject at all, and afterwards he was his usual cool, collected self."

Amanda stared straight in front of her in complete silence for a few moments. At last she roused herself, and exclaimed vehemently: "Bella, you — you idiot!"

"Whatever can you mean? I —"

"Do you not see," asked her sister, scornfully, "what a chance you missed? You could have told him then that love between you was impossible, and put an end to the engagement; or, if you were still determined to go on with it, you could have made an effort to — to build upon the fascination which you say he has for you, to try and turn it into — something deeper, more permanent. You tried to steer a middle course, Bella, and 'pon my soul, I feel you were scarcely fair to the man! He was honest with you, at all events!"

"I didn't try to do anything, Mandy, I tell you — I was taken by surprise — I didn't realise how deeply I should detest his embrace!"

"Then how do you think to marry him?" asked her sister, bluntly.

"I was taken unawares — there is time enough, and I shall become used to the notion —"

"I wonder?" said Amanda, thoughtfully. Then with a change of tone: "Bella, did you find his kiss so very dreadful an experience?"

Isabella shuddered. "It is impossible to make you realise!"

Amanda sat down upon the bed, and drew her knees up until they touched her chin, a favourite attitude of hers when deep in thought.

"That is odd," she said slowly. "Do you know, Bella, in spite of the fact that I think Mr. Barsett the most detestable creature alive, and I'm determined to prevent your marrying him, still — I —" She broke off, and brooded, clasping her knees firmly in her arms.

"Yes — what?" asked Isabella, impatiently.

"I should imagine that to — to be — embraced by him — could not be so very disagreeable an experience — it might even have — a certain attraction," finished Amanda, jerkily.

"You can say that, Mandy? *You?*" asked her sister, incredulously.

Suddenly Amanda laughed.

"To be sure," she said, airily. "But then, you are always telling me that I have by far too much imagination!"

Chapter XII: The Ball

The days slipped past, and no more was said of Charles Barsett between the sisters. Once or twice he came to the house, though not nearly so often as Roger Thurlston. It seemed that Isabella had put her doubts and fears resolutely behind her, and was now completely reconciled to the match. However this might have been, she appeared in excellent spirits, entering into the business of choosing bride-clothes with suitable enthusiasm. Amanda had her own reasons for avoiding the subject: at any time now, she was expecting Mr. Thurlston to tell her that their plans were ready to be put into execution. Moreover, for some reason that she could not quite define, she found herself reluctant to speak of Charles Barsett to anyone. She could not altogether avoid meeting him, but whenever she did nothing but the barest civilities passed between them.

A few days before Amanda's ball, John Webster returned to Town. He paid a formal call upon the Twyfords which passed off without undue awkwardness. Isabella was politely distant, Lady Twyford watchful, and my lord and Amanda warm and welcoming. Lord Twyford asked John to dine with them; it was perhaps fortunate that Isabella had an engagement which took her from home that evening.

During the course of the evening, Amanda managed a few words in private with John.

"Mama said you would be sure to return for my ball," she began, "but I had almost given up hope of it."

"You may be certain I should not miss that occasion!" he replied gallantly: then added, with irrepressible honesty — "But in any case, I could not bring myself to stay longer away!"

She lowered her voice. "I am glad of it, because before long I hope to embark on an enterprise that will need your help to ensure its success. You are arrived just in the nick of time!"

"What enterprise?" he asked, suspiciously. "If it is anything akin to those others — egad, I almost blush now to recall them!"

She shook her head. "No, this one will be more certain, for it is not being planned by myself alone. I have aid, this time —"

"What are you talking of, Amanda?" asked Lady Twyford, across the tea-cups. "I am sure it must be vastly disagreeable, for John looks so very serious!"

"We were speaking of my ball, Mama," replied Amanda, hastily and not altogether untruthfully. "John is to lead me out for the first dance."

"Very suitable," approved my lord. "I was thinking that the duty might fall on me, and I fear my dancing days are over. But this is better; who will look to dance with her father, when she may command a fine young fellow to partner her? Eh, miss?"

He pinched Amanda's cheek, and she dimpled at him roguishly. Lady Twyford produced something between a smile and a frown; she rated John's claims very low as a suitor for either of her daughters.

Talk nowadays tended to revolve around the forthcoming ball. Dress was discussed with a frequency that drove Lord Twyford to seek shelter in the clubs; and the ordering of food, flowers and other adornments kept my lady in constant consultation with the housekeeper. Amanda found half her thoughts upon her plot, and, in spite of herself, half upon this other occasion which was to launch her into the Polite World. Child though she was in many ways, she was yet completely feminine, and the prospect of her very own ball aroused in her all the pleasurable anticipation which was to be expected from a young lady of her age.

The day at last arrived, and with it countless gifts for Amanda. Shortly after breakfast, the morning-room was already strewn with torn wrappings and costly objects, some of which were totally unsuited to their recipient.

"Only fancy, Mama," she said, with a pout, "my aunt Matchett sending me this china figure! It is very pretty, of course," she added, doubtfully, handing it to her mother.

Lady Twyford took the trinket, and turned it over in her hand, revealing the inscription 'Josiah Wedgwood' on its base.

"It is well enough," pronounced her Mama, "though not of any great value, and certainly not the kind of thing to appeal to you, as Matty must surely have realised! However, a time may come when you will care for such trifles. Gracious, here are more flowers! I declare, I need not have been at the expense of ordering any for the ballroom, so many have you had!"

This remark was occasioned by a footman entering, bearing a huge wreath of pure cream roses, small tight-lipped buds with heads set close together. Amanda gasped with pleasure, and flew across the room to receive them.

"Are they not beyond anything perfect, Mama? Who can have sent them, do you suppose?"

She was fumbling for the card as she spoke. It was found at last, small and unobtrusive, and inscribed 'To my little sister-to-be, in affectionate congratulation'.

"Oh!" she said, and blushed.

"Who is it, Mandy?" asked Isabella, curiously, and gently took the card from her sister's relaxed fingers.

"Why, Mama, it's from Mr. Barsett! And he has put the drollest message —"

"Very handsome, I'm sure," nodded Lady Twyford, "and in perfect taste. Anything else would have been — but there, one would not expect Charles Barsett to err in such a matter. What exactly is the shape supposed to represent, child? It looks like some kind of hook — the upper part of a shepherd's crook, mayhap?"

But Amanda knew better, and the flush of pleasure left her face. Her eyes flashed. "It is a mark of interrogation, Mama," she answered quietly enough.

Both my lady and Isabella stared at her.

"You mean to say the kind of thing one writes to mark a question?" asked her mother, amazed. "Well, to be sure, that is a very odd shape to choose! A star, now, or a crescent — a heart shape would not, of course, be suitable in this case —"

"It is — it is a kind of — jest which he has with me," stuttered Amanda, feeling foolish.

Lady Twyford glanced sharply at her face, and decided for once to be merciful. It was not often that she was privileged to see her younger daughter in a state of embarrassment. Somehow the sight brought out all her latent maternal instincts.

"Oh, well, jest or no, it is a very pretty gift," she said, dismissing the subject.

Amanda agreed, with compressed lips, and passed on to her other gifts.

The rest of the day passed in a flutter of excitement and preparation. Only ten minutes before the first carriage drew up outside the house did Amanda's abigail pronounce her mistress to be ready.

"I should think so, too, Mary, for I've looked so often in the mirror that I quite detest myself!" said Amanda emphatically. "Still, I believe I shall contrive to do you credit, if only I may manage to avoid entangling myself with these hoops! Thank goodness I am not obliged to wear them every day. Thank you for your pains — you have been a deal more patient than I should have in your place."

The girl coloured with pleasure, and looked admiringly at her young mistress as she passed out of the door of her chamber, and began to descend the staircase. Lord and Lady Twyford were already waiting in the flower-banked hall: they turned as they heard Amanda's step on the stair. There was a sharp intake of breath as their eyes lighted upon her.

Her gown was of white silk, falling softly over the formal hoops, and cut away at the front to reveal an underdress of white, embroidered with large pink roses. The corsage was low, and her white neck, encircled by the simple necklet of pearls which had been her father's birthday gift to her, rose from it with proud grace. The honey-gold curls were brushed and tended until they sparkled like a new-minted guinea; and Isabella thought that she had never before seen her sister's eyes look so blue.

"My little girl," murmured his lordship, with feeling, and hastily blew his nose.

Amanda finished the rest of the stairs at a run.

"Will I do?" she asked naïvely.

"Do?" answered my lady, laughing. "La, child, you will set the Town by the ears tonight, I'm thinking! But none of your hoydenish pranks, mind. In such a gown you must be all demureness."

For once this was Amanda's intention. With her inborn sense of drama, she had put on the role with the clothes, and would continue to play to perfection the belle of the ball just so long as it pleased her. She succeeded so well in sustaining her part during her first dance with John Webster that poor John was quite overawed, and found himself bowing over her hand as though she had been a captivating stranger.

Roger Thurlston noticed it, and drew Isabella's attention to the circumstance. Charles Barsett, like a good many others, had not yet arrived; and, as Isabella could scarcely stand up for the first dance with anyone other than her betrothed, the two were sitting together, watching the dancers.

"Your young friend from the country appears to be quite taken with your sister," he remarked, smiling.

Isabella's eyes, which had been fixed on the pair since their first moment on the floor, narrowed slightly.

"Would you say so?" she asked lightly. "They have known each other since childhood, do not forget."

"That is just what I find so remarkable," he answered, leaning towards her in a confidential manner. "One would expect childhood playmates to have a free and easy manner together, but only see how he glances at her — and she at him."

Isabella watched more closely. The dance was ending: low over Amanda's hand bowed John, and just brushed it with his lips. Amanda glanced at him in reply from under her long lashes — a coy, teasing glance that seemed to hold a depth of promise.

A cold hand touched Isabella's heart. Could it be possible that John would look at another — so soon? And Mandy, of all people... But no, it was the effect of the June night, the music, Amanda looking so adorable. Everyone said that Amanda was very like her sister, only more roguish. She forced a little laugh.

"Mandy is playing a game," she said huskily. "She is such a child at heart." He looked at her. Did she imagine it, or was his glance a pitying one?

"That is just what I should have supposed," he answered gravely, "had I not known that —" He paused, and removing an elegant snuff box from his pocket, flicked open the lid.

"Yes?" Isabella, although she did not realise it, at that moment sounded very like her sister. There was the same impatient touch. "You were saying, Mr. Thurlston —?"

Once more the compassionate look, this time more easily recognisable.

"It is of no moment," he said, and took snuff deliberately.

Isabella mastered an almost over-powering impulse to stamp her foot. "But you cannot leave your sentence thus unfinished, sir!" She affected a light tone. "I am all suspense."

He shut the box with a snap, and returned it to his pocket in a leisurely manner. "Dear lady, I would not willingly cause you one unquiet moment," he said solicitously. "Allow me to wield your fan for you: your cheeks are hot."

Isabella repressed a sudden desire to slap his face. Really, she had never until this moment understood how like Amanda she still could be.

"Mr. Thurlston, my sister is in many ways younger than her years," she said persuasively. "If you know anything of her with which you feel her family should be acquainted, you may safely tell me."

"But that would be tale-bearing!" he protested.

Isabella felt her temper rising, but made a last valiant effort to restrain it. "You need not fear to carry tales of Mandy to me. If it were Mama — or Papa — now, but Mandy and I have few secrets from each other. Never fear, I shall not betray her, whatever it may be."

"I daresay you are right." He hesitated a moment more, then went on quickly "Perhaps, after all, you ought to know of it, for there is no saying where it may eventually lead."

He paused again. Isabella caught her bottom lip between her teeth, to prevent herself from crying out in impatience. He went on slowly, deliberately, as if intent on prolonging her suspense.

"You may perchance recall an occasion not long since when I called upon you one morning at your house, and happened to mention my habit of riding early in the park?"

A second's thought, and Isabella nodded, still biting her lip.

"I have seen them there on several occasions — oh, they have not observed me, for I took good care to keep out of sight when I realised who it was. Your sister was unattended by any servant: they were quite alone."

A lump came to Isabella's throat, but she seemed unable to rid herself of it; her long white fingers twined together restlessly in her lap.

"Ah, my esteemed cousin! And filling my place nobly, I see. I can always depend upon you."

The lazy drawl floated across Isabella's agonised thoughts. Roger Thurlston rose somewhat hastily, and offered his chair to Charles Barsett, who stood before them resplendent in black and silver, a diamond glistening on his finger, and another in the fall of lace at his throat.

"Thank you, cousin. It is perhaps only fitting that I should take my rightful place."

The gentle words brought a faint tinge of colour to Mr. Thurlston's cheek, but he managed a wintry smile. Isabella sat on, like one dazed.

"A thousand pardons, my love, for my lamentably tardy appearance," Charles said, bowing over her hand. "I declare I am a positive slave to that valet of mine; damme if the fellow doesn't feel himself insulted if he is expected to dress me in anything under four hours! If you could but see —" He broke off, and eyed Isabella sharply.

"You will pardon me, I am sure," said Roger Thurlston hastily. "I see that Miss Dunster is without a partner."

"Good God, that pudding-faced female!" ejaculated Charles, but his eyes were still on Isabella. "By all means, my boy, lead her out; she will have none of me — fortunately, she has never been able to forgive me for my engagement."

Roger departed unnoticed. Charles sat down at his betrothed's side. "There is blood upon your lip, child," he said gently. "Here, take my handkerchief. What has that —fiend — been saying to you?"

"Thank you," said Isabella, taking the handkerchief, and dabbing at her mouth. "I — I cannot think how that can have happened. I — I must have — caught it with my fan."

He picked up the trinket, examined it briefly, then raised his eyes to her face. "You must permit me to buy you another one," he said smoothly. "But what did my esteemed cousin say to you?"

"He — we — just talked of — of Amanda," was the halting reply.

His eyes searched her face. There was more here, he knew, but evidently she was not to confide in him.

"I have not greeted your sister as yet," he said. "She was dancing when I entered the room. I observed that she looks very beautiful tonight — I have never seen her appear to better advantage."

Isabella choked a little. "Yes, doesn't she? So — so ethereal, and not a bit like the little girl she usually seems. But I forget — she is grown up, after all... "

Her voice trailed off. There was silence for a moment, then he leaned over, and lightly touched one of her hands. "You do not feel that you can confide in me?" he asked softly.

She drew her hand hastily away, and affected a laugh.

"Confide? What nonsense is this, sir? What should I have to confide? Had you not best go and greet my sister, for it is her evening, and all must do her homage, you know."

He shrugged lightly, and his expression closed in again.

"You do well to remind me of my duty. I shall not be long away, and then perhaps you will do me the honour to dance with me?"

She assented, and in a moment he was lost from her view.

Amanda had rejoined her parents when Charles Barsett finally ran her to earth. He made his bow solemnly, and offered congratulations. She thanked him with a hint of reserve in her manner.

"You must allow me to compliment you upon your looks, little sister," he said ironically. "Such beauty holds me spellbound."

"It could not, however, bring you here in good time, sir," she retorted with a sarcastic smile.

"You have me there," he answered, in mock dismay. "But the blame lies at my valet's door — I shall dismiss him instantly when I return."

"That would be a pity, for your absence has not put me about in the slightest."

He looked at her reproachfully. "But you must not assume such cruel looks, Miss Amanda. I protest, they do not accord with your attire, which is that of an angel."

The compliment was ironically under-lined. She sketched a little curtsy. "I thank you, sir. No doubt you know well how an angel should look. I must thank you, too, for my gift from you."

"Gift? Ah, my roses — an offering at the shrine of beauty. Dare I hope that you approved them?"

"Vastly." She dimpled. "But I fear the Greeks even when they bring gifts — more particularly in such sinister shape!"

He raised an eyebrow in the way she disliked. "So you had the advantage of a classical education? I congratulate you."

"Miss Brown taught me most things, sir, except perhaps how to — get the better of a rogue!"

"And that," he said, smiling, "your own native wit can teach you, I'll be bound. But may I hope for the honour of leading you out in the dance at some time during the course of the evening?"

"Alas, sir," she said, with apparent regret, "you are come so late that I am promised for the duration of the ball! It is melancholy, is it not?"

"It is indeed," he answered, and there was a tinge of real regret in his voice. "Is there not the smallest chance —?"

"Why, here is one of my partners come to claim me!" exclaimed Amanda, not letting him finish. "You will excuse me, sir?"

He watched her go off on the arm of some young dandy; there was a twinkle in his eye. Of a certainty, these sparring matches did give a certain zest to his occasional meetings with Miss Amanda.

"Mr. Barsett!"

He turned at the sound of his name, and groaned inwardly when he saw who it was who addressed him.

"Why, Mr. Barsett!" cooed Miss Dunster. "We have not met in an age! I must congratulate you upon your recent engagement: it was such a surprise."

"You are most kind, madam," he murmured, looking about him for some way of escape. At the present moment it appeared hopeless; there was no one in sight to whom he could present the lady as a partner, for the dance was just about to begin, and all about him were already leading their partners out.

"Can I perhaps procure you some refreshment?" he asked, in desperation.

"I declare that is *most* thoughtful in you!" she gushed. "I should like a glass of lemonade of *all* things — but do not be too long away — there are so *many* things I want to say to you."

This remark echoed his own fears, and he made his way to the refreshment table with alacrity, thankful for the respite, and on the look-out for some way out of his difficulty.

As he was procuring the promised glass of lemonade, he came across his father, sampling the punch with every evidence of satisfaction. "My dear sir, you are well met," he said, clapping his hand upon his parent's shoulder. "There is someone here to whom I positively must present you."

"Have a care, Charles!" warned Lord Barsett, as some of the liquid spilt from the glass he was holding. "This stuff's too good to waste. I want to see you, too, my boy. When's this wedding to take place, eh?"

"We'll discuss that later, father. Just now I have urgent work for you to do."

He took up the glass of lemonade, and propelled my lord gently but firmly in the direction of the waiting Miss Dunster.

"Damme, boy, let be!" protested his lordship. "I'm as well here as anywhere, give you my oath."

"Doubtless, but there are duties to be performed."

"Duties? Nothing to do with me Twyford's affair," stated Lord Barsett decidedly. He had found the punch excellent, and was reluctant to leave it.

"But we must consider ourselves in some sort connected with the family," coaxed Charles, as he led him onwards relentlessly. "We must help to make Miss Amanda's ball a success, eh, sir?"

"Fine little girl," commented my lord. "Like your mother, Charles. I thought the other one was, but this girl's got more spirit — nearer your mother's colouring, too."

Charles made no comment to this, for by now they had reached Miss Dunster's side, and he was busy with the presentations. His father cast him a reproachful glance, which deepened as Charles presently took the opportunity to slip away.

Ditched, b'God! thought his lordship resentfully. If it isn't all of a piece with that precious whelp's behaviour —!

He applied himself to Miss Dunster, however, with all a gentleman's courtesy, and presently was enabled to escape from her side by his nephew, Roger, coming to his rescue. He noticed that his graceless son was now dancing with Isabella, and paused for a moment to watch them, a frown between his eyes.

They danced well enough together, but seemed to derive precious little enjoyment from it. Yet she was a strikingly handsome girl, the Twyford female —

His thoughts were interrupted by the discovery that Amanda Twyford was at his side. She, too had her eyes upon her sister and Charles.

"Well, my dear?" he addressed her. "Why ain't you dancing? Are all the young men blind?"

She dimpled at him, and sank into a nearby chair.

"I am fatigued, my lord; I would as soon watch for a while."

"They make a handsome couple, do they not?" he asked, following the direction of her gaze.

"Ye-es," she admitted, doubtfully. "But not, I think, a very lively one, sir!"

"What d'ye expect?" he asked jovially. "Love is a serious business, my dear."

"Love?"

There was a trace of scorn in her voice. He looked at her, surprised. "You don't set much store by it, eh?"

"On the contrary," said Amanda emphatically, "I am a great champion of love! But I fail to observe much of the grand passion in this case."

"Hrrmph! No, maybe you're in the right of it there. He's a cold fish, that son of mine."

"I wonder?" asked Amanda, reminiscently.

"Eh?"

"You know him best, my lord," she said impetuously. "Tell me, is he really as cold and — detached as he appears to be?"

Lord Barsett shook his head. "Don't ask me, child. I know him less than anyone, it seems."

"How can that be? You are his father."

My lord gave an embarrassed cough. The influence of the punch was making itself felt, however, and loosened his tongue.

"There has been little sympathy between Charles and myself, I fear. Some fault may have been on my side — my wife died when the child was born, and I had little time to spare for him."

"Poor infant," said Amanda, softly. "To lose a mother and a father at one fell blow."

He glanced at her quickly. "Mayhap you feel that I should have taken more interest in the child? Well, perhaps so. During these last months, for some reason, I have taken to asking myself the same question. At that time, I felt that I had done what was necessary in providing a substitute mother and a brother for the child, in the shape of my sister and her boy. It worked well, too, for a while. Charles was fond of his cousin — in fact, fond is too mild a word —"

"Yes, of course," said Amanda, musingly. "Of course, it would be don't you see, sir? For there was no one else to whom he could give his affection —"

"I —" He stared at her, bereft of speech. "You go too fast for me, m'dear," he said, after a pause. "What are you trying to say?"

She hesitated in her turn. "I — I'm not sure myself," she answered slowly. "For a moment I felt that I had made some discovery — but it is gone before I could properly lay hold of it." Her expression changed, and she smiled. "Would you not like some punch, my lord? I see my father is by the refreshment table, and I must soon leave your side, for I am engaged for the next dance."

Chapter XIII: A Summons

On the evening immediately following the ball, Mrs. Thurlston sat opposite her brother in the drawing-room at St. James's Square. There was a faint air of suffering on her thin, angular face, and several times she stifled a yawn.

"I declare I must be getting beyond these late hours, James, for I find myself overcome with fatigue today after the Twyford's ball last night. An insipid affair, don't you agree? But, of course, one had to attend."

My lord stifled a yawn, in his turn. His sister's company was never stimulating; fortunately he was seldom at home to endure it.

"Oh, I don't know. The punch was excellent. Of course, our dancing days are over, Fanny, but the young people seemed to be well enough entertained. The Twyford chit — little Miss Amanda — was here, there, and everywhere. Pretty little thing — plenty of spirit, too —"

Mrs. Thurlston made a gesture of distaste. "A hoyden!" she said waspishly. "How her mother can tolerate such conduct passes my comprehension. If she were my daughter I should place her upon a diet of bread and water for a few days, or else pack her off to the country until she had learnt her manners!"

"You've always been critical of other people's children, haven't you, Fan? Only your own son could ever win your approval."

"I flatter myself that I am not easily pleased," said Mrs. Thurlston complacently. "I am not so readily taken in as some people appear to be. As for Roger, has he not always been everything that is desirable in a young man?"

"Yes," answered my lord slowly. "I suppose so —and yet —"

"Yet what?" she asked sharply. "Is there any count on which you can justly offer criticism?"

"That's just it. Damme, Fanny, I wonder sometimes if the boy's human! He doesn't seem to have any faults."

"You should be very glad of it. Your own son has enough, in all conscience."

My lord's eyes flickered towards the portrait hanging over the mantelshelf. His sister noticed the movement, and a spasm of irritation crossed her features.

"True," he said. "But it occurs to me that I may perchance be somewhat to blame myself in that."

"To blame — you?" She stared at him incredulously. "I'm sure you have always given him every opportunity — from childhood upwards, he has been denied nothing —"

"Except perhaps the most important thing," answered my lord, quietly.

She made a gesture of impatience. "Pray, what has come over you, James? What important thing could he possibly have lacked?"

"Affection," replied Lord Barsett, tersely, avoiding her wide opened eyes. "The interest of a truly loving parent — he never had that, Fanny."

"What nonsense is this?" she asked scornfully. "I think you must have sat too long over the wine, James!"

He shook his head. "I am as sober as you, sister. It's taken me close on thirty years to see my error, and even now I doubt if I should have done so, but for a chance word from a slip of a girl."

"What girl? Do you speak of Isabella Twyford?"

Once again he shook his head. "No, but of the other one —
little Amanda — the one you called hoyden."

"Oh, she!" Mrs. Thurlston said tartly. "What has she been
saying to you, pray? Something vastly pert, I'll be bound! She is
for ever putting herself forward."

"I can't recall her exact words anyway, they don't signify: it
was the tenor of her speech. She said something to the effect
that Charlie lost both his parents at one blow. I tell you, Fan, it
made me think. If — if Kitty had lived, that boy would have
been the apple of her eye — ay, and of mine, too, I don't
doubt."

"How can you be sure that he would not have disgusted
her?" said his sister contemptuously. "This is maudlin
sentiment, brother, if ever I heard it."

Her words brushed past him, seeming to make no impact.

"I blamed him for Kit's death," he said, in a low, despondent
tone that was very unlike him. "He was a babe — helpless —
and I turned my back on him, swallowed up in my own selfish
— yes, I see it now — selfish grief. She would have found
such a thing hard to forgive."

"Nonsense!" said Mrs. Thurlston briskly. "You should take
one of those powders I told you of — whenever I have the
vapours they do me a power of good. It is very likely all these
late nights undermining your constitution. You are not a young
man, you know. I will have Thomson fetch you one of them
immediately."

She rose as if to summon the servant, but he stayed her with
a gesture, and himself rose from his chair, moving towards the
door. "Spare yourself the trouble, Fanny. There is more here
than a powder may cure. I'll bid you good night."

After he had gone, she sat on for a while, a worried frown on
her thin face.

Presently she heard Roger's step, and rose to greet him.

"Still up, Mother?" He bent to kiss her cheek. "Where is my uncle?"

"He's retired — or so I think. Roger —" She caught at his arm urgently. "He is in a very odd humour."

"What kind of humour?" he asked, frowning.

She repeated as nearly as she could remember it the conversation which had taken place between herself and her brother. He heard her out in silence, brow lifted.

"So Miss Amanda Twyford grows upon him, does she?" he said at last, softly. "So much the better."

"What do you mean? Roger, I am alarmed for your future. It has never been very secure, and now that James has found this sudden new tenderness for your cousin —"

"Never fear, Mother," he smiled at her reassuringly. "I know a trick worth two of that."

"What do you mean to do?" she asked, alarmed. "I pray you, go carefully, Roger. You have nothing of your father's gambling streak as far as money is concerned, but I sometimes wonder if you do not play for too high a stake with your fate. If all your expectations fail, son, you could wed that West Country heiress — the plain one — what is her name? I noticed yesterday evening that she seemed very taken with you, and there is no one else in the field for her."

He grimaced. "Miss Dunster? Charles calls her the suet pudding, and, on my oath, he's in the right of it! I should need to be desperate indeed to consider such a step, and all is not yet lost. Like you, I am coming to rely less upon my uncle's goodwill, but I fancy I know a way, Mother, to hook a fortune and a pretty face into the bargain."

"You don't mean Amanda Twyford?" she asked quickly. "I cannot abide the female, but if you think there is a chance —"

"I did have the notion, at one time, but now I have more knowledge of how things stand, and an altogether better plan. I do not mean to tell you what it is, Mother, and then there is no danger of your betraying me."

"I betray you!"

Her tone was bitter and incredulous. He put an arm about her, soothingly. "Not wittingly, I know, but it is easier for you to be in complete ignorance of my affairs."

"I have seldom known what you were about," she said, complainingly. "You were ever one to keep your own counsel."

"And have I not so far managed our affairs well enough?"

She nodded, grudgingly. "I suppose so; we have been comfortable here all these years. But that is not all to your credit."

"I grant you that; you have contrived wonderfully. But only trust me now, and we shall both reap the benefit, you'll see."

Over a week passed, and nothing of moment occurred, save that the weather suddenly took a turn for the better, and became very hot. Charles Barsett escorted Isabella to the play; the lady was gay, vivacious, but aloof, the gentleman ironically gallant. Amanda contrived a clandestine meeting in the park with John, and explained the plan she had in mind. Mr. Thurlston had as good as indicated that he did not wish Webster to know who was helping her in the affair, but she inadvertently let it out before she could stop herself. John received her communication dubiously.

"You can't go about sneaking into other people's houses, Mandy. It's not at all —"

"The thing," Amanda finished for him, in mocking tones. "I refuse — yes, positively refuse — to argue this point again. Are you with me, John, or are you not?"

"I can't think," he objected, "what this other fellow is about to contemplate embroiling a female in such a — a hare-brained scheme. Either he must be wanting in his wits or else —" He paused, and relapsed into thought.

"Or else what?"

"Damme if I know! Is he taken with you, Mandy?"

A little colour came into her cheeks. "No, of course not, nothing of that kind. What can have put such a notion into your head? But he is willing to help me — possibly out of kindness — because he, too, feels that Mr. Barsett is not worthy of Bella — possibly —" She broke off.

"What is it?" he asked. "There's something troubling you, Mandy."

She seemed ill at ease. "Oh, nothing: only it did occur to me that — that he bears no love to his cousin."

"By all accounts that feeling is reciprocated."

"Yes, but —" again the hesitation — "I fancy that Mr. Barsett is not exactly looking to do his cousin an injury."

"And you feel that Thurlston might be?"

She nodded uncomfortably. "It is only a notion of mine, and must be wrong, by all we have heard. Anyway, what do his motives matter to us? The thing is, he is willing to get me into the Abbey — how, I know not — to see for myself what goes on there, and the part taken in it by Mr. Barsett, so that I can report to Bella."

"Well, I don't like it," said John, emphatically. "And what's more, I've a good mind to put a stop to it."

She looked at him in horror. "John, you could not — you don't mean to peach on me? Surely you could never be so base!"

"It might be the best thing," he said, his face grim.

Two hands seized his arm urgently, and a pair of blue eyes gazed imploringly into his. "John, you would not."

He grinned sheepishly. "Never fear, I could never bring myself to give you away. But I've a mind to have a word with this fellow Thurlston."

"You had much better not," she said quickly. "I'm not perfectly certain that he wishes you to know of his part in the affair."

He frowned. "How does he know so much? He tells you that what goes on at this Abbey is a closely guarded secret, yet he himself seems to have a reasonably exact knowledge concerning the doings there. How does he manage it?"

"He said something about having sources of information," replied Amanda dubiously.

"Sounds like spying. Egad, Mandy, I don't know that I care much for the sound of this Thurlston fellow. Barsett may be a rake, and a thought wild, but he doesn't strike me as the kind of chap to spy on another."

"All the same, he's not going to marry my sister," stated Amanda, firmly. "And unless I am to think you a craven for the rest of my days, you are going to help me prevent him."

"Put like that, of course —"

He was reluctantly persuaded, and they parted on the understanding that she would get word to him when the moment was ripe for putting their plan into execution.

On the evening following his visit to the theatre with Isabella, Charles Barsett received a letter. It did not come through the post, but was delivered to him by a pot-boy from a tavern in Covent Garden; and the manner of its delivery was unusual. Charles had taken a chair to the house of a friend who was expecting him for an evening of cards. As he alighted, having paid off the chairmen, a youth came flying round the corner of the street, all but colliding with him. With an oath, Charles Barsett put out his hand to restrain the lad; a folded paper was thrust into it, and the boy vanished.

Only one person whom Charles knew was at all likely to have a note delivered in such a melodramatic style. He smiled wryly, and stowed the paper away in his pocket, to be read later. He had almost forgotten it by the time he returned home in the small hours of the morning. A moth fluttering at his candle for some reason recalled it to his memory; he drew it forth, and read the brief message.

'The most noble Order of St. Francis is to assemble as usual for the Summer Solstice, in the place of which you know. All Friars of the Superior Order are asked to attend, and each may introduce a Lady of cheerful, lively disposition to join the ranks of the Nuns. Look that you fail not your Holy Prior.'

His smile changed to a frown. He tossed the paper carelessly on to a side-table. Typical of Francis, this dramatic message delivered in a roundabout way: he was a strange fellow, with his odd pranks and mysteries, and all the mummery of this secret society of his.

What drove him to it, a man of taste and intellect? For that matter, thought Charles Barsett with a shrug, what drove himself to it?

The question pulled him up short. He was not normally the man to indulge in introspection. Long ago, he had put by the temptation to do so, fearing what he would find. Certain essentials of life had failed him, and he had tried to distract his attention from the gaps by filling his time with any diversion that offered, however wild. For some years now, the Order of the Monks of Medmenham had tickled his impish fancy. Why then did the thought of it suddenly fill him with impatience, almost a sense of shame?

He decided that he would not attend this meeting. He was done with all that. He was soon to marry a lovely lady, who — he paused in his reverie — who undoubtedly despised and loathed him. There was no disguising the fact that this was so: Isabella Twyford had shrunk from his embrace in horror. On a sudden, he thought of the other sister, the little hoyden who had struggled in his arms some few days since, in her dreadful stable-boy's disguise. She, too, had said that she hated him; but there had not been the shrinking disgust, the sense of outrage in her repulses, which had been shown him by his bride-to-be.

The past had offered Charles Barsett no affection: it would seem that the future was to be equally barren.

He stood up, and took his way to his bedchamber, on his face the look which Amanda detested. His mind was quite up; he would attend the Summer Revels of the Order, after all.

He had been gone some time, and the house was dark and quiet, when presently a footman came by, soft-footed. He was about to extinguish the solitary candle which had been left burning in the room when his eye chanced upon the paper lying on the table.

He carried it to the candle, and scanned its contents with some labour. Not for the first time in his life did he thank the relentless mother who had forced him to Sunday School as a lad, so that he might have the advantage of learning to read. It had seemed to be a useless accomplishment until these last few years, when fate had put him in touch with someone who had need of a spy in the service of the Honourable Charles Barsett.

Since that time, his early toil over the alphabet had been amply rewarded.

He pocketed the paper, and stole softly away, bearing the candle with him.

Chapter XIV: Amanda Prepares for Action

"What urgent family business can he possibly have that will take him from the side of his affianced bride for more than a se'enight?" asked Lady Twyford, scornfully. "It is what I warned you of, Isabella; you have not been sufficiently oncoming, and now he grows tired of you even before you are wed."

"Pray, hush, Mama," implored Isabella, her cheeks flushed, and her eyes suspiciously bright. "Mr. Barsett and I do not want to be for ever living in each other's pockets!"

"Small danger of that, it seems," retorted my lady tartly. "But did he not tell you where exactly he was going?" she continued, after a pause, evidently unwilling to let the subject drop.

"I believe he said Buckinghamshire, but I cannot be sure," replied Isabella, casually. "Mama, should we not call upon Brownie and our aunt in Richmond, one day soon? Amanda, you will like to see Brownie again, I know."

Amanda, thus appealed to, readily assented, willing to aid her sister in changing a distasteful subject; but her thoughts were upon this information concerning Charles Barsett's movements, which Isabella had that moment divulged. So the gentleman was to go into Buckinghamshire, was he? It was possible, she thought, with a stirring of excitement, that he had in fact gone to the Abbey, and this might be the moment for which she had been waiting so eagerly.

"Oh, yes, to be sure, we will go over to Richmond one day soon," promised my lady. "Amanda, do not frown so, child. I declare, I do not know what is to be done with my daughters! One is determined to wreck all her chances of marriage by unpretty behaviour, while the other has not wit enough to hold a suitor when she finds one!"

"Mama, I think you should try one of those powders that Mrs. Thurlston was recommending to you the other day," remarked Amanda, her tongue in her cheek. "You seem sadly out of sorts; it must be the heat."

"Nonsense!" snapped her mother, moving over to the window. "Though I must confess that this sudden warmth does take one unawares — and, of course, it seems more oppressive in London than in the country. Well, I declare!" she exclaimed, breaking off — "if it isn't Mr. Thurlston calling upon us again, and you and I, Amanda, not fit to be seen, dressed in our morning wrappers! You must entertain him, Isabella, until we shall have changed into something more suitable — unless we deny ourselves to him."

"Oh, no, don't do that!" exclaimed Amanda hastily. "He may have something I mean, he must realise that we are within, for he cannot have failed to see you standing at the window, Mama. After all, it is wide open."

Lady Twyford gave her daughter a keen glance, then, with a shrug, decided that she probably had imagined the eagerness in Amanda's tone.

"Come away, then, child, since we are to admit him. We shall not be long away, Isabella."

She whisked Amanda before her out of the room. Scarcely had they left than Roger Thurlston was announced.

Isabella had not seen him for a few days, though he was a very regular caller, and they were always encountering him at social events. She greeted him warmly, for he was quite a favourite with all the family, and for a few moments they chatted of the weather and other trivial topics of the day.

"I have heard something today which I can scarcely credit," he said, after a time.

"What is that, sir?" she asked.

Her glance was easy, merry, interested. She did not often look so at Charles, he thought, with a little surge of triumph. His look was sober, however, when he answered her.

"I heard that my cousin was to leave Town for an indefinite sojourn in the country."

"And so?" She gave him a challenging glance.

"It cannot be true? He does not leave you so soon after your betrothal?"

Isabella tossed her head carelessly.

"Oh, as to that, our betrothal is full a month old, Mr. Thurlston! We are become quite accustomed to it now."

He looked at her gravely. "You speak lightly," he said, in a low tone, "but I fancy I know what you feel."

"Indeed, sir?"

Her voice had a slight edge to it. Isabella might like Mr. Thurlston, but she would permit no one to take a liberty with her, and she considered that his present remarks bordered on the impertinent.

He paused, sensing her antagonism, and weighing what was best to do. But such an opportunity as this might not come again for a long time: he could not afford to be too circumspect, and must risk a throw.

"Believe me, Miss Twyford — may I say Miss Isabella? — you cannot realise how I suffer with you. To be so slighted —"

"Enough, sir! This is rank impertinence!"

"Do not say so," he implored, in a passionate tone. "If you could only know the depth of my feeling for you —"

She gasped, and put her hands before her face.

"What are you saying?"

"Charles does not love you," he said quickly, while she was still too stunned by his outburst to interrupt, "nor you him. I have watched you both, loving you as I do, and it is all too plain. But, in spite of this, you cannot care to be humiliated and neglected for his gross pleasures. Break off this shameful engagement, I implore you. Isabella — dearest — there is one who has a true heart to offer you, one who would gladly die in your service —"

"Hush," she hissed, her face pale, her eyes glittering. "I hear Mama and Amanda on the stair. Do not speak of this again. I wonder that you should dare — it can never be."

She turned away to the window to compose herself a little before facing her mother and sister. He, consummate master of dissimulation that he was, began at once a light-hearted commentary upon the passers-by, which was soon interrupted by the entrance of the other members of the family.

He did not stay long afterwards.

Amanda tried hard to manoeuvre an opportunity to be private with him, but she was not successful. She watched his back retreating down the street with strong feelings of frustration. She had been so sure that he had called for one purpose only.

Her disappointment remained with her throughout the day, and a musical evening which she attended with the others seemed inexpressibly tedious. She was undressing in her bedchamber, with many yawns and expressions of impatience, having dismissed her maid to bed, when there came a gentle tap upon the door. She opened it, half expecting to see her sister, who had been unusually silent all evening: but it was one of the abigails standing outside, a pretty little girl who had a fondness for Tom, the stable-boy.

She bobbed, and handed her mistress a note, carefully sealed.

"Tom gave it me for you, Miss," she whispered. "A gentleman gave it 'im."

Her brown eyes were sympathetic: she fancied she scented romance.

Amanda thanked her, and softly closing the door, went over to the candle. She tore the note open impatiently.

'*Tomorrow at seven in the park.*'

That was all it contained, and it was unsigned; but she never doubted for one moment who had sent it. At last events were coming to a head. With a feeling of elation, all her tiredness and boredom gone, she carefully held the paper in the candle flame until nothing was left but a tiny heap of ash. She was an altogether more accomplished conspirator than Charles Barsett.

As she had expected, Roger Thurlston was awaiting her the next morning in the same secluded spot as before. She felt a little thrill of excitement as she recognised him. He did not appear to share her feelings, however, and seemed as ill at ease as on the former occasion, and just as anxious to come to the point without delay.

"You may perhaps have guessed," he began, once the brief formal greetings were over, "that my cousin has left Town in order to be present at a meeting of the society in Medmenham. He will be there for close on a fortnight. Now is the time for you to make your attempt to gain an entry to the Abbey. I have formulated a plan for doing this, and managed to obtain a disguise that should serve to keep you reasonably safe from discovery. But you alone can find a way to absent yourself from your home for a space without alarming your parents. Have you any notion how this may be done?"

"A disguise!" exclaimed Amanda, much struck by this. "Pray, whatever can it be? It does sound exciting, to be sure."

He handed her a parcel which he was carrying. "You will find it in there. It is the robe and mask worn by the — ladies of the society. Pull the hood well down over your head, and on no account remove the mask. You will find yourself in no way remarkable there — every female present will be dressed in this way."

"Whatever can this society be, sir? 'Pon rep, it sounds the queerest affair I ever heard of."

"It is indeed, but you will see for yourself shortly, I trust. At present, the most vexed question is how to spirit you away to Medmenham. Your absence from home for more than a few hours would, I imagine, raise the alarm, and it is possible that you may have to stay away for a night. Is there any possibility of your parents spending a night out of Town at any time during the next two weeks? I suppose it is scarcely likely; they would not leave their daughters unchaperoned — and then, there is your sister to think of —"

Amanda frowned, deep in thought. "No, I fear it is not at all likely. What can we do? There was some mention made yesterday of a visit to my aunt at Richmond, but I suppose we should all go there. Indeed, I should like to see my old governess who is now there, and Mama would scarce believe me if I said that I did not wish to accompany her. Indeed, I cannot think of anything."

"Well, something may turn up," he said soothingly. "Very often in these affairs chance is more valuable than arrangement. If an opportunity should present itself, you may get word to me by way of your stable lad. I shall use the same method to convey a message to you. Do you still intend to take your friend Webster with you on this expedition?"

Amanda nodded. "Yes. I — I would prefer to have a companion, and it won't be the first time that John and I have adventured together. Besides, he is more nearly concerned in this than anyone, as I explained to you before."

"Very well, but I advise you to keep him outside the Abbey grounds. I have no disguise for him, and I imagine that a male spy might meet with short shrift there."

Amanda nodded again, and tried not to look alarmed at this remark.

"And now I must leave you. Take care that no one sets eyes on your disguise until you need to use it, and inform me at once when your chance comes to slip away from home."

"Suppose it doesn't?" asked Amanda, in sudden doubt.

"Then we must contrive something; but I've often found in the past that opportunity will play into one's hand if only one is patient enough."

In the event, he was proved to be right. When Amanda returned home, she found her mother prostrated with the headache. Lady Twyford put the blame for her indisposition on the sudden heat which had fallen over London in the past week. All day long, the sun poured down out of a cloudless sky, parching the gardens and turning the leaves of the trees to a shrivelled brown; heat shimmered over the stone buildings, and the cobblestones of the streets burned into the feet of the pedestrians.

"Lovely weather for the country," said one to another, and some left Town early for their residences in the shires.

At midday, the doctor called to see my lady, and prescribed a similar course of action for her. Lord Twyford announced his intention of taking her back to Berkshire on the following day, and his daughters with her.

Alarmed, Amanda protested. Once safely back in the country her hopes were lost indeed. "Papa, I am only just arrived in

Town! And surely Isabella and I may be trusted alone for a few days."

"If you ask me, I should say that you couldn't be trusted alone for a few minutes," replied her father, with a grin. "However, I'll speak to your Mama about it."

To Amanda's intense relief, Lady Twyford agreed to leave the two sisters in Town for the present. She insisted, of course, that they would require a chaperone. It was decided, after some discussion, that my lord should bring back Mrs. Matchett to act in this capacity. This would mean that they need be alone only for the two days it would take their father to make the journey to Berkshire and back.

Amanda sighed with relief; it had been a near thing. She took the first opportunity of despatching a brief note to Roger Thurlston by way of Sally and Tom, and prepared, with a beating heart, to await early developments.

Early next morning, Lord and Lady Twyford departed for the country under a brilliant sun. They had not been gone many hours when Mrs. Thurlston and her son were announced. The lady seemed desolated at having been denied the pleasure of seeing my Lady Twyford.

"Your Mama gone to the country! I am vastly sorry to hear of her indisposition, but no doubt a few days in the fresh air will soon restore her to her customary health. But how will you go on, without any matron to chaperone you to the balls and other diversions? I pray you, call upon me if you should be in any difficulty; I don't in general go much into company, you know, but I am always ready to put the needs of others before my own wishes, and especially those of Isabella, who is soon to be connected to me by a closer tie than that of friend."

Isabella thanked her politely, but explained that they were soon to have their aunt staying with them. In the meantime, they would be content to remain quietly at home.

"But you will find that so dull, I am persuaded," persisted Mrs. Thurlston. "Do come and take tea with me this afternoon, I beg. It will be better than staying at home, though, of course, I can offer you no grand entertainment; just a quiet afternoon's chat. I shall brook no refusal, I do declare."

Isabella did not well see how to refuse this invitation, and accepted for both of them, before Amanda could speak. The younger sister had opened her lips to plead a prior engagement, or some other excuse, but just then she caught Mrs. Thurlston's eye upon her in a meaning way, and she desisted.

Shortly afterwards, the visitors rose to leave. At the last moment, Mrs. Thurlston engaged Isabella in earnest conversation upon the subject of her embroidery, which lay neglected on a stand close to the window. The two ladies moved over towards it, and Roger Thurlston took the opportunity this presented of a hurried word with Amanda.

"Do not come with your sister this afternoon," he said, in a low tone. "A headache — any excuse that will serve to make her willing to leave you behind. Get word to your friend —" he glanced fleetingly over his shoulder at Isabella and his mother, but they were absorbed in a discussion of colour and design — "to meet you at the entrance to the park. A coach will be waiting there to take you both up — the coachman will wear a yellow rose in his coat. He will drive you as far as the Castle Inn; there you will find horses waiting. You must ride, so wear suitable clothes. Follow the road through Maidenhead — but here is a paper, with minute directions written upon it."

He gave a screw of paper surreptitiously into her hand as he spoke; Amanda secreted it in the front of her gown, this time thrusting it well out of sight. She did not mean to repeat her former mistake.

"You know your way to the ford," he went on, hastily, and only just audibly. "It is the way you took before, on your journey to Town. Do not rouse the farm. Can you row a boat?"

Amanda nodded; she had lived close to the river all her life.

"Good! Then you can leave your friend Webster with the horses, for you may need to escape quickly. There will be a boat waiting at the ford, but no ferryman. You must do the best you can. I wish you good fortune."

"Bella!" whispered Amanda, struck by a sudden thought. "When she returns home and finds me missing, what —?"

"Leave her a note: say you have gone with John, so that she may know you are in safe hands, but not one word of the Abbey, I caution you. You must hint at some other reason for your absence."

Amanda nodded, and, seeing that Isabella was moving away from the embroidery frame, made haste to bid Mr. Thurlston goodbye in a slightly raised voice.

When the visitors had left, Amanda prepared the ground for her refusal to accompany her sister. She had quickly decided that it was safer to be frank with Isabella.

"I cannot think why you should have agreed to go to St. James's Square this afternoon," she reproached. "You must know how cordially I dislike Mrs. Thurlston."

"Well, I don't care for her above half myself," agreed Isabella. "But it was difficult to refuse without incivility and, anyway, her son will be there also. You like him well enough, it seems."

"Not well enough to compensate for my dislike of his Mama," retorted Amanda. "I don't think I shall go, after all."

Isabella protested at this, but found her sister surprisingly stubborn for once.

"Very well," she said at last, seeing that Amanda was not to be moved. "I feel that I am obliged to go, as I am soon to be one of the family. But it is vastly disobliging of you, Mandy."

Amanda felt a twinge of conscience, but held firm, as she must if she was to carry out her plan.

"I shall say that you have the headache, then," said Isabella, "since you are not to be persuaded. It should scarcely surprise anyone in all this heat. I think we shall most likely have thunder before the day is out. I mean to leave their house early, Mandy; I shan't allow them to persuade me to remain to dine. Perhaps it is just as well that you are not coming, for otherwise there would scarcely be a good reason for refusing if they should ask. Take care that you don't get up to any of your mad starts in my absence, mind. I shall be away only an hour or so — just so long as is civil."

It was by that time close on noon, and Amanda was anxious concerning John's part in the affair. For all her show of bravery, she did not care to undertake this adventure without his support, and she had yet to send a message to him. Suppose he should not be at home when it arrived? It was with anxious feeling that she handed a quickly scrawled note to Sally, with instructions for Tom to deliver it at Mr. Webster's lodging immediately.

More than an hour went by. Isabella and she partook of a cold collation, and her sister went to her room to change her dress for the afternoon's visit. There was still no answer from John. Alone in the drawing-room, Amanda fretted, uncertain what to do. If only Bella would hurry up and go out. Then she could go round to John's house and find out what was keeping him. She paced the room anxiously, glancing from time to time out of the window. The sun beat relentlessly down; occasionally, sparks struck off the wheels of the carriages as they rumbled past. A perspiring old woman in a grey homespun gown stood on the corner of the street, on her arm a large basket of wilted flowers, which she was vainly inviting passers-by to purchase. Preoccupied as she was, Amanda knew a brief moment of pity, and, leaning from the window, tossed the old flower-seller a coin.

As she did so, a coach drew up outside the house. Amanda watched Roger Thurlston alight, and mount the steps to the house.

"Heavens, Amanda!"

Isabella had entered the room, and exclaimed in dismay at seeing her sister leaning from the window.

"If you are to make the excuse of a headache, it will never do for you to be seen there by Mr. Thurlston!" she whispered urgently. "Away to your bedchamber, silly girl."

Amanda started, and reproached herself for carelessness. Of course it did not matter if Mr. Thurlston saw her there, for he was privy to her secrets; but she had almost forgotten that there was a part to be played for Isabella's benefit. It was borne in upon her suddenly that a conspirator must be a very accomplished deceiver indeed. She fled to her room.

She listened at the door until the quiet of the house suggested that Isabella and her escort had departed. Cautiously she crept from her room, and was about to steal downstairs when she encountered Sally. She hailed the abigail with relief.

"Has Miss Isabella left?" she asked quickly; then, as the girl assented, "Have you a message for me, Sally?"

The abigail blushed, and handed her a note.

"Wherever have you been till now?" asked Amanda, as she took it. "It is not ten minutes' journey to Mr. Webster's lodging."

The girl looked more confused than ever. "Beggin' your pardon, Miss, but Tom — he had something very partic'lar to say to me, an' it hardly seemed to be a minute —"

Amanda glanced sharply at her, then twinkled. "Very particular — oh yes, I am sure. But just you tell your Tom, mistress, that when he has an urgent message to deliver to me —" She broke off at sight of the girl's crestfallen face. "There!" she said soothingly, and laughed softly. "I daresay you can think of better things to tell him for yourself! And he's a good lad, too. Here's for your bride-clothes."

She handed a coin to the blushing abigail, and turned away.

"Oh, thank you, Miss. And — may I make so bold as to wish you happy, too?"

Amanda stopped in the act of unfolding the note, and stared at the girl. "Wish me —? Oh, I see! Well, perhaps everything is not quite as you suppose — but never mind that."

"Yes, Miss," replied Sally, dutifully, and went about her business, puzzled.

Amanda tore open the note, which was brief and to the point. "I will be there at three. John."

She glanced at the mantelshelf; the clock showed just a quarter short of the hour. She closed the door of her room, and changed hastily into travelling dress. That done, she crossed to a writing-table, drew paper and quill from its interior, and began a note to Isabella.

After the opening words, she paused, chewing thoughtfully on the end of her pen. What should she say? She had no wish to alarm Bella, but it must be made clear to her that her sister might not return home until the small hours: also, Mr.

Thurlston had set certain restrictions upon the letter which made it difficult to phrase.

A moment's thought produced the right words. She wrote swiftly, sealed the note, closed the desk, and, taking up her parcel from the bed where she had left it lying, tiptoed from the room. Softly, she opened the door of Isabella's adjoining bedchamber, and crossed over to the dressing-table. Here she propped up the note in a prominent position before the mirror, and quietly left the room.

She hesitated only long enough to ascertain that there were no servants about, then swiftly descended the stairs, and let herself out of the house.

Chapter XV: Medmenham Abbey

"There is a gate farther along," whispered Amanda. "I remember it from when I was here before. We will do better to take our way over the fields, for there's a farm at the end of this lane, and we shall be bound to rouse the dogs if we go that way."

John nodded briefly, and urged his mount forward. In a little while they came to the gate. He dismounted to open it, then swung back into the saddle. Against the sky of pearl and daffodil the trees were sharply etched in black; the river gleamed silver in the distance.

"It's a lovely night," breathed Amanda wistfully. Strangely, the beauty of the night seemed all at once to move her to sadness.

"Yes, but there's a great black cloud coming up from over yonder, and the air's demmed oppressive," said John, in low tones, mopping his forehead as he spoke. "I fear there's a storm brewing."

Amanda shook her head, and glanced anxiously in the direction which he had indicated. A storm now would complicate everything. She pressed her horse forward.

Presently they came to the river at a point not far from the ford. They halted amongst the thick trees which bordered that part of the river bank, and dismounted.

"There's the boat," whispered John, looking towards the ford. "There doesn't seem to be anyone about. I'll tether the nags, and row you across."

Amanda hesitated for a second: Mr. Thurlston had been insistent that John should remain on this side of the river. Still, she herself could see no reason why he should not take her over, provided that he came back straight away afterwards. She nodded.

They approached the boat. The June light was deteriorating rapidly under the approach of the ominous black cloud; the trees on the opposite bank loomed heavy and dark on the horizon. She shivered as she stood motionless for a moment, surveying the scene.

"Well, come on, then!" urged John, in an undertone. "Jump in!"

She obeyed with more caution than his words suggested, and he bent his back to the oars. He rowed for the opposite bank to a point just beyond the small landing-stage which served the village, the point which Amanda had indicated as giving access to the Abbey grounds. He fetched up under the leafy screen of a dipping willow, and deftly tied the boat to its stoutest branch.

In silence he helped Amanda out, just as a low growl of thunder was heard in the distance.

"You must go back, John! The horses may take fright if there is to be a storm."

He hesitated. "I suppose so," he admitted reluctantly. "But I don't altogether relish leaving you here alone, Mandy, and that's a fact. Egad, you're a female, after all, and defenceless."

"I have my disguise," she reminded him, tapping her package. "While I wear that, Mr. Thurlston assured me that there could be no trouble. Besides, Mr. Barsett is there."

"What does that signify?" he asked, amazed.

She hesitated for a second. "I can't somehow believe that — that he is altogether bad," she answered reluctantly. "I don't think he would let any harm come to me —but what harm could there be, after all?"

"I don't know," replied John uneasily. "That's what's so deuced uncomfortable in the business."

He lingered uncertainly beside the boat, obviously reluctant to take himself off: another distant roll of thunder recalled him to the matter of the horses.

"I suppose you are right; we cannot afford to risk the loss of our mounts. Tell you what, Mandy — I'll leave you the boat, and swim back. Then you can make your escape quickly, if need be."

"No." She caught his arm. "You will be soaked through, and we may have some hard riding to do afterwards! Take the boat — watch for my signal — when I am ready to return, I'll stand over there —" she pointed to a nearby clearing in the trees. "You should see me readily enough from the opposite bank, for I shall be dressed in white — anyway, the lightning will aid you, for we are obviously not to escape the storm. We must trust to chance — go now, quickly!"

He pressed her hand. "Good fortune go with you, little playmate," he said softly, and turned towards the boat.

She heard the soft plash of the oars, and, without looking back, hurried deeper into the belt of trees. Once in their dark shelter, she paused, and drew forth the garments which Roger Thurlston had provided. She donned them swiftly; the white cloak fell about her in soft folds, completely covering her travelling dress.

She slipped on the mask, and pulled the hood of the cloak over her curls, tying it firmly in place. That done, she felt more secure; surely her own mother would not have recognised her in such a guise.

All the same, for a moment her feet refused to carry her onwards. What lay before her? Roger Thurlston had thrown out dark hints concerning the secret society which had its headquarters here, but he had given her no clue as to the nature of its proceedings. She guessed that there would be wild doings, possibly, even — her heart contracted at the thought — black magic. She asked herself if she was afraid; dared she go on?

Even as she stood pondering, the air was suddenly rent by loud shrieks. A sharp flash of lightning had illumined the sky, and now the cries were drowned in a low, ominous rumble of thunder. When this had died away, the shrieking was replaced by wild catcalls of laughter. A chill ran through Amanda's blood, and she grasped at the trunk of a nearby elm, striving to steady her trembling limbs. Her eyes strove to pierce the gathering gloom, and she dimly discerned, at some distance ahead through the shadowing trees, glimpses of white figures flitting across the lawn. She shuddered as the blacksmith's words came sharply to her memory; spectres, he had said, ghostly shapes that shrieked in the night. Almost she turned, and ran from that place.

But some quality, part courage, part curiosity, held her firm in spite of her alarm. Her racing thoughts began to rationalise what she had seen and heard.

Of course these were not spectres, but men or women dressed in the same garb which she herself was wearing: no doubt if she could have appeared to the blacksmith in her present guise, he would judge that she, too, was a spirit risen from the grave. The notion brought a shaky smile to her lips, and she felt a sudden upsurge of courage. Decidedly, if slowly, she continued on her way towards the house.

When she finally came out on to the lawns, there was no one in sight. In the dim light, the house looked sinister and foreboding. Another brilliant flash of lightning added to the macabre effect; Amanda once more found herself torn between fear and curiosity. Should she go back? There would almost certainly be a heavy downpour of rain before very long, and she would be soaked if she did not seek shelter.

She set her chin obstinately. She had ventured so much in order to find out what went on in this place; she did not intend to return now without having succeeded in her self-appointed task. Another quick glance assured her that there was still no one about. She decided to make a brief tour of the buildings, and see what she could discover.

She skirted the cloisters, and approached the east wall of the house. A short walk brought her to the main door of the building; she was surprised to see that the windows on either side of the low, square stone entrance were unlit. With guests in the house she would have expected a blaze of light, but all was quiet and dark. A sudden, blinding flash of lightning illumined some words which were painted up over the door — '*Fay Ce Que Voudras*'.

She paused, considering the legend. That meant "Do what you will". Could John be right, after all? It would make a very suitable motto for a bagnio. If only that were the worst, she thought, with a sudden spasm of pain; bad as it was, she could bear it...

She arrested her thoughts in sudden panic. She felt as one in danger of being pulled down into a quagmire. Why had she come here? To find evidence of Charles Barsett's ignominy, to be sure; and also simply because she was curious about the doings at Medmenham Abbey. Well, then, let her proceed to her task.

With renewed resolution, she left the dark, deserted house, and made her way back to the cloisters. The sky was now completely overcast; the thunder rolled ever nearer, while the lightning gained in intensity, but still the rain did not come. A vivid flash of light forking its way down the sky, showed her a flight of stone steps winding upwards from the cloisters. After a moment's hesitation, she began slowly to mount them, her heart beating fast.

At the top, there was an oak door, which stood slightly ajar. Amanda peered cautiously round it. It gave on to a long, stone-pillared room which was at present unoccupied. Greatly daring, she edged inside and looked curiously about her.

The room was richly decorated in classical style, and dimly lit by chandeliers hung at infrequent intervals from a painted ceiling. There were a number of statues of pure alabaster, and sofas were set about the room, luxuriously covered in green silk damask. Amanda paused before the nearest statue, and considered it in horrified surprise. She felt the slow red mounting to her cheeks as she stood there, for the moment motionless with amazement. Then she gave an outraged exclamation, and turned hastily to quit the room.

At that very moment, a door at the far end of the apartment opened, and two or three females dressed in white, exactly as she was, came in, chattering. Amanda gave a little, involuntary cry, and fled their presence. They looked after her curiously, but made no attempt to follow her.

In a flutter, Amanda ran swiftly down the stone staircase, and out of the shadowy cloisters on to the lawn. Her one immediate thought was to put as much distance as possible between herself and those others. She ran blindly, and did not stop until she found herself breathless, and unable to continue for the moment. She pulled up, panting, and took her bearings.

The house was left some distance behind; ahead, not a stone's throw away, lay the building which she had fleetingly noticed on her first visit here, and which she had then thought to be a domestic chapel. She was near enough now to notice the winking light of candles illumining stained glass windows, imparting a holy glow to the otherwise grey and slightly forbidding edifice.

Her first thought was that here, if anywhere in this weird place, she would be safe. She paused for a few moments longer until she had quite recovered her breath, then stepped into the porch of the chapel. The door of the building was tight shut. A round handle of twisted iron hung from it; hesitating a little, she finally lifted this, and slowly turned it.

The door yielded, and swung noiselessly open a few inches. Amanda peered cautiously round it before entering, then halted, surprised. Amazement turned rapidly to horror, as her roving eye took in the details of the interior decoration of the building.

There were statues here, too, and painted frescoes on the ceiling as grotesque, as indecent and unholy as those in the room which she had just left so hurriedly. Her horrified gaze quickly dropped away from these, and travelled the whole length of this mockery of a chapel, then halted. At the far end, grouped about a travesty of an altar, were gathered some dozen or so monkish figures, in robes of purest white. Their backs were towards her, and they were gazing up earnestly at one of their number who stood on a raised dais, his face turned unseeing in her direction. He was dressed like the rest, save for the red hat, similar to that of a cardinal, which crowned his round, heavy jowled face. His vacant, slightly protuberant eyes seemed to glare with an unholy light, as he mouthed some words which she could not catch.

His whole attitude struck terror into her very soul. The air of the chapel, heavy with the scent of some weird incense, assailed her nostrils, making her feel that she must swoon if she remained there a moment longer. A sudden gust of wind through the open door blew out the candle nearest to her. The man in the red hat ceased his mutterings, and glanced in her direction.

With one accord, the rest turned, too, and instantly discovered her before she had time to conceal herself behind the door.

"A nymph! And prying!"

The cry came first from one of the monks who had a particularly debauched, vicious countenance; he ran towards her, the others following close behind.

With an involuntary sob of fear, Amanda took instantly to her heels, holding up the skirts of her long robe so that it should not impede her movements. A fork of lightning twisted across the sky; she blinked, and nearly stumbled, but, recovering herself, ran on with renewed vigour. Her white hood blew back from her head, and her fair curls tossed about her face. Swift as her legs could carry her, she ran in the direction of the river. If once she could gain the clearing that she had indicated to John, help would be forthcoming. She glanced swiftly back over her shoulder. Nimble as she was, her pursuers were gaining on her, their longer limbs carrying them at greater speed than she could hope to make.

With the desperation born of fear, she put on an extra spurt. It was not far now to the clearing, and then there would be John to protect her. But there must be an interval, she thought frantically, before he could row across from the opposite bank; and meanwhile... meanwhile?

She put out the last ounce of her strength as she heard her pursuers pounding hard on her heels. She could never do it — her lungs would burst... She stumbled, sobbing.

"What's this?"

A pair of arms encircled her, raising her up from the ground where she would have fallen. She was clasped close to a man's chest, and never in the whole of her life had she felt so certain that she had found refuge. And yet from his voice, she knew that the man was Charles Barsett.

"A prying Nun, Brother Charles! She has broken the rule, and must pay the penalty!"

The tones were those of the monk who had first raised the alarm. The others applauded, laughing, and gathered round the pair like vultures circling their prey. A fierce clap of thunder broke suddenly overhead. Amanda's grip on her rescuer tightened convulsively.

When the noise had died away, Charles Barsett stayed the monks with a gesture. The old cynical smile curved his lips as he spoke.

"By all means," he said, smoothly. "But this is my prize. I brought the lady here, and therefore claim first right. You may safely leave the honour of the Order in my hands."

"Aha!" said the other, with a leer. "So now we have come at the reason of your refusal to join in our diversions during these last few days! Damme, I thought it seemed odd that we should scarce have set eyes on you since we arrived! You were ever a sly dog, Charles! But by all means carry on with the good work; do not let us hinder you, Brother. *Fay ce que voudras!*"

A lascivious laugh ran round the assembly. After a barely perceptible pause, Charles Barsett joined in it; but his face was set.

Amanda sensed rather than saw all this; her face was buried in Charles Barsett's coat, for he was not wearing the monkish garb. She felt ready to drop with shame, but other emotions, not so easy to define, were stirring within her.

And then the rain broke from the sky with piercing suddenness. Steel shafts of water beat about the heads of the assembled monks, who turned as one man for shelter, flinging back as they went a lewd jest, which fortunately was drowned by the crash of the storm.

Charles Barsett drew Amanda's hood over her hair, and, putting an arm about her waist, ran with her in the opposite direction from that taken by the others. Their feet slithered on the drenched grass, a moment since so parched, and very soon, Amanda's white robes flapped wetly about her.

At last they gained the shelter for which Charles had been heading. It was a small temple in the Grecian style, with a floor of mosaic, and furnished with marble benches covered in red velvet cushions. Towards one of these he led her.

Inside the temple, the light was dim; she could not but be thankful, for at first a strong sense of shame was her chief emotion. He, too, was glad of the obscurity, but for different reasons: all the statues and buildings at Medmenham Abbey were such as must be considered unsuited to ladies of Miss Amanda Twyford's quality.

He began gently to divest her of the wet robe, but shook his head when she would have torn off the mask.

"No," he said quickly. "You will do better to retain that until we are safely out of this place."

"I must go now, at once!" exclaimed Amanda, starting for the entrance. The shame had vanished, and other bewildering feelings taken its place. Her state of mind defied understanding: she only knew that she wanted to set a distance of half the universe between this man and herself.

He restrained her gently.

"Presently," he said quietly. "When the storm has abated a little. I have a carriage here, and will conduct you to a place of safety."

She recoiled in horror.

"You! Do you think that I would go anywhere in your company? After all I have learnt of you after all I've seen here —!"

"What have you seen?" he asked, quickly.

"Those — those arch-fiends," stuttered Amanda, words spilling out incoherently in her haste and confusion, "mouthing dreadful incantations — in that unholy place — conjuring up the devil —"

"You must first believe in a devil before you can conjure one up," he reminded her, gravely. "Those men you saw — I, myself — have long since ceased to believe in any power — for good or evil. What you saw, child, is mummery — an empty jest."

"Jest!" she flung back at him, scornfully. "How can one jest on such a subject?"

"A grim jest, I grant you," he said, with a shrug, "but still, a jest. Once, such things amused me, too; but now —"

"Now?" she challenged him.

"Now," he said, slowly, as though the words were dragged from him; "now, it would appear that I have lost my sense of humour."

"Then you have little left to you!" she taunted him, her blue eyes flashing. "For you must long since have lost your self-respect, to visit this haunt of — of wickedness, and — and vice!"

His mouth twisted. "True," he answered wryly; and paused for an instant. "What else did you see?" he continued, with a shade of anxiety in his voice.

The colour flooded her face. "Everything of the most bestial and — and debauched! Statues and paintings, pictures — I cannot tell you! But you know it all — those females — you know them, too —"

Her voice choked, and died away. She lowered her head, and the wet curls veiled her face. Had she but been able to see it, the man's expression was one of relief: bad as these sights were, Miss Amanda had yet managed to escape the worst indignities that the Abbey could offer.

Outside, the rain lashed down in unabated ferocity, but the lightning was now growing feebler, the thunder more intermittent.

"I am sorry," he said, in a subdued tone, "that you should have been exposed to such sights. But you must realise that you brought it upon yourself; on a previous occasion, I endeavoured to spare you. What moved you to come here again? Was it that unbounded curiosity which has formed so large a part of our relationship?"

Her head came up at that, and the anger returned to her eyes.

"You know well why I came!" she flashed. "I warned you that I would do everything possible to prevent your marriage to Bella! And at last I have succeeded! When she learns from my own lips, and not from hearsay, how you conduct yourself — what debauched pleasures —"

Something suspiciously like a sob escaped her. He regarded her gravely, without speaking.

"John is awaiting me," she said, suddenly, with a change of tone. "He will take me back home. He must be anxious by now, wondering at my long delay. I must go at once; it does not rain so hard as before."

She took a few steps towards the entrance, but he gently arrested her. "Where is your friend, Webster, then? Did he bring you here? Why did he not accompany you into the grounds of the Abbey?"

There was more than a hint of grimness in his tone.

"He is across the other side of the river; we came on horseback from Salt Hill, and then the storm came, and we feared the horses might bolt, so he remained with them. In any case, I don't see what concern it can be of yours! Let me go, sir!"

She shook off his restraining arm, and turned to go: but he still stood in her path.

"Out of my way!" she stormed, clenching her fists.

"Wait," he said, standing his ground. The quietness of his tone calmed her for the moment. "Have you thought where you will go now? You cannot reach London before the small hours; and you will be the centre of God knows what scandal if you should travel unchaperoned with a man through the night."

Amanda shrugged, and pushed the wet hair from her face.

"I can see no help for that. I will not waste any more time in this place; let me pass at once!"

"But I do see a way out," he said, quickly. "I have a proposal to make which may yet save your reputation."

"My reputation?" she echoed, with biting scorn. "What can that be to you, pray?"

"I will defend it against anyone with my sword," he answered, quietly. "But please hear me out. I have an old servant — the woman who nursed me when I was a child — living at Maidenhead, not far from here. We may reach her home in less than an hour in my carriage. She is a creature of unimpeachable honour, and you may safely pass the night under her roof."

Amanda paused, and thought rapidly. "I will not go there alone with you," she said, at last.

"Webster will accompany us," he persisted. "After we have seen you safely lodged with Nurse, he and I will journey to Town and endeavour to concoct some tale that will satisfy your parents though God knows what!"

"Oh, there is no need to concern yourself over that," put in Amanda, quickly. "Mama and Papa are staying in the country for a few days — there is only Isabella, and I left her a note, in some sort explaining —"

"Poor Isabella!" he said, with a wry smile. "She must be sorely troubled."

"You need not trouble yourself about my sister," said Amanda loftily. "She will soon have no thought to spare for you, that I promise you!"

He bowed slightly, but made no reply to this. The rain had almost stopped, and the sky was growing lighter with the pale radiance of a June night.

"Very well," said Amanda, suddenly. "I agree to your plan. I'll go and signal to John."

"I'll go with you."

She made no demur, but set forward without waiting for him. He kept pace with her, and silently, an arm's length apart, they made their way through the dripping trees to the clearing near the water's edge.

As they came out in the open, a shadow moved suddenly from the shelter of the trees. Amanda started, and ran to clutch at Charles Barsett's arm. It tightened about her; the other hand rested on his sword.

The shadow resolved itself into the figure of a man.

"Mandy!" An urgent whisper came to her ears. "Is that you? Who is with you?"

It was John. She heaved a sigh of relief, and quickly thrust Charles Barsett's arm away from her.

"Oh, John!" Both men noticed the catch in her voice. "What are you doing here? What of the horses are they safe?"

"Once the rain began, I begged shelter for them at the farm, and came straight here. It seemed the best thing to do, though it took longer than I hoped — are you all right, Mandy? Who is it — oh, I see. Mr. Barsett."

His bow lacked dignity from the damp, dishevelled state of his garments, but even so, was noticeably curt. Charles Barsett acknowledged the grudging salutation, and spoke urgently.

"There is need for haste. It will scarce be necessary to explain to you, Mr. Webster, that Miss Amanda's presence here is — to say the least — compromising. One cannot avoid the conclusion that anyone who had her welfare at heart must have forbidden this escapade."

The last sentence was delivered sternly. For a moment, John Webster was reminded of certain uncomfortable periods passed in the headmaster's study during his schooldays. His hand automatically tugged at his bedraggled cravat.

"Yes — well, I would agree with you, sir. But Mandy had made up her mind to come here, anyway, and I thought it better she should do so accompanied by me."

"There is not time now to argue that."

Briefly, he outlined his plan to John; after a word with Amanda in a low tone, John agreed to it.

"Take Miss Amanda in the boat to the landing stage," instructed Charles Barsett. "Tie the boat up there, and walk to the top of the lane, where it joins the road to Marlow. I will have my carriage waiting there to convey you both to Maidenhead, where we can leave Miss Amanda in Nurse's charge, and also procure some dry clothes."

Without more ado, he turned away. They entered the boat in silence, and rowed across to the jetty.

"What is to be done about the horses?" asked Amanda, as they were tying up the boat.

"We can arrange with the farmer to keep them until they are collected from the inn where we hired them," said John, easily. "That does not signify, now. But tell me, what happened in that place, Mandy? Were you discovered? How came you to be in Mr. Barsett's company?"

Amanda shuddered. "I would rather not talk about it now," she said, listlessly.

He glanced at her curiously. "You might take that demmed mask off; it gives me the creeps!"

She shook her head, but without any vehemence. "He said I had best retain it until I was safely in the carriage."

"I see. Perhaps that's wise. I collect that you were discovered, by Barsett, at any rate."

She nodded. "It was dreadful, John! That is a — wicked, evil place!"

"Is it as bad as you feared?"

She shuddered again. "Worse!"

"You make me curious," he said, with a trace of envy in his tone.

"Never let me hear that word again!" said Amanda, passionately. "I am convinced now that curiosity is a vice, like — like thieving, and lying, and all the other sins!"

"All the same, I wish I'd been with you. I suppose you wouldn't care to describe just what — but no, never mind! You did find what was necessary for your purpose, though, Mandy? You will be able now to convince Bella that this man Barsett is not a worthy husband for her?"

"Yes," she answered, and the word was a sob.

He looked at her curiously. "What ails you, Mandy? You seem very low in spirits for someone who has done what she wanted! This is not your usual style when you have succeeded in an enterprise!"

She did not answer. He glanced at her again, but the mask concealed her expression. He thought, however, that he caught a glint of tears in her eyes. She had no doubt had a trying time of it in that place, and the hour was late; probably she was tired. He would not question her further tonight.

But it was not weariness of body, but of spirit, that assailed the intrepid Amanda. She was discovering for the first time how hollow a thing victory can be. She had found evidence of Charles Barsett's unworthiness, indeed: but, she wondered in sudden panic, was it, after all, what she had wanted?

Chapter XVI: The Making of a Rake

The three travellers in Charles Barsett's coach presented a sorry spectacle. Water dripped from their clothes, their foot-gear was muddy, and their manner far from animated. For some time, there was no conversation; Amanda kept her face, now relieved of the concealing mask, studiously turned away from the gentlemen, and they appeared to be immersed in their own thoughts. At last, Charles Barsett broke the long silence.

"I hesitate to trouble you with questions, Miss Amanda, at a moment when it is all too obvious that you are fatigued, and in need of rest; but there is something in this matter that puzzles my understanding. How came you by the white garments which you were wearing?"

"I do not mean to tell you," stated Amanda, flatly, "so you may spare yourself the trouble of questioning me further."

The sudden spurt of spirit seemed to revive her a little, for she corrected her hitherto drooping carriage, and sat upright in the manner taught her by Miss Brown.

"No matter," he said, grimly. "I fancy I know the answer already. You obtained them from my cousin, Roger Thurlston, did you not? And, unless I am very much mistaken, this whole exploit was planned by him, not by your friend here, Mr. Webster."

Amanda turned with dignity to John.

"You will be good enough to inform Mr. Barsett," she said, coldly, "that I do not desire any further conversation with him. I accept his assistance because at the moment I have no choice; but after tonight, I wish never to set eyes on him again!"

John looked uncertainly from one to the other. He was recalling the moment on the river bank when he had stepped in their path out of the shadows. Amanda had clung then to Barsett as though she looked to him for protection; now she was as good as asking John to call him out. If the fellow had insulted her, b'God, thought John, then he was only too ready to oblige: but did Mandy really know what she wanted? Odd creatures, females... John sighed heavily, and for the moment, held his tongue.

Charles Barsett had bowed to them both at conclusion of Amanda's words. His face was taut and withdrawn, and he looked momentarily older than his years. Damned if he was not a better fellow than his cousin, thought John, suddenly, in spite of all.

A long silence fell over the carriage, broken only by the sound of the trotting horses on the road. Presently, Amanda lowered the window nearest her, and leaned out. The storm had quite passed over, and the night air was sweet and fresh. She inhaled it gratefully. There was a pain at her heart that she had never experienced before, and could not at all understand. It would be good to be back with Bella, she thought, to tell her the whole story, and then be able to put the wretched affair out of her mind. She quite saw that it was a wise plan of Charles Barsett's to take her to spend the night with his old Nurse; if she had journeyed to London alone with John, there would have been complications, for sure. She did not fear for her reputation, as Mr. Barsett had seemed to do, but rather was she afraid of any rub being put in the way of Bella's being united to John. There had been hindrances enough already to their happiness, goodness knew. But now, at last, all seemed set fair for them: as for Mr. Barsett, she reflected passionately, she wanted never to see him again. But, of course, she never would. Bella would soon send him about his business when she knew all — she would wed John, and they would all return to Berkshire. Everything had worked out just as she had planned it — everything... At the thought of her triumph, the suppressed tears stung her eyelids.

Ahead, the winking lights of scattered homesteads appeared and, in a short time, the carriage was pulling up before a fair-sized cottage set in a flower-scented garden.

Mr. Barsett stood to one side in order to allow John to assist Amanda to alight. A muscle tautened in his cheek as he watched them. The stone-flagged path, strewn with rose petals brought down by the recent storm, shone white in the moonlight as they opened the gate leading to the cottage door. Charles Barsett knocked thrice when they reached it, and then called out in soft tones, evidently with the intention of allaying any alarm that his summons might have caused to the occupant of the house.

In a few moments, the door opened, and framed in the doorway stood a round, motherly body with white hair set neatly under a lace cap trimmed with lavender ribbons.

"Why, Master Charles!"

The matron's surprise deepened as she saw that he brought company, but she asked no questions, hospitably bidding them enter.

"This is Miss Amanda Twyford and Mr. Webster, Nurse. As you may observe, we are all very wet. May I crave your kindness for Miss Twyford? I desire you to supply her with a bed for the night, if you will be so good."

"Gracious goodness, how did you come to get so soaked?" The old lady clucked, and straightway swept Amanda upstairs to her own bedchamber. Without more ado, she opened a drawer, and took out a grey muslin gown, which she laid on the bed.

"If you'll give me your wet garments, ma'am," she said, busily arranging a screen so that Amanda might disrobe in privacy, "I'll have them dry in a trice before the kitchen fire."

Amanda struggled thankfully out of her wet clothes, and donned the grey gown. She found that it fitted tolerably well, when Nurse had found her some pins with which to take up some of the fullness over the bosom. She followed the old lady downstairs feeling a little less bedraggled, and found that the gentlemen were there, having likewise changed out of their wet garments. It would appear that Mr. Barsett was a frequent visitor to the house, as he could command changes of raiment and a bed at a moment's notice.

Nurse paused to see that Amanda was comfortably seated, before bustling into the kitchen to prepare some refreshment for her unexpected guests. Thither Charles followed her, leaving John and Amanda together in the parlour.

"'Tis only the young lady who is to have a bed?" asked Nurse, as she expertly carved slices from a large ham. "What of you and the other gentleman?"

"We ride to London."

She raised her brows, and eyed him keenly for a second.

"Is this the young lady you are to wed?" she asked. "She's pretty, even though she looks fagged to death, poor dear! She puts me a little in mind of your poor Mama."

"No." His answer was abrupt, and she looked up again, surprised. She did not often hear that tone from him. "I am affianced to Isabella Twyford. This is the younger sister, Amanda."

She stopped her work for a moment, and looked into his eyes, noting the deep unhappiness there.

"Yet this is the one you love," she said, quietly.

He drew in his breath sharply. Not even to himself had he admitted so much.

"Small matter what I think," he answered, bitterly. "She holds me in abomination —and with good reason! Moreover, I believe that she and young Webster —" He broke off.

"Maybe you'd better tell me all about it," invited the old lady, in the way familiar to him ever since he could remember.

He told her rapidly, in an undertone. She was the one repository of all his secrets. She shook her head when he had done, but began placidly to slice bread on a wooden platter, as though they talked of trivialities. Her unruffled composure a little soothed his troubled spirit.

"This Abbey, now," she said, calmly. "No doubt it will be — a disgraceful place?"

He nodded, lips tight set. She made no comment, but indicated a tray standing on the dresser, close to his hand.

"Be good enough to pass that over, my dear. I think a glass of warm milk for the young lady — she looks fair done up, poor little thing"

She accepted the tray from his hands, and stacked the various items upon it. Before opening the door to carry them into the next room, she paused.

"Don't worry, trust old Nurse. And, Master Charlie — do nothing foolish: there has been folly enough."

"Good God, I know it!"

There was a world of bitterness in his tone.

She said no more, but carried the tray through into the parlour.

The meal was hasty, and perfunctory on the part of two of the visitors: John Webster alone ate with good appetite. Soon the two gentlemen rose to leave.

"I will be here again tomorrow around noon," said Charles Barsett, addressing Nurse. "Perhaps I may prevail upon you to be ready to accompany Miss Amanda to her home in Town? I will make arrangements for your lodging there overnight — or for a longer period, should you desire it."

"Thank you, Mr. Barsett," replied Nurse, who was always very circumspect in front of strangers. "I promise to be quite ready to accompany the young lady wherever and whenever she chooses."

"It — it is very good of you," stammered Amanda, realising for the first time that she might possibly be putting the old lady to great inconvenience. Normally, such a thing would have readily occurred to her, for she was the last person to take a service for granted; but since leaving the Abbey, she had been completely immersed in her thoughts, and scarcely knew what was going forward. "I — I am sorry to be putting you to so much trouble on my account."

"There now, I like to be useful," affirmed Nurse. "It puts me in mind of old times. Drink your milk, ma'am, before it gets cold, pray do!"

John bent over Amanda's hand in taking leave, and was able to whisper in her ear.

"You'll be all right and tight here, Mandy — the old lady puts me in mind of my own nurse, and she was the rightest one that ever walked! Do you wish that Barsett shall come for you tomorrow, or shall I?"

"No," whispered back Amanda, hurriedly, "you stay within reach of Bella. It cannot signify whether he comes or no — I shan't need to speak with him: Nurse will be there."

Mr. Barsett contented himself with a low bow in her direction. She responded distantly, with averted face.

As soon as the door closed behind them, she abandoned all pretence of eating, and slumped back into her wing chair with a gesture of utter weariness.

"I'll away to slip a warming-pan into your bed," said Nurse, inspecting her closely while appearing to be about the business of clearing the table. "There's nothing like a good night's rest for restoring the spirits."

Amanda shook her head.

"I'm not tired: I don't believe I could sleep if I tried."

"At your age, my dear," replied Nurse, forgetting that this was not one of her charges, and instinctively taking a motherly tone, "you should drop off as soon as your head touches the pillow!"

"I do, in general," said Amanda, dispiritedly. "But not tonight."

"And what's so special about tonight?" Amanda looked up from her rapt contemplation of the hearth-rug. Her blue eyes showed the trouble that lurked beneath. Nurse's heart stirred with compassion. Poor lamb — poor young thing! She herself might be an old woman now, but she could still remember a time in her life when griefs had been sharp and poignant, before the gift of resignation had come to mellow even despair. How they did suffer, these young ones! It would do the pretty creature good if she could confide her trouble, thought the old lady, and wondered how she could persuade Amanda to talk to her. Perhaps, if she were only handled gently enough, she might come round to it in time.

Amanda did not answer Nurse's question, however, but instead asked another one.

"Did you —" she hesitated a second — "were you with — Mr. Barsett when he was a child? I collect that you were."

"I helped bring him into the world," answered the old lady. "Ay, and held my lady's hand as she breathed her last. His lordship was on her other side: as God is my judge, I thought that he must die, too, so pale and stricken he was!"

Amanda moistened her dry lips.

"I have heard it said that — that my lord Barsett took his son in dislike because of his wife's death."

Nurse's mouth set firmly.

"I remember that when I took the child to him, he said he never wanted to set eyes on it again. I thought it was but the shock of the moment; for he loved her as a man loves a woman only once in a lifetime. Theirs was no marriage of convenience, but a love match."

She paused for a moment, and came over to sit down on the other side of the hearth from Amanda. There was a reminiscent look in the faded grey eyes.

"But he never did recover from the shock, and — God forgive him — he never took to the child. He was a sturdy, healthy little boy, too, such as a father might well be proud of. He sensed his father's dislike — you can never fool a child, though you may succeed with a full-grown man or woman — and in his little, innocent way, he tried to overcome it. Many's the time I've watched him run to my lord eagerly with some piece of news which the child thought might please him — there was the day when he'd mastered his alphabet, and later on, when he'd taken his pony over a fence for the first time without a spill — and to see him come away again, with all the light gone from his little face, I tell you, it fair broke my heart!"

She fished in a pocket for her kerchief, and blew her nose vigorously. Amanda said nothing.

"Then there was the aunt, Mrs. Thurlston," continued Nurse, sniffing slightly. "She never cared for Master Charles from the first. But she had the interests of her own boy at heart — I suppose you can scarce blame her for that! She made sure that any boyish exploits that Master Charles got up to, lost nothing in the telling to my lord! But worst of all, there was Master Roger."

She stopped, and a grim look spread over the gentle features.

"They were very attached to each other, weren't they?" asked Amanda.

She might not wish to see Charles Barsett ever again, but nevertheless, she was finding this account of his past life interesting in the extreme. For once, it was not only curiosity which moved her: she found herself possessed of a burning desire to find some justification for his actions, some mitigation of the dreadfulness of his offence. Vaguely, it was borne in upon her that this was a new feeling.

"No brothers were ever closer," replied the old lady. "Everything was done together, every secret shared. At least, on one side, it was. Master Charles believed for many years that his cousin confided completely in him, but he was to find otherwise. On that worthless boy my poor young master lavished all the affection that, in a happier home, he would have given to mother, father, brothers and sisters: and, in return, what did he gain? Nothing but the worst kind of treachery!"

"Treachery?" asked Amanda.

"Too weak a word," said the old lady, in a trembling voice, "too weak a word for the betrayal of a single-minded affection such as his! For he is possessed of an intense nature, my dear; don't be deceived by that languid, sneering manner of his! That is the face he shows to the world."

"But what did Mr. Thurlston actually do?" asked Amanda, with a trace of her usual animation.

Nurse pursed her lips. "Everything that he possibly could to discredit Master Charles. No secret was safe with him; it would go straight to Mrs. Thurlston, and she would see that it found its way to my lord — presented in its worst possible light!"

"But surely it was only natural that Mr. Thurlston should have confided in his parent?" asked Amanda, dubiously.

"That was just what was so cunning in the scheme! For a long time, Master Charles believed that it was all as you say, and that his aunt was really the one to blame. And then came the day when he could not mistake any longer — when it was brought home to him just what his cousin's character was."

"What happened?" Amanda leaned forward in her chair, interest shining in her eyes.

Nurse hesitated, and considered the girl dubiously. She looked such a child in the grey gown that was too large for her, and with her honey-gold curls drying in tight little ringlets round her head. But something must be done for Master Charles, unless his heart was to be broken a second time. It might be of no avail, but all Nurse's maternal instincts forced her on to make the trial.

"Properly speaking, it isn't a story for your young ears," she began, cautiously. "But perhaps you should know of these matters, after all."

Amanda was surprised. "I should? Why do you say so?"

"Your sister is betrothed to Master Charles, is she not?" asked Nurse, artfully.

Amanda nodded; she had almost forgotten that fact herself.

"Well, then, since I haven't the pleasure of Miss Twyford's acquaintance, it may be as well to tell her sister of these things. Mayhap you can explain them to her, my dear, and then she may be persuaded not to think so hardly of him for — for follies which I dare swear are past, never to be committed again!"

Amanda looked thoughtful, and nodded silently.

"It happened this way," went on the old lady, watching her carefully, ready to stop her narrative at the first sign of affront; "There was an abigail in my lord's service — a pretty, silly wench up from the country, and no better than she ought to be. It was discovered that she was with child, and the housekeeper was for packing her off home again. But she made a stir, declaring that Master Charles was responsible for her condition, and that my lord should pay for it, and handsomely, too. At that time, the young gentlemen were close on eighteen, and I had long since outlived my usefulness in the household, but still my lord would keep me on, for I had been nurse to his dear wife. Master Charles came to me one night, full of trouble. He swore that he was not to blame; but what really troubled him was that he knew for a fact that his cousin was responsible. It seemed that my young master had seen the wench coming from Master Roger's room on several occasions. Yet this precious cousin had stood by and said nothing when my lord had given Master Charles the dressing-down of his life over the business. However, my boy could not believe that his cousin would not eventually confess; he thought that Master Roger had been taken unawares, and been too afraid to speak up there and then, in face of the first transports of my lord's wrath."

"The thing is," said Amanda, judicially, "why did the abigail tell the lie?"

"You may well ask!" replied Nurse, with scorn. "Of course, it was a put-up thing between Master Roger and herself. But Master Charles kept waiting and hoping that his cousin would speak; and as the days passed, and nothing was said, he seemed to grow older all at once, until he was a man instead of a boy. In the end, he taxed Master Roger openly."

Amanda sat up suddenly. "What — what happened?" she asked, eagerly.

"The rogue denied it!" exclaimed Nurse. "He expressed sorrow that Master Charles should try and shift the blame of his own misdeeds on to him, and said — hypocrite that he is — that he only wished he was in a position to render such a service to his cousin, but that Master Charles must know that it would quite ruin him, Roger, with his uncle!"

"I never heard anything so base in my life!" exclaimed Amanda. "But are you quite certain — there could not be any possibility of a mistake?"

"If you knew my master as I do," said Nurse, indignantly, "you could not ask such a question! But there, I suppose you will judge him from the wild reputation that he has — it's only to be expected!"

"No, I don't think I will," replied Amanda. "I beg your pardon for seeming to doubt your word. Had he been other than you represent him, I feel sure he could not have gained your respect!"

"Indeed he could not, Miss," said Nurse, looking somewhat mollified. "Even for my lady's sake! But the fact is that I never knew him to tell a lie of any magnitude, even as a child. I think he was too proud for such shifts!"

"I can believe that," said Amanda, thoughtfully. "Well, I can only hope that Mr. Thurlston felt thoroughly wretched at playing so base a part! I dare say he may have, you know, for I remember once, when John Webster tried to take the blame for me over some escapade, I felt so utterly unhappy, that I was obliged to confess the whole to Papa!"

"Is John Webster the young gentleman who was with you and my master tonight, Miss?" asked Nurse, momentarily diverted from her tale.

Amanda nodded. "Yes. He is our neighbour in the country, and a very old friend of my family."

"Begging your pardon, Miss, for the liberty — but are you and he, by any chance —?"

Amanda stared at her for a moment, then realising her meaning, coloured.

"No, nothing of that kind. In fact —" She paused. Nurse waited without speaking, her hands motionless in her lap. "To tell you the truth," said Amanda, candidly, "he is in love with my sister always has been. But do tell me what happened next, Nurse! Did the truth come out, after all?"

Nurse shook her head sadly.

"It never came out: the girl was sent away, she had her child, and my lord provided for them both. No more was heard of her from that day to this."

"And — Mr. Barsett?" asked Amanda, hesitantly.

"He was punished, of course; his allowance was stopped for a time, to pay the girl's dues. But that was the least of his troubles. From that time forward, he changed."

"Changed?" Amanda breathed the word.

"Yes. I told you that he had become a man in a few short days. He even looked different — his mouth took on that disagreeable sneer which it has worn ever since."

"I know it," said Amanda, and shivered.

"He began to gain a name for wildness, especially after I left the house —"

"You left? Why was that?"

"I went to my lord," said Nurse, grimly, "and gave him a piece of my mind. I told him the truth. He would not believe it, so I said that I felt I could no longer remain in the same house that sheltered such a perfidious rascal as his nephew. That did it, of course! For old time's sake, he would not cast me off, but bought me this cottage, and pays me an annuity. At first, in my anger, I did not want to take anything of him: but in some sort, he pleaded with me, for my dead lady's sake and because I'd spent my life in the service of the family. Master Charles was insistent with me, too; and later, when he came into his own money at one and twenty, he added a further annuity of his own. So I came here, and only heard from a distance of the path my poor lamb was treading."

"I suppose," said Amanda, thoughtfully, "that he considered he might as well play the game, as simply own the undeserved name for it."

"He felt," said Nurse, defiantly, "that there was no more honour, no more love, no more trust in the whole world. I know well what he felt."

"He did have you," said Amanda. Her lips were trembling.

"An old woman, powerless to serve him in his need. A hired nurse instead of the loving parents every child, even the poorest, has a right to."

"Oh, Nurse!" cried Amanda incoherently, bursting all at once into tears. "I feel so unhappy I can't think why."

But Nurse fancied that she could, and, as she gathered the girl into her warm, motherly arms, she breathed a silent prayer of thankfulness.

Chapter XVII: The Toll House

Isabella Twyford went to St. James's Square with small expectation of enjoyment. For one thing, ever since his unexpected and unwelcome avowal of love, she had felt reluctant to be in Roger Thurlston's company. However, as she had remarked to Amanda, it was difficult to refuse the invitation of the woman who was soon to be related to her by marriage, without appearing uncivil.

My Lord Barsett was not within, and she was entertained solely by the Thurlstons, mother and son. The time passed pleasantly enough, but a growing feeling of uneasiness for which she could in no way account made Isabella curtail the visit beyond what she had originally intended. She pleaded her sister's supposed indisposition as an excuse.

To her chagrin, Roger Thurlston insisted on accompanying her home. She had no choice but to invite him within doors, but hoped that his sense of propriety would force him to decline the invitation. She soon saw that such was not to be the case. Not only did the gentleman enter the house, but sat on for some little while, chatting as though he intended to make a protracted stay. He seemed quite impervious to hints, so at last she looked pointedly at the clock.

"Heavens, it is five o'clock already! If you will be good enough to excuse me for a moment I will go and see how Mandy does. I left her lying down in her room; I was hoping that I might have found her recovered from her headache again by now, and downstairs to greet us."

Truth to tell, she was genuinely puzzled by the non-appearance of her sister. It was unlike Amanda to keep to her room when there was company in the house, and a pretended headache was of all things the easiest to dispel. She must have noticed their arrival by now, thought Isabella uneasily. Did she perhaps wish to avoid Mr. Thurlston for some reason known only to herself? Or had she — the notion caught suddenly at Isabella as she went on her way upstairs, making her quicken her steps — had she disobeyed Mama's injunction, and ventured abroad alone?

She pushed open the door of her sister's bedchamber, calling out her name. A quick glance showed her that Amanda was not there. With an exclamation part annoyance, part consternation, she hurried to her own room, and opened the door. Amanda was not here, either.

Alarmed now, trouble clouded her face. Foolish girl, where could she have gone? Perhaps the housekeeper might know.

Her train of thought broke off abruptly. At the far end of the room, propped against her dressing-table mirror, she espied a small square of white. She flew across the room towards it.

In a moment, the note was in her hand and she had torn it open. She devoured with her eyes the short message it contained.

My dear Bella,

I am gone out, though I may not tell you where. I think it only right to warn you that it is possible I shall not return home until tomorrow, but you need have no alarms. I shall be with John, and I know you will agree that I could not be in safer hands.

Do not fret, my love, all is well.

A.

Isabella read these words twice over, scarcely able to take in their full meaning on the first reading. She sank on to a stool, and gazed at her now haggard face in the mirror.

"Dear God," she breathed to herself, "what can it mean? She has gone with John —could it be possible...?"

She dared not finish the sentence; recollection brought back in a flood the secret concerning John and Mandy which Mr. Thurlston had confided to her on the night of the ball. She rose unsteadily, and clutching the note convulsively in one hand, made her way back to the drawing-room.

Roger Thurlston rose politely as she entered, then paused at sight of her distraught looks.

"My dear Miss Twyford," he said, in a voice full of concern. "Is anything wrong?"

She could make no reply for a few moments. The conclusion which she had been obliged to draw from Amanda's note had brought her to a sudden, unwelcome understanding of her own feelings. She pressed a hand to her temples, and sank wearily into a chair.

He repeated his question, his eyes fixed anxiously upon her. "I don't know. I — I — have had some disturbing news —"

"What news, my dear young lady? May I not help? Can you not bring yourself to confide in me? Rest assured, if I can serve you in any way, I shall count myself fortunate."

She hesitated for a long space, during which he watched her carefully. Her thoughts were racing round her head until it ached with the effort of disentangling them. If what she feared was indeed true, what ought she to do? Had her parents been here —but could it be possible that she was reading too much into this note of Amanda's? Her sister had given no certain sign...

She felt that she must have another opinion on the matter. It was too grave an issue to decide alone. But there was no one available except Mr. Thurlston, and he...

Reluctantly she handed him the note. He took the paper, and studied it attentively.

"What — what do you think it can mean, sir?"

Mentally he applauded Amanda: she had carried out his instructions to perfection. Nothing could better serve his purpose than this letter. He handed it back to Isabella with a grave face.

"I fear there is only one conclusion to be drawn from it," he said, shaking his head.

"You mean," said Isabella, slowly and painfully, "that Amanda and — and John have — eloped?"

He nodded, watching her carefully. The faint ray of hope which had illumined her face while he read the note now died away, leaving her expression full of misery.

"Miss Isabella!" he said, softly and compassionately.

She ignored the ejaculation, and going over to the window stared hopelessly out into the street. The old flower seller was there, with her basket of faded flowers. To Isabella, the wilting beauty was a painful reminder of her own situation. She turned away again, her eyes blinded by tears.

"What ought I to do?" she asked desperately, rousing herself a little. "Oh, if only Papa were here to guide me!"

"Surely there cannot be much doubt of what your course of action should be?" he asked. "Surely you will follow her, and bring her back?"

He waited with bated breath for her answer: on it his plans depended.

"I suppose that is the right thing to do."

Her voice was indecisive, lifeless.

"You cannot let her make herself the centre of a scandal," he replied gravely. "We must set about it immediately. It should not be too impossible a task to trace their movements —"

But she broke in upon him suddenly in a vehement tone that was foreign to her hitherto undecided manner.

"No! I have changed my mind. After all, why should I try to prevent their union? Mama, I know, will never consent to the match — that is why Amanda has taken this course. She is wiser than I, for all we call her schoolgirl and child! I have quite ruined my own hopes of happiness through my blind folly, but that is no reason for destroying hers, and — and — his."

Her voice broke on the final word, and she buried her face in her hands, sobs shaking her frame.

It was as well for Roger Thurlston that she did so, else she must have observed his chagrin at her decision. She had foiled one carefully laid scheme by her answer; there yet remained another way.

"Isabella!" he said in a low, pleading tone. "Forgive me, I cannot help but be aware of the regard in which you have held Webster. Now that he is removed from your life and heart for ever, do not — my dearest — be content to replace that feeling by the mockery of a marriage of convenience. Will you not accept instead the homage of a heart that truly loves you, and does not entirely despair of one day kindling love in your bosom, in return?"

She raised her head, and dried her eyes. She began to laugh, a dry, short laugh that did not touch her compressed lips. He shook his head reproachfully, but his look was gentle.

"I implore you not to mock at me, beloved, but give me leave to teach you that love begets love. That sneering cousin of mine is not the man to do it; you have not touched his heart, as you have mine."

She shook her head, and something of the bitterness died out of her face. "I ask your pardon: I did not mean to mock at you.

Heaven forbid that I should make game of any man's honest affection. I believe I have told you before this that my answer must be no. I can never love you — I can never love any man — again. I sought a marriage of convenience, rather than the happy union I might have had... I shall keep my word to your cousin, and go on with it."

Roger Thurlston bowed low, and reflected that it had been worth a try, at all events. His agile mind leapt swiftly to one last, desperate throw with fate, win or lose.

"Forgive me," he said humbly. "I shall never again importune you on this subject, believe me."

Isabella murmured something which did not signify to either of them. He took a measured pace or two about the room, as though in deep deliberation. Presently he halted, and turned towards her. "I wonder," he said, musingly, "if all is as it appears?"

"What do you mean?" asked Isabella, her attention caught.

"Suppose they have not eloped after all?" he continued. "Suppose they have simply embarked on some escapade — oh, I know that their attachment is obvious, but your sister would not, I feel sure, allow your mother to stand in the way of a marriage to Webster. Do you not yourself feel that Amanda would face it out with her Mama, and wed whomsoever she chose, without the hole and corner affair of an elopement? Is it not more in her character?"

Isabella had winced at his reference to the supposed attachment between Amanda and John, but she forced herself to consider this point.

"Ye-es," she said doubtfully. "Unless, of course, the romantic side of an elopement should have attracted her. That is possible."

"But your friend Webster," he said, masking his impatience, "is surely not the man to behave so dishonourably? From what you have said —"

"No." Isabella was thoughtful. "No, I do not feel that even Mandy could persuade John to such a — an unchivalrous action. He is — everything that is upright and — and honest."

Her voice shook on the words.

"Quite," he said curtly. He wanted to waste no more time on John Webster's perfections, or on the supposed elopement. She must be made to consider the truth — or part of it.

"I have been turning over the possibilities in my mind, Miss Isabella," he said, frowning thoughtfully. "And I believe that I have hit upon an explanation that more nearly accords with the characters of both these young people."

"What can that be, sir?"

"The more I contemplate it, the more likely it seems. Tell me, has your sister always been as insistent to you as she has to me, that she would never permit your marriage to my cousin?"

"She has said that to you, too?" asked Isabella, shocked.

"She is a forthright young lady, and has from the first honoured me with her confidence — you may perhaps recall that I was once able to render her some small service."

"Yes, of course — how could I forget?" replied Isabella, forgetting his recent offence, and warming to him a little.

"I don't know how much she has recounted to you of her adventures on her journey from Berkshire to Town," he went on, tentatively.

"Everything, I should imagine. Mandy and I have few secrets from each other, as I believe I told you once."

He nodded. "In that case, you may perhaps recall her mention of a mysterious Abbey which she tried to explore?"

Isabella started, and gave a nod.

"This may be painful to you, but it must be said. It is a place of — bad repute — and I know for a fact that my cousin is staying there at the moment."

Isabella's face crimsoned. "So that is where —"

He nodded gravely. "Yes, I am sorry that you should need to know. He is but let us leave that; I cannot trust myself to speak on that subject, holding you in the regard that I do. The point I wish to make is that I believe your sister may have followed him there, and taken Webster along with her."

Isabella gasped. "But why? What can they hope to do there?"

"Gain knowledge of what goes on in that place — knowledge which your sister hopes may make you turn from Charles in loathing and disgust. Believe me, if she should succeed in entering the Abbey, she will certainly find sufficient there for her purpose."

"Dear God!" exclaimed Isabella faintly. "Do you mean —?"

"That it is a stronghold of depravity and debauchery, and no fitting place for a young girl."

"Then we must go at once!" cried Isabella, distracted. "Why do we linger here, when already Mandy may be in the midst of dear knows what terrors? Take me to this place, I beg of you!"

His face was devoid of expression as he answered her.

"My carriage is waiting below; when you say the word we may go at once."

Afterwards, Isabella had no very clear memory of her journey in pursuit of Amanda. A pulse in her head seemed to echo the beat of the horses' hoofs on the roads. The streets and buildings, coaches and sedan chairs were left behind: in their place appeared trees and hedgerows, the country taverns, the toilers in the fields. Gradually the fierce June day waned, giving way to an opalescent twilight which threw into relief dark shapes of foliage against the skyline. The coach rolled on, stopping only to change horses; and in all that time she had not moved, and scarce spoken a word.

The silence was broken at length by a low rumble of distant thunder.

"I feared we should have a storm," muttered Roger Thurlston, mopping his brow. "No matter, we have not far to go now."

Isabella said nothing, but shrank into her corner every time that a flash of lightning lit the sky. Country-bred as she was, she had yet a strong dislike of storms. This one was slowly gathering in intensity: the rain was long in coming, but finally burst against the sides of the coach in a metallic tattoo.

Presently, far along the road, a light winked. The coach began to slacken pace.

"Is this the place?" asked Isabella, starting to life as the vehicle stopped.

"As near as we may get for the moment," answered Roger Thurlston, and threw his traveling cloak about her shoulders and head. "Come, my dear, we must run for it if we are not to be drenched."

She noticed the familiarity with a vague resentment, but was too preoccupied to take him up on it. He helped her from the carriage, and putting his arm about her, broke into a run. A vivid flash of lightning illumined the building for which they were making. It was a round toll house, built of stone and with a thatched roof.

The rain lashed about them as they stood by the door, while Mr. Thurlston produced a key. He unlocked the door, and urged Isabella gently inside. Half dazed, she removed his cloak from her shoulders, and looked about her. They stood in a small room, sparsely furnished with a deal table and chairs, and an old wooden settle which stood over by the fireplace. On either side of the small chimneypiece were shelves, on which stood cooking utensils, plates and mugs. The stone floor had no other covering than a layer of clean straw.

A lantern was set in the small, uncurtained window. Roger Thurlston removed this to the table, and closed the wooden shutters which were set at each side of the window. As he did so, Isabella noticed that the carriage was moving away from the front of the toll house. The sight shook her out of her apathy.

"Where is the driver taking the coach?" she asked in surprise. "Are we not going to this place that you spoke of — this Abbey? What of my sister — we must go to her at once."

For answer Mr. Thurlston moved over to the door, and turned the key in the lock. This done, he deposited the key in a pocket. Isabella watched him in startled surprise.

"We are going nowhere, my dear, for the present," he replied coolly. "As for your sister —" he shrugged — "she must do the best she can."

"What do you mean?" cried Isabella in alarm.

"Sit down, my dear."

He indicated the settle, and tried to draw her towards it. She shook him off angrily, though panic was in her heart. He went and sat down, leaving her standing in the middle of the floor.

"My meaning should be plain," he said calmly. "I made you an honourable offer of my heart and hand: I was willing to be patient for a while, if you would promise to be mine. You gave me no hope. Wed you I must, so this —" he shrugged again — "was the only way."

"Are you mad?"

She tried to keep her voice from shaking, but only partially succeeded.

"Never more sane, I assure you. Come and sit here beside me, and I will endeavour to teach you to love me, after all."

"How dare you!" she stormed, lashing herself into a fury in order to hide the terror that now assailed her. "Let me out of here at once!"

He laughed softly, and shook his head. "Oh, no; not now. Tomorrow, if you wish — but you will not. You will be only too glad, then, to accompany me to a reverend of whom I know, who will wed us without asking any questions. He would murder his own mother, that one, for a fee!"

"Tomorrow?" gasped Isabella, turning pale as the significance of this word dawned upon her reeling senses.

Again he nodded. "Tonight you stay here with me," he said softly. "I fear I cannot offer you luxury, but we shall be snug enough together."

She stood stock still with horror for a while. Outside the storm was abating, but she noticed nothing.

"You can't do this," she stammered, through bloodless lips. "Papa —"

"How is he to know?" he asked easily. "Your sister is not at home to give the alarm, remember. In any event, by the time help reached you it would be too late."

She threw herself on her knees beside him. "Mr. Thurlston!" she begged, with tears in her eyes. "You can't do this to me — if you pretend to have any feeling for me at all — if you have any claim to the name of gentleman —"

"What use are my claims to that title without money to back them up?" he asked bitterly.

"So that is it!" said Isabella, starting to her feet, and fixing him with a look of withering contempt. "Your avowal of love was a falsehood. All this is to force me to wed you so that you may enjoy my fortune."

"Precisely," he said, coldly. "But I see no reason for you to be in such a heat on that account. Was it any more noble that your parents would have sold you for the sake of Charles's title, and position in the world? Were you any more virtuous than I when you agreed to marry a man you could not love?"

She hung her head. "No," she whispered. "No, I was not. Mayhap I deserve some punishment for that. But not this!" she cried vehemently. "Not to be tied for life to a man such as you! 'Pon rep, they give Mr. Barsett a bad name, but he is as an angel beside you. At least he is no hypocrite!"

He rose, and came menacingly towards her. Far away, a last faint roll of thunder sounded.

"We have talked enough," he said, fixing his eyes upon her. "The time has come for action."

"Oh, yes, indeed!" cried Isabella defiantly.

Suddenly she was quite calm. She knew that she meant to fight him to the last ounce of her strength. Desperately she prayed for release.

He continued to advance upon her, and she moved away, putting the table between them. He laughed softly, and made as if to move round it.

With the strength of desperation, she put both hands under the table, heaved, and succeeded in overturning it in his path. The lamp which stood upon it went crashing to the floor, exuding a gush of oil. A tongue of flame licked hungrily along the stream of dark liquid; in a moment the nearby straw was blazing merrily.

"Good God!" he cried, alarmed as he saw the fire rapidly spreading to other parts of the floor, "you hell-spawn, you!"

He began stamping his feet upon the crackling straw in the vain hope of extinguishing the blaze. He soon realised that this was not to succeed, however; the dry straw made perfect kindling, and already the whole floor was alight, while tongues of flame crept round the legs of the table and chairs. If something was not done quickly the whole room would be ablaze.

He looked wildly about him: Isabella was for the moment too stunned by the unexpected result of her action to move. His eye chanced upon his wet travelling cloak, slung over one of the chairs. With an exclamation of satisfaction he seized it, and began a frantic attempt to beat out the flames by holding it in both hands, and wielding it about him. He began to gain a little ground, but as fast as he extinguished the fire in one part of the room it gained a hold in another. Out of the corner of his eye he noticed that the settle by the fireplace had caught alight.

He moved over to that part of the room, and raised his cloak to deal with this new menace. A wild flourish of the garment caught at a large stone ewer which stood upon one of the shelves. It wobbled uncertainly for a second, then plunged into space, landing upon Roger Thurlston's head. From thence, it rolled to the floor without sustaining a single crack: but Roger Thurlston dropped in a heap, senseless.

Isabella let out a frightened exclamation, and, seizing his cloak, tried to continue his work. But the room was now a mass of quickly starting flames, and one person unaided could not hope to cope with it. She beat about her desperately, panting and afraid.

She paused, breathless, for a moment, and all at once noticed that the hem of her gown was alight. With a little cry of fear, she stooped to beat out the flames with her hands, dropping the cloak in order to do so. She succeeded in extinguishing the flame, and leapt wildly towards the door. She must escape quickly, before it was too late. There was no more to be done to save the building from total extinction.

She tugged desperately at the handle, before recollecting that the door was locked. The key! She must have the key! But where had he put it?

Sobbing now, she ran to Roger Thurlston's side. He lay where he had fallen in a crumpled heap, the flames licking perilously about him. She raised her skirts about her waist, and tied them, as she had been wont to do in the far-off days when she had climbed the apple trees with Amanda and John in the orchard at home. Swiftly she bent over him, and began her search.

She turned out his pockets ruthlessly, flinging down the unwanted articles which she unearthed from them. At last, her fingers closed over something metallic in a waistcoat pocket: with a thankful sob she dragged forth the key.

She was beside the door in an instant. Her trembling fingers made several fumbling attempts before finally she succeeded in turning the key in the lock. With a wild exclamation she flung wide the door, and ran into the road.

From behind her rose an angry sound, as of a giant sigh. She turned to look. The sudden draught of air admitted by the open door had added fury to the fire. The toll house was now a blazing inferno.

She turned and ran, her skirts dropping once more about her ankles. She neither knew nor cared where she went; she was unconscious even of movement. Some deep instinct carried her on, away from the dangers of the toll house.

She fled over a little wooden bridge which spanned the nearby river, and came to the coach road, gleaming white in the moonlight. The rain had stopped, and the night was set fair, but she did not notice. Along the road she stumbled, unseeing, unthinking, her mind a whirl of horror.

The distant sound of horses' hoofs recalled her a little to herself. She gazed anxiously ahead of her. Far down the wet road the winking lights of a coach were drawing even nearer. She paused in her flight, her bosom heaving, her breath laboured.

As the vehicle drew nearer, she could hear that its horses were at the gallop. Dimly, she realised that she must stop these travellers, and ask their help. She stood still in the path of the oncoming vehicle, like one turned to stone.

The coach thundered onwards. Nearer it drew, and even nearer, and still Isabella did not move, or call out. Now she could see the outline of the horses: they were almost on top of her.

Suddenly the coachman saw the immobile figure standing in his path. With a fierce oath, he reined in his horses violently.

A head popped out of the window as the vehicle drew to a sudden halt.

"What's amiss, Smith?" asked an impatient voice. "Why the delay?"

"There's a pesky female in the road, y'r honour, and she don't move out o' the way," replied the man. "Seems women are takin' to the High Toby nowadays!"

There was a startled exclamation, and the door of the coach was opened. Isabella, coming suddenly to life, ran towards it. She opened her lips to appeal for help.

Before she could utter a word, someone had leapt from the coach with a bound, and was taking her arm, to turn her face towards the light.

"Bella!" cried John Webster's voice, in accents of amazement and love. "Oh, Bella, my dear, what on earth are you doing here?"

For answer, she fell into his arms, sobbing.

He began to draw her into the coach tenderly, and Charles Barsett came forward to help; but all at once she shook them off, and gasped, "Mr. Thurlston! You must save him!"

"Roger?" asked Charles Barsett quickly. "Save him from what? Where is he?"

"The toll house!" panted Isabella, pointing down the road. "Over there — in flames — he is unconscious — I —"

She collapsed on to the seat of the coach, spent for the moment. John settled her as comfortably as he could in the corner, then joined Charles Barsett, who was standing in the road, peering anxiously in the direction she had indicated. The toll house was now a beacon in the night sky.

"Good God!"

Charles Barsett broke into a run.

"Look to this lady, Smith," ordered John tersely, and followed him.

Isabella leaned back wearily in the corner of the carriage.

"Be you all right, ma'am?" asked Smith. "Mebbe you'd like a nip o' something — there's a flask o' cordial in the carriage —"

"No, I thank you. I need nothing but rest."

She closed her eyes as she spoke.

Pray heaven she don't go after faintin', thought the man uncomfortably. That would be a fine kettle o' fish, an' no mistake!

But Isabella was no longer in danger of a swoon. She felt curiously drained of emotion, and almost at peace, after living through what seemed to be the feelings of a lifetime. John was near — she was in his care — nothing now could harm her ever again…

It was not above a hundred yards to the toll house, but it seemed a very long time before at last she saw the two men returning. They bore a body between them. Isabella knew a sudden stab of returned fear. Was he — would he be — dead? She had never looked on death before, and scoundrel though he was, she did not wish it for Roger Thurlston. Her new-found calm deserted her, and her heart began to pound uncomfortably.

Silently the two deposited Roger Thurlston gently inside the carriage, placing a cloak beneath his head to serve as a pillow.

"We must get skilled attention for him at once," said Charles Barsett crisply. "We'd best take him to the 'Bear' at Maidenhead — it's less than a mile back, and they may know of a doctor."

"Is he — is he — much hurt?" asked Isabella, fearfully.

"He's conscious, at any rate," said Charles Barsett abruptly. "But he's badly burnt, I fear."

He bent over the injured man, a furrow between his brows.

Roger Thurlston stirred, groaned, then spoke faintly. "So you got me out, did you, Charlie?" he said. "How like you! I doubt if I should have done the same in your place."

It was years since he had called the other by that name. Charles Barsett winced, and his frown deepened.

"You'd best not talk now," he said gently. "Try to conserve your strength for the journey; I fear it may be — painful."

He gave the coachman the order, and the vehicle turned back along the road to Maidenhead, the horses at the gallop.

John had seated himself by Isabella, and she leaned a little towards him. Charles glanced at them curiously. There had been no mistaking the way in which Isabella had turned to Webster in her need, instead of to the man she was to wed; nor was there any doubt of the affection and concern that had tinged John's voice when he spoke to her. It was obvious to the most casual observer that these two were in love.

A sudden sharp misgiving twisted Charles Barsett's mind. What of Amanda? If he had read the signs aright, she also had fixed her affections upon this young man. Was she, then, that bright, fearless child, doomed to a fate similar to his own?

Roger Thurlston moaned slightly, and recalled his unhappy thoughts to the present need. He bent over his cousin to try and ease his suffering, but there was little he could do. He lowered the window, and shouted to the coachman, "For God's sake, hurry, Smith!"

"I'm givin' 'em their heads, y'r honour!" Smith shouted back. "They can't do more!"

There was a faint sigh from the recumbent form on the floor. Charles saw with relief that his cousin had once more relapsed into unconsciousness. At least he would feel no pain for the time being.

His gaze wandered from the inanimate form, and fixed itself upon his two travelling companions. They were still sitting close together, without speaking, but a little colour had returned to Isabella's face.

"If you should now feel sufficiently recovered, Miss Isabella," he said quietly, "would you be good enough to try and tell us what happened?"

Until this moment Isabella had been conscious only of the balm of John's presence, after the horrifying experience through which she had recently passed. Charles Barsett's question recalled sharply to her mind the cause of it all. She sat up in sudden alarm.

"Mandy!" she exclaimed, in agony of spirit. "Where is she? Her note said she was with you, John. Can it have been —"

"Hush, dearest," interrupted John, smoothing her rumpled curls with a gentle hand. "Mandy is safe enough; she is staying with Barsett's nurse."

Unconsciously he had dropped the formal title. Charles Barsett looked up, momentarily surprised.

"With —?" asked Isabella, in puzzlement.

"With the old woman who was nurse both to my dead mother and myself," explained Charles quickly. "But do you feel able to explain the cause of all this commotion? At present, Webster and I are sorely puzzled to know how you and my cousin come to be here; we had thought you safely in Town, and were on our way to reassure you as to your sister's safety when we chanced upon you just now."

Haltingly, and with many promptings, Isabella told her story. At the conclusion of it, John's expression had hardened. "Well for that rogue that he does lie there helpless!" he said grimly. "Otherwise I should kill him for this."

"The duty would have fallen to me, I believe," said Charles expressionlessly.

John met his eyes squarely. "Look here, Barsett," he said purposefully. "You cannot wed Isabella."

"No?" asked Charles, with the ghost of a smile.

"No!" answered John firmly. "We can settle the matter when and where you will, hereafter, with any weapons you choose: but this much I want understood here and now."

Charles turned to Isabella.

"And what has the lady to say to this?"

Isabella hung her head. "I — I have acted very wrongly," she said in a voice only just above a whisper, "and I — deserve your censure, I know but — but — sensible as I am —"

"— of the honour which I have done you," finished Charles, ironically, "you beg to be excused from marrying me. Is that the gist of what you wished to say?"

Isabella nodded in silence, and shrank against John, the red flaming in her cheeks. He put a protective arm about her, and glared at the other man.

"Really, Webster," complained Charles gently, "there can be no need to give me such black looks. Miss Twyford, I release you from your promise to me; I am persuaded that we should not suit. I am quite unworthy of so much beauty and virtue — Webster must be far more deserving than I."

"You — you can give her up so easily?" asked John, amazed.

"She was never mine to renounce, my dear fellow, but yours. The whole affair was a mistaken notion of our parents, and is best forgotten."

John considered this for a moment in silence. Relief showed on Isabella's face. "Then you don't wish me to meet you?" asked John at last.

"I should be sorry," said Charles, "to make such a poor beginning to what I regard as a promising friendship. May I wish you both all the happiness you so richly deserve?"

He extended a hand. John seized it firmly.

"Egad!" exclaimed John, elation flooding over him. "I always knew that Mandy was mistaken in her judgment of you."

Charles Barsett shook his head, and the smile vanished from his face.

"No," he replied austerely. "I fear she was right."

Chapter XVIII: Amanda Surprises her Family

When they arrived at the 'Bear', Roger Thurlston was quickly transferred to a bed. By great good fortune, it happened that there was a doctor of some reputation staying at the inn, and he immediately placed himself at the service of the sufferer. Charles Barsett had bespoken a parlour: here he left Isabella and John together, while he attended the doctor at his cousin's bedside. Presently he returned with a lighter countenance.

"The medico says that he does not entirely despair of Roger," he said, entering the room suddenly, and taking its occupants by surprise. They started guiltily apart; Isabella blushed, and John straightened his hopelessly crumpled cravat.

Charles flung them an amused glance before continuing, "There is no danger of his life, it seems, though he has had a severe shock; but his looks will be impaired."

"One cannot but feel that it is a judgment," said John sternly. "But what are we to do now, Barsett? Do you suggest we still return to London?"

Charles frowned thoughtfully. "I think it may be wiser to remain here for tonight. Perhaps we might take Miss Isabella to join her sister at Nurse's cottage — there are beds enough, and they will like to be together, apart from the greater propriety of such a course. My coach will be available for them to return to Town tomorrow, and we could accompany them on horseback. What do you say?"

John agreed to the plan, and Isabella was straightway conducted to Nurse's home. If the good lady wondered a little at the constant stream of visitors, she controlled herself admirably, merely remarking in an aside to Mr. Charles that he must remember that she had only a limited number of beds in the house.

Isabella and Mandy, after the first surprise, were well content to be together again; each had much to relate to the other, but on her side, Amanda anticipated no joy in the telling of her story. The gentlemen soon returned to the inn, where they had bespoken beds for the night, and Nurse quickly and efficiently installed the sisters in a dainty bedchamber, with instructions to be sure and get a good night's rest.

There seemed little likelihood of this for some time, for there was too much to be discussed and explained between them. Isabella was the first to tell her story, and give her sister the glad news of her engagement to John. Nothing this time was to come in the way of it; John meant to approach Papa, who had always favoured his suit, and he had strong hopes of gaining Papa's consent at once. If not, stated Isabella boldly, then they would think of some plan — maybe even elope. This time there would be no mistake.

"And what of Mama?" asked Amanda, wondering a little at this new Isabella.

Her sister's face clouded a little. "To be sure, that is a difficulty," she began uncertainly. Then she tilted her chin in a resolute way. "But we must and shall surmount it! Mama will never force me, Mandy, of that I am persuaded and if Papa is on my side —"

"All will be well," finished her sister with a laugh. "Bella, you know very well that he eats out of Mama's hand! But I'm confident that you will carry the day, if only you are resolute."

Her voice changed. "What of — Mr. Barsett, Bella? What has he to say to all this — or haven't you yet told him?"

"Oh, yes, we have, and he was so understanding, you would scarce credit it. John offered to meet him in a duel, you know —"

"Bella!" said Amanda faintly. "To have a duel fought over you! It is of all things the most romantic."

"Perhaps, only I'm glad that it isn't to take place after all," replied her more practical sister. "For I should not like either of them to get hurt — and especially not John! But there was no need, for Mr. Barsett said that he could see we were not suited, and he made a vastly pretty speech about not deserving me, and then he released me from my promise."

Amanda received this news in silence.

After a pause, she asked, "What did John have to say?"

"Oh, I think he was glad to be relieved of the necessity of calling Mr. Barsett out. Not for any cowardly reason — you know I could not mean that of John! — but because he has taken a fancy to — to Mr. Barsett. He says that you are mistaken in your opinion of his character. He actually told Mr. Barsett so."

"You mean that John told him that I — was mistaken in my opinion of him?" asked Amanda.

Isabella nodded.

"And what had Mr. Barsett to say to that?" asked Amanda in a subdued tone.

"He is the strangest person, Mandy. He said that he thought you were right."

"He — he did?" asked her sister in a strained voice.

Isabella glanced keenly at her, but could make nothing of her expression.

"What happened to you, Mandy?" she asked, having for the moment exhausted the topic of paramount interest to her. "Tell me the whole. Mr. Thurlston — what a rogue he is, after all, and how we have been mistaken in him he said that you and John had gone to this Abbey that you talked so much of. I was half mad with fright for you. Was it one of his dreadful lies, or did you in fact go there?"

Amanda's face was sober. "Yes," she admitted reluctantly. "Yes, we did go there."

"How you could bring yourself to do such an improper thing —" began Isabella, then broke off, frowning. "But I suppose you felt that it was for my sake," she continued, after a pause for reflection. "You always did say that you would never rest until you had proved that Mr. Barsett was not worthy of me."

Her sister made no reply to this remark.

"What — what kind of place is it?" asked Isabella, doubtfully.

Amanda looked uncomfortable, and shrugged with a show of nonchalance. "Oh, it is all a hum!" she said hurriedly. "They — the gentlemen — have a secret society of some kind there, but — but it is just a lot of mummery."

"What kind of secret society?" pressed Isabella, her curiosity aroused in proportion to Amanda's evident reluctance to satisfy it.

"Oh, I do not know the whole! But they dress up in white robes, and — and conduct ceremonies — and the females wear masks —"

"Females? Mandy, are they —?"

"I don't know," replied her sister hastily. "Yes, I daresay they may be, only I was not there long enough to find out all that. Mr. Barsett —" she choked a little — "soon discovered me, and brought me away from there to this house, in company with John, of course."

Isabella considered this for a moment. "John says that it was Mr. Thurlston who made the arrangements for you to go to that place," said she, frowning. "What a villain he is, Mandy! He planned to injure us both."

Amanda shook her head. "I have been turning it over in my mind, and I feel convinced that his original plan was to injure his cousin. He meant to smuggle me into the Abbey, and somehow contrive to blame it on to Mr. Barsett. I feel sure that was the real reason why he was unwilling for me to tell John who was helping me in the affair, and also why he said it would be better if John did not accompany me into the grounds. He hoped to implicate his cousin, but I spoilt that by confiding in John."

"He must have surely realised that you might," replied her sister. "But only fancy, Mandy! The wretch actually made me a declaration."

Amanda stared. "Did he? But I'm not surprised, after all. Bella, I recollect now that I once let slip to him that you were possessed of a handsome fortune. You may be sure that he was after it."

"I had realised that — earlier this evening," said Isabella, shuddering. "He tried to make me think that you and John had eloped together — and offered me his hand and heart in consolation. He must have got wind somehow of — of my feelings for John."

She looked inquiringly at Amanda as she said this, and the other girl coloured. "I daresay I may have dropped a hint or two," she confessed sheepishly. "I was so upset at your persistence in maintaining your engagement to — to Mr. Barsett. I knew all along that it was John you really loved."

"Oh, well, I forgive you," replied Isabella magnanimously. "But I must say, Mandy, that you would do better to be more on your guard in future. True, it is not every day that one meets with such a rogue, but it's as well to be prepared, and you are a deal too free in your manner at times."

"How did he persuade you to go with him?" asked Amanda, ignoring this homily.

"He finally told me that he believed you had gone off to the Abbey, and he painted a lurid picture of what kind of place it was. It sounded so likely a tale, and I was so wild with concern for you, that I never gave one thought to the impropriety of going off with him alone. Who would, in a like case? Which, of course, was exactly what he had anticipated. I played right into his hands," concluded Isabella ruefully.

"And then instead he took you to this toll house?"

Isabella shuddered violently. "Don't let us speak of that any more. I shall never forget it — never!"

At this point in the conversation there was a gentle tap on the door. Amanda opened it, and Nurse came clucking into the room.

"What, not abed yet?" the old lady asked, in pretended horror. "Come, now, my dears, you've both had a trying day, and must be astir betimes tomorrow for your journey to London. If we're to keep the roses in those cheeks, we must get a good night's rest."

The two sisters responded automatically to the authority of her kindly voice, and were reminded of similar reproofs delivered when they were much younger than now. Within five minutes of her quitting the room they were safely between the lavender-scented sheets, and the candle was extinguished.

"Mandy," whispered Isabella, before she turned over to go to sleep.

"Mmm?" was the sleepy answer.

"You did not find this Abbey so very shocking a place, then?"

Amanda, roused by this question, hesitated before replying to it. Not for worlds could she bring herself to confess her real sentiments on the subject, even to Isabella. "It — it is not at all the thing," she said at last, borrowing a phrase from John. "But I think that the rumours concerning it may be a little exaggerated. All the same, we must not speak of it in company, and so I warn you, Bella!"

"Of course, I realise that," replied her sister, turning to plump up her pillow.

There was a pause, then Isabella said thoughtfully, "Mr. Barsett behaved towards you in a gentlemanlike way, however, even if he is a member of this odious society."

"I — I think he is finished with it now," said Amanda hastily. "He told me that it had amused him to belong to it at one time, but that he had since found it tedious. I remember, too, that the — the others — said that he hadn't joined in any of their activities on this occasion."

Her face flamed crimson as she recalled the scene in the grounds of the Abbey; it seemed to her that it would be for ever engraved on her memory. Fortunately the room was dark.

Isabella yawned. "Perhaps he is not so black as he is painted," she said sleepily. "I'm glad of it, for John appears to like him. He says that it is his intention to ask Mr. Barsett to be chief groomsman at our wedding."

In spite of herself, Amanda went off into peals of subdued laughter at this information. "Oh, Bella, that will indeed be odd. Why, only yesterday he was to be the groom!"

"Life is full of surprises," stated Isabella in a drowsy tone. "I wonder whom you will wed, Mandy?"

There was no answer to this. After a moment, Isabella fell fast asleep to dream of John.

At an early hour the next morning the two gentlemen presented themselves at Nurse's cottage. They brought with them an indifferent account of Mr. Thurlston. He had passed a restless night, and was in some pain.

"However, he has someone to console him," said John, with a grin. "It appears that Miss Dunster — you will recollect her, Bella, she is the fat, white female who gushes — was staying the night at the 'Bear' on her way back to the West Country. She came downstairs this morning all prepared for an early start, together with her travelling companion. No sooner does she learn who it is who is lying injured in the inn than she cancels all her arrangements, and begs the doctor to allow her to assist in the nursing of him. It seems that nursing is her one passion! When we left, she was preparing a soothing posset in the kitchen with her own hands! The landlady and the doctor didn't like it I can tell you, but she is so rich no one dares to offend her!"

"However, I believe that we will not leave him entirely to her tender ministrations," said Charles Barsett. "When we reach Town, I shall instantly inform my aunt of his condition. No doubt she will post here at once."

This was the first time he had spoken, except to murmur a formal word of greeting to the sisters on arrival. Amanda stole a covert glance at his face. It wore a grave expression, and there were dark shadows under his eyes, as though he had not slept. No doubt he was concerned for his cousin. She knew a moment's sudden anger: why should he worry over one who had always sought to injure him? Not that she cared what he did, she told herself hastily. For her part, he could lie awake worrying over all the cousins in Christendom.

She patently ignored him while preparations were being made for the journey to Town. These were slight enough, as neither sister was equipped with any luggage: Nurse had lent them all that was needful. They both thanked her now sincerely for all her kindness, and said goodbye with real regret.

She retained Amanda's hand for a moment longer than was necessary. "Look well into your heart, my dear," she whispered, as that young lady was about to step into the coach. "God bless you."

Amanda pondered this cryptic utterance, but some impulse prevented her from confiding it to Isabella, who, in any event, found it difficult to talk of anything but her new engagement, and how she was to break the news of it to her parents. After a time, Amanda gave up suggesting ways and means, and relapsed into her own thoughts.

These were confused and unhappy — quite a new thing for Amanda. She found herself hoping that her parents might decide to remove permanently to their home in Berkshire. The prospect of returning to a round of social pleasure held for her no appeal; besides, if she remained in Town, she might possibly encounter Charles Barsett. This was the last thing she wanted. When she thought of him, it was with a strange mental shrinking, as though somewhere in her mind was an open wound which must be protected at all costs.

The journey was uneventful, and shortly after one o'clock the two sisters were deposited safe and sound at their own door. Mr. Barsett took his leave of them immediately, but John entered the house, and sat on with them for a little time. It was decided that he should call on the following day, when my Lord Twyford would have returned to Town, and seek her father's permission to pay his addresses to Isabella.

"But you have paid them, have you not?" laughed Amanda, diverted by this. "And you have already had your answer!"

"Do not jest, Mandy!" reproved Isabella, with a look of apprehension. "I do not quite know how I am to tell Papa that I have decided to wed another man than the one to whom I am promised. I feel sure you would not care to be in such an awkward fix."

Amanda refrained from saying that she would not have allowed herself to become so involved, and merely contented herself with the consoling remark, "Don't worry, Bella. I am certain that it will all pass off a deal more easily than you suppose at present."

In the event, she proved to be right, at least as far as Lord Twyford, was concerned. He arrived in the late afternoon of the same day, bringing with him a cheerful account of their Mama. She had recovered her usual health very quickly in the country air, and was determined to quit it no more this season.

"And we would all do better to follow her example," he finished, "particularly since your Aunt Matchett was not at liberty to come and stay with you here in Town. Even your Mama feels that it will not be possible for you to remain under the circumstances. She thought that perhaps later on, when Isabella has fixed a date for her wedding —"

Here Amanda quickly interrupted, saying how glad she would be to return to Berkshire, and the conversation was turned for the moment. But later on, Amanda managed to leave her sister alone for a space with my lord. She caught Isabella's eye as she quitted the room, and held up two fingers crossed for luck, behind my lord's back.

She did not return for some time to the drawing-room. When she did, it was with the liveliest expectation of finding that all had gone well. A glance at Isabella confirmed her hopes: her sister was flushed, but her eyes sparkled with triumph.

"Well, Mandy, so your sister has thrown over her grand new suitor, eh?" asked her father, with a quiet chuckle.

"She's a fickle lass, ain't she?"

"Not fickle, precisely, Papa," returned Amanda, with a smile. "Bella's only trouble is that she doesn't know her own mind."

"And you do, I'll be bound," he retorted. "Well, I can't pretend that I'm not glad of the change. Barsett is one of the best, an old and valued friend; but that boy of his —"

He stopped, not caring to say more in the presence of his daughters.

"You do Mr. Barsett an injustice, sir," said Amanda, impetuously. "If you could know him better, I feel convinced that you would think differently of his character."

He directed a sharp glance at her, and raised his brows.

"You do, do you?" he asked. "Since when, may I ask, have you been an advocate of his? I would have taken my oath on it that you disliked him extremely!"

Amanda positively blushed. Isabella eyed her in astonishment.

"I — I am not invariably right," she stammered, awkwardly. "Brownie used often to warn me of the danger of yielding to hastily formed opinions — not without some justification!"

Lord Twyford stared hard at his younger daughter, bewilderment in his eyes.

"Egad, here's a change!" he exclaimed. "'Pon oath, I never thought to hear you admit to such a thing!"

Amanda's colour deepened. She hastily muttered some incoherent excuse, and fled from the room, leaving both her relatives staring after her in utter astonishment.

Chapter XIX: My Lord Barsett is Beset by Doubts

After Charles Barsett left the two sisters, he drove at once to St. James's Square. His father was from home, but he found his aunt sitting alone in a shady room at the back of the house. She did not attempt to conceal her surprise on seeing him, and told him at once that she could not imagine what he should want with her.

It was an unpromising start to a difficult interview. He cast about in his mind for some way of breaking his news to her without inflicting too great a shock to her sensibilities. He could feel very little affection for one who had never shown him any at all; but common humanity urged him to be gentle in his dealings with her on this melancholy occasion.

"I am the bearer of a message from my cousin," he began, at last.

"From Roger?" Her brows shot up: this was indeed an unlikely messenger from such a source.

He nodded briefly. "I have something of an unpleasant nature to communicate to you, Aunt. Roger is not well —"

She started from her chair on these words, and a cry of alarm escaped her.

"Do not concern yourself, I beg," he said. "There is no danger of his life. There is a doctor with him who says that he will do very well in a little time."

She sank back again on to her chair, relief on her face.

"Thank God!" she breathed. "But what has happened — you — what have you done?"

He could not fail to notice her assumption that he was somehow responsible for Roger's misfortune. He passed this over, however.

"What I have to tell you must go no further," he said, with a stern air, "but you, at least, must know the truth. Yesterday, for some purpose of his own, my cousin tried to abduct Miss Twyford."

She started violently, and the colour drained from her face.

"You are no doubt aware that this was made easy for him by the absence from Town of her parents and myself," he continued. "I don't propose to labour you with all the details of the affair indeed, some of them are not yet clear to me. Suffice it to say that he took her to a deserted toll house on the road to Maidenhead, which appears to have been a haunt of his for years. A struggle ensued, in which Miss Isabella overturned a lamp, and started a fire. During the upheaval which followed, Roger was knocked senseless, and Miss Isabella made her escape. Roger was left there unconscious in the midst of the flames."

She began to shiver at these words. He rose to pass her a shawl which lay over a chair close at hand. She accepted it wordlessly, drawing it about her thin shoulders, and cringing, as if from an expected blow. He looked at her compassionately.

"By great good fortune, a friend and myself chanced to be travelling along the road where Miss Isabella ran for help. Between us, we were able to pull Roger out, and found immediate medical attention for him nearby, at the 'Bear'."

Her trembling had stopped, but she sat still, watching him.

"As I said before, you need have no fear for his life," he said, soothingly. "He will recover; he has the best of attention. This medico has a notable reputation."

Her expression had changed. He looked appalled at the hard, ruthless lines of her face.

"The fool!" she said, in a high, unnatural voice. "He is his father's son, after all! I knew that one day he would overplay his hand!"

He made no reply to this, but his voice was less sympathetic when he next spoke.

"Miss Twyford," he said, coldly, "was returned to her home today, and her parents are none the wiser. I am sure you will agree, Aunt, that it would be as well to keep them in such a state of blissful ignorance. No doubt you will wish to join your son without delay. If there is any way in which I can assist you to this end, you may command me."

She passed a hand over her eyes, and once more her voice changed.

"Is he — much hurt?" she asked falteringly.

His glance was gentle again.

"He has been badly burnt, I fear: but he is conscious, and has the best attention."

She rose hastily. "I will go to him. I don't doubt that you will be only too ready to explain to your father where I am gone, and why."

He had risen, too, and now bowed gravely before her.

"As for your help, I want none of it. I shall manage very well alone!"

"That is as you please, of course: but I think you know that my father will never hear this story from my lips."

He left the house without more ado.

Later that afternoon, when Mrs. Thurlston had departed for Maidenhead, and Charles Barsett was sitting broodily in his room in Albemarle Street, a carriage drew up outside the house in St. James's Square. A young lady and an abigail alighted, and, mounting the steps, knocked upon the door. They were admitted, and presently the young lady was shown up to his lordship, who was sitting alone.

Surprise showed on his face as he rose to greet her, but he carefully kept all trace of it out of his manner.

"You do me a very great honour, Miss Amanda," he said, setting a chair for her. "I trust I see you well?"

She answered him absently in a few low words, and, seating herself, lapsed into silence.

"It is some days since I had the pleasure of meeting the rest of your family," he continued politely. "They are also in good health, I hope?"

"Yes — yes, thank you, my lord," replied Amanda. "That is to say — no, not quite all; Mama found the heat very oppressive, and has been obliged to quit Town for the country. Papa is but just returned from accompanying her there, and says she is already much recovered."

My lord clucked his tongue in concern. "I am sorry to hear of her indisposition," he said. "The weather is certainly hot, though a little improved, I think, since the recent storm."

Beneath his urbane manner, he was agog with curiosity. Certainly Miss Amanda Twyford had not come here to exchange the courtesies with him: what could the chit want?

"We are all to return to Berkshire in a few days' time, my lord," continued Amanda, with a trace of uneasiness in her manner. "That is why I felt that I must seek you out immediately. You see —" she swallowed nervously — "there — there is something I must tell you!"

"Indeed?" he said, smoothly. "However that may be, I am delighted that you did not leave Town without affording me the opportunity of bidding you Godspeed. Though we shall soon meet again, I trust?"

"I do not think it likely, sir," said Amanda, regretfully.

"I — I beg your pardon?"

My lord was puzzled.

"Perhaps I had better first tell you my story, sir. Then you will better understand. But I am puzzled where to begin; my — my mission is rather a — a delicate one."

"Mission — delicate?" echoed my lord, feeling out of his depth.

Amanda tilted her chin in the old courageous gesture.

"I must be plain, my lord. My purpose in coming here is to place before you evidence which should serve to right a wrong. If in so doing, I should seem to be meddling in affairs which are your own private concern, or — or questioning your judgment, I beg that you will forgive what may perhaps appear as an impertinence. Please believe that I am compelled to speak — my conscience will not acquit me of the duty — common justice requires it!"

By now, his curiosity was thoroughly aroused.

"Have no fears, Miss Amanda," he said, courteously. "I acquit you readily of any charges of impertinence, and give you leave to meddle and to question with impunity! Take your time, my dear young lady, and say what you will."

Amanda drew a deep breath of relief.

"Thank you, my lord. Do you perchance recollect a conversation between us at my birthday ball — a conversation concerning your son?"

Lord Barsett nodded, his eyes alert. He had thought often enough of that conversation since, with a troubled spirit.

"You told me then that there had been little sympathy between you and — and Mr. Barsett in the past," continued Amanda, hurriedly. "But I collected — more from your manner than from any words that you spoke — that you were beginning to think better of his character. What I have to tell you now must surely convince you that you were utterly mistaken in him — that he is essentially noble!"

My lord could not repress a start. Noble — Charles? That was coming it a bit strong, surely? But he would hear the girl out.

"We shall see, my dear," he replied, diplomatically. "But by all means, tell me your story."

Amanda hesitated for only a second.

"In telling you, my lord," she said, with a blush, "I am obliged to betray myself. I have been guilty, I must confess, at times, of — of what can only be described as — unmaidenly conduct."

"Nothing you may tell me, Miss Amanda," he said, gently, "can in any way alter the esteem in which I hold you. Rest assured of that."

She smiled tremulously, and shook her head.

"When you have heard me out, I fear you will think otherwise. However, that cannot alter my duty. You see, my lord, it was like this…"

She plunged determinedly into her tale. She told everything, not sparing herself: how her determination that Isabella should not wed Charles, added to her curiosity concerning the Abbey and its doings, had made it easy for Roger Thurlston to inveigle her into going to Medmenham.

At this point, my lord started to his feet, exclaiming, "The villain! Do you tell me that my own nephew —"

She nodded emphatically, and he subsided, not wishing to put her off the rest of her story. She went on to tell of how Charles had eased her out of her predicament; and then she retailed Isabella's part in the affair. Once again, Lord Barsett showed considerable emotion; but Amanda plunged on, and came to the business of the fire, and Charles Barsett's rescue of his cousin. She wound up by telling of his renunciation of her sister in favour of John Webster.

When she had finished, there was a long silence in the room. Her cheeks burned, and her heart was beating uncomfortably fast, but she knew a strong feeling of relief. At last she had done what justice demanded.

"Am I to understand," said my lord, at last, "that you have told me this in order to show me that I have all this while been mistaken in the characters of my nephew and my son?"

She nodded, apprehensive but steadfast. "Not only you, my lord, but all the world."

He raised one eyebrow in a way that reminded her painfully of Charles.

"Yet," he said gently, "you have — pardon me for reminding you of it — yourself seen proof of — his wildness."

She could not meet his eyes.

"Yes, sir," she answered, almost in a whisper. "But I have also learnt something of the reasons for it."

"You find that to understand all is to forgive all?"

She nodded, not trusting herself to speak.

"How much of this story is known to your parents, Miss Amanda?"

She looked alarmed. "At present, merely the part concerning Bella's engagement."

"Do you intend to confide the rest to them?"

She shook her head.

"Bella, John and I have discussed it thoroughly, and we believe it can serve no useful purpose, for the present, anyway. Indeed, it may prejudice John's chances of obtaining Mama's consent to the match. She — you must understand, sir, that she was very set on Bella's marrying your — son. One day, perhaps, it may be possible to tell them all — or nearly all," she added, with a shamefaced look. "I must say, I do not find it comfortable to be obliged to keep a secret for very long."

"That I can believe," he said, with a smile. "Yours is an unusually candid nature."

She blushed, and rose to go, unwilling to prolong an interview that had been attended for her by so much embarrassment. Lord Barsett, too, came to his feet.

"It is difficult to find adequate words to thank you for coming forward in this way, Miss Amanda. Believe me, I am fully sensible of the courage required to take such a step."

He took her hand, and saluted it, bowing low.

"May I say that what you have confided to me leaves me with an even higher opinion of you than I held formerly?"

He saw the tears start in her eyes at his words. His own were gentle.

After he had seen her to her carriage, he came and stood before the portrait over the mantelshelf.

"She loves him, Kit," he whispered, "though I think she doesn't yet know it herself. Can she be right, think you? Have I misjudged our son all these years?"

He gazed earnestly into the blue eyes of the portrait. Was it fancy, or did they seem to hold a hint of wistfulness tonight?

"The evidence was all against him," he said, aloud, defensively. "And there can be no doubt that he has been wild enough since then, in all conscience! But, small sympathy as I held for the child, I never in his life knew him to persist in a lie until that day. I wonder —" He broke off, musing silently for a while. "But she is young, and a prejudiced witness, after all!" he exclaimed, after pacing the room for a while longer. "'Twould be a fine thing for him, though, if he should wed her: I do believe she is the very girl for him!"

He stared earnestly at the picture again. "Damme if I won't know for sure!" he exclaimed. "What was the name of that wench again? Baker — Blunt —? No, its gone! No matter, my lawyer will know. I'll settle this, once and for all!"

He crossed again to the fireplace, this time to ring the bell.

Chapter XX: Reconciliation

Two days later, Charles Barsett received a message from his father asking him to call in St. James's Square. He fancied that he knew the reason for the summons, and went at once, anxious to have done with the business.

My lord looked up as his son was shown into the drawing-room, and studied his face attentively. Charles was dressed with his usual care, but he looked tired and drawn, and the sparkle had left his eyes.

Lord Barsett extended a hand, but Charles declined ruefully, indicating a bandage on his own which was partially concealed by his ruffles.

"How came you by that?" asked my lord, with studied carelessness.

Charles shrugged. "A trifling affair; some straw caught alight in the stables."

Lord Barsett made no reply to this, but indicated a chair, and rang for some wine. When they were served, they sat drinking for a time in melancholy silence.

"Well, Charles," said my lord, eventually. "I learn that you and Miss Isabella have broken off your engagement. A pity, but I collect that the lady's affections are engaged elsewhere."

"You've seen Twyford, then?" asked Charles.

His father nodded. "He was apologetic, but firm. It appears that you did not employ your time with that young lady to good enough advantage, my boy. It should have been a simple enough matter to fix your interest with her, an accomplished gallant like yourself!"

He fancied that his son winced a little at this, but Charles's voice was level enough as he replied.

"I think her affections were too firmly placed already for any efforts of mine to signify. In any event, it is all for the best: we should not have suited."

"No," answered Lord Barsett, reflectively. "Too demmed proper for you, ain't she? We should look for someone with a less guarded temperament, mayhap, someone a shade more impulsive. I wonder — now, what say you to the other sister, the little one?"

Charles Barsett set down his glass with an abrupt movement that spilt the wine. His mouth was grim.

"Clumsy!" reproved my lord, facetiously.

"We will leave aside the question of my marriage, if you please, sir," said Charles, stiffly. "It may be that I shall choose to remain a bachelor. In any event, I prefer not to discuss the matter."

"As you wish," replied my lord, indifferently. "But don't neglect your wine, even if you are to forswear women."

"No," said his son, with a twist of the lips. "No, I shall not do that."

He picked up his glass again, and there was a short silence.

"I made a brief journey yesterday," offered his father, in conversational vein. "Into Kent."

"Indeed?" murmured Charles, politely. "A pleasant country."

"I did not go for the scenery," replied my lord, rising to refill the glasses. "Let us drink a toast, my boy."

"By all means. What shall it be?"

Lord Barsett raised his glass aloft. "Let us drink to our better understanding, my boy."

"Willingly," replied Charles, with a tired smile, and raised his glass in turn.

There was a pause. My lord glanced surreptitiously at the picture over the fireplace.

"As I said, I did not go into Kent to admire the scenery. I went to interview a female."

His son made a polite murmur of interrogation, but it was obvious that his mind was elsewhere.

"You may perchance remember her," continued my lord, watching the other keenly, "though it is a long time since you met. Her name is — was — Brent."

There followed a tinkle of glass, and a muttered oath. Charles Barsett looked at the wine glass lying splintered in the hearth.

"You are uncommon careless today. I'll ring for another."

"Don't bother," replied Charles, looking his father full in the eye. "What is all this, sir?"

"You recall the name, do you?" asked Lord Barsett, softly. "I thought you might. She marked a turning point in your life, did she not? But today I had the truth from her, Charles."

His son's mouth twisted.

"She might have spared herself the trouble. Her work was done long ago — and his — too well to be undone now."

My lord placed his hand gently on the other's shoulder.

"Charlie."

The familiar name was uttered in a tone quite unlike any that Charles Barsett had been used to hearing from his parent. He looked up, and the expression in his eyes went to the older man's heart.

"There is something else I discovered today," went on Lord Barsett, "something that also throws a new light upon the characters of you both."

Charles could not entirely conceal his surprise.

"I know," said his father, glancing significantly at the bandaged hand, "just how you really came by that injury."

Charles started. "How do you know?" he shot out, swiftly.

My lord twirled his glass thoughtfully in his fingers.

"A day or two since, my boy, I had the honour of a visit — from Miss Amanda Twyford."

"Amanda!" Charles started to his feet. "She came here? Why?"

"To put me right on one or two matters where she considered I had erred," said his father, with a reminiscent smile. "She gave me a full account of her — escapade at Medmenham, and of the sequel that involved her sister. I now know everything, Charlie."

"The devil she did!" exclaimed Charles, his brow darkening.

He began to pace restlessly about the room. His father was silent, watching him closely. At last, he swung round to confront Lord Barsett, accusingly.

"I trust you used her gently, sir. Only conceive what courage it must have taken, to confess to such an exploit — not that she understands to the full the impropriety of it, innocent child that she is! And to be prepared to face such an ordeal for the pure cause of justice!"

His father smiled. "Not quite, my boy."

Charles' brow darkened. "What do you mean — not quite? Do you deny that she acted with great bravery, and from the highest motives?"

"No, I don't deny her courage, Charles. She is as plucky a one as I ever met. If you could but have seen her standing here before me, with that little chin thrust well up, and no doubt her limbs shaking like aspen leaves!"

"I can well imagine it," replied Charles, and a smile of great gentleness lit his sombre face.

His father noticed this phenomenon with wonder: if Amanda Twyford could produce such a change in his son's expression, then more than ever did it become apparent that she was the girl for him.

"No, it is not the lady's courage that I call in question," he repeated.

"Then what?" asked Charles, with a trace of aggressiveness.

"Her motives," was the smiling reply.

"Do you suggest," said his son, acidly, "that Amanda Twyford could possibly have a dishonourable motive for anything she does?"

My lord backed away, in mock alarm.

"Egad, here's a pother! Damme, I fear you'll be calling me out, next! But you mistake my meaning. What I would say is that I doubt if the lady herself realises her true motive for coming to me with this tale."

Charles frowned. "I don't quite follow you, sir. Be plain with me."

"Why do you suppose that she was so anxious to clear your character in my eyes?" asked Lord Barsett.

Charles raised one eyebrow.

"Why, if you know her well, that is obvious enough. She is the soul of integrity, and could not bear the thought of anyone being misjudged, however much —" He paused.

"Yes?" prompted his father.

"However much she disliked the person concerned," concluded Charles, with a wry smile.

"You are a fool, Charlie! But in one thing I have been wrong — and grievously wrong in my judgment of you, and for that I humbly ask your pardon, if you feel that you can grant it. Though you may be a fool, you were never a rogue, and once I thought you so. Can you find it in your heart to forgive me, my boy?"

Charles grinned, and readily extended his uninjured hand.

"Say no more, father. There have been faults on both sides."

Lord Barsett gripped his son's hand tightly, and for a moment neither man spoke. Involuntarily, both glanced up at the portrait. To my lord's eyes, the lady's smile had never looked so roguish.

"She would have been glad," he said, speaking his thoughts aloud.

Charles nodded. "Until now, I never really understood just how you felt about her," he said. "I can easily see how it was that you — resented me."

"I was blind," replied his father, regretfully. "But love makes a man blind to many things."

There was a pause, then Charles suddenly asked: "Why did you say I was a fool?"

His father gave him a quizzical look.

"Because you said that Miss Amanda disliked you."

"And so?" asked Charles, with lifted eyebrows.

"My dear boy, can you not see?"

Chapter XXI: Amanda Falls into Happiness

Amanda was walking in the orchard, away from the fierce glare of the August sun. She had discarded her bridesmaid's dress for one of less delicate hue, and shaken her curls free of the becoming lace cap that had framed her face during the recent ceremony. Most of the guests had long since left, and she had been impatient for solitude, and the chance to give rein to her confused thoughts.

She paused when she came to the wall that separated her father's land from that of their neighbour, Mr. Webster. An old tree grew here, one which spread its branches over the wall, and had offered an illegal, quick means of entry to the young people. A reminiscent smile touched her lips. She and John had climbed this tree many a time in that past that now seemed almost as if it had never been.

Her thoughts wandered to the ceremony she had so lately left. She recalled the picture of Isabella, beautiful and ethereal in her white gown, standing beside their father in the little church where both sisters and John Webster had been baptised as infants; of John, handsome and just a little nervous, as Charles Barsett had handed him the ring. John and Isabella were man and wife now: another chapter of their lives was over. They had departed, and of the three who had been together for so many happy years, only Amanda was left.

There was nothing in this to make her feel sad, she told herself, with inward impatience. John and Bella loved each other, and would presently return. But, all the same, in a sense it was the parting of the ways.

She looked up at the tree, and her eyes filled suddenly with tears. It was a symbol, this old friend, a symbol of the childhood she had lost. She dashed the tears away angrily, and told herself not to be fanciful. Everything was as it had always been, save only that John and Bella were together for always. Then why should there be this weight upon her heart, this strong feeling of loss?

She knew suddenly that she must climb the tree once more. Up there in the boughs, amongst the sun-dappled foliage, she might perchance recover the peace of mind she had once known. There was one branch with a crook in it, that had always made a cosy nesting place, where she had been wont to retire when anything troubled her. She could see it now, from where she stood; it would be a moment's work to reach it.

She hitched up her skirts to knee height, tied the ends securely round her waist, and began the ascent.

She soon discovered that she was surprisingly clumsy at something that had been ease itself only a few short years back. Twice she slipped, and almost fell, recovering herself with difficulty, and scraping the skin from her arms; before she had finally, with great perseverance, attained her objective, she had lost one shoe, torn her gown, and dirtied her white stockings to an alarming degree.

Breathless but triumphant, she took no heed of these mishaps, but curled herself into the crook of the branch with a sigh of content, and leaned her back against the rough gnarled trunk as though it had been pure goose down.

Peace settled over her. The familiar scent of apples and dusty bark, the slight rocking motion of the branch beneath her, combined to soothe her troubled spirit. Her thoughts drifted, wandering idly back over the happenings of the past few weeks.

There had been serious trouble with Mama over Isabella's decision to wed John. Amanda wriggled a little on her perch as she recalled a particularly prolonged, unpleasant scene, which had reduced poor Bella to tears. It had ended in a way that had succeeded in surprising everyone, most of all my lady. Lord Twyford had listened to the diatribes of his wife for some time, interposing every now and then some gentle, ineffectual remonstrance. When Isabella suddenly burst into a flood of weeping, however, he was immediately metamorphosed.

"Have done with this!" he commanded, in a strangely authoritative voice. "No daughter of mine shall be coerced into a loveless marriage! I will not play the tyrant, no, not even to please you, Margaret!"

Lady Twyford opened her mouth to protest, but before she could utter a syllable, he had concluded, "She shall marry John Webster! I say so, and I am master here. You'd do well to recollect that, wife!"

Amanda recalled with a smile that her mother's mouth had remained open for quite two minutes. When she had shut it, it had been with the meek words, "Yes, of course, my lord; just so, as you say."

She had been quiet after that, offering no further opposition to the match. Then, as the weeks passed, and the date appointed for the wedding drew nearer, somehow the breach between herself and Bella had healed. The business of buying bride-clothes, the issuing of invitations, all the fuss and excitement of planning a wedding, had done much to reconcile her, no doubt; but she had a genuine affection for her children, and this, together with her strong commonsense, urged her to take her daughter to her heart once more.

Amanda clasped her hands behind her head, to ease the discomfort of the pressure of the apple tree's rough bark. Her thoughts turned to Mr. Thurlston. He had made a good recovery from his burns, although his looks had indeed suffered; no longer could he be truly described as handsome. It was evident, thought Amanda, that my Lord Barsett's eyes had now been fully opened to his nephew's villainy, for she had heard from John that my lord had forbidden Mr. Thurlston the house. He had made some provision for his nephew's future by the purchase for him of a commission in one of the Line Regiments. Perhaps this had been the worst kind of suffering for Roger Thurlston; his pride would find it hard to swallow the ignominy of a regiment of the Line for my Lord Barsett's nephew.

Mrs. Thurlston, too, was to leave her brother's house; he had taken a house for her in Bath, that haunt of fashionable widows. No doubt the waters would ease some of her imagined complaints.

For a time, it had seemed that Roger Thurlston was to redeem his fortunes by a match with Miss Dunster, the West Country heiress. There had been an unexpected turn of events, however, that had quite ruined his hopes. Through her ministrations to him, the lady had discovered in herself a totally unsuspected vocation for nursing. Talkative, awkward and gushing in the social scene, she was in the sickroom, quiet, practical, and efficient. The doctor who was attending Roger Thurlston was much struck by her abilities. As Miss Dunster did not consider him at first in the light of an eligible bachelor she made none of her disastrous attempts to captivate him. The result was that, by the time Roger Thurlston was sufficiently recovered to leave the 'Bear' and the ministrations of doctor and nurse (for Mrs. Thurlston had been careful to allow Miss Dunster every opportunity of tending her son), the medico was in a fair way to being in love with the young lady from the West Country.

There had been certain difficulties in the way of their coming together.

At first, Miss Dunster's relatives had been convinced that the man was nothing but a fortune hunter. Enquiry established, however, that he was not only of good family, but possessed of a reasonable income of his own; moreover, a short acquaintance was sufficient to show that he was a single-minded person to whom his calling meant everything, and money very little. His affection for the lady was undoubtedly genuine; and she, grateful for the first sign of interest she had ever succeeded in raising in a member of the opposite sex, was only too ready to love in return. It was rumoured that they were to be wed in November, and use some of Miss Dunster's fortune for the building of a hospital.

It had been such a strange, eventful summer, thought Amanda; it had changed the lives of all her own small circle and many more besides. What would happen now, she wondered, to Mr. Barsett?

He was reconciled to his father — that much she knew, for John had told her so. John and Charles Barsett were fast becoming firm friends, now that Isabella was no longer an issue between them. Mr. Barsett had been groomsman for John; he had looked very grave there in the church, she remembered, but not, she felt convinced, for love of Isabella. She supposed that he would go out of her life for ever now. He was to stay the night with John's parents, and to make the return journey to London tomorrow. They had hospitably pressed him to remain longer, but he had refused politely, according to John's report. No doubt he was eager to escape to the world he knew, to leave behind him this tiresome Twyford family, who had caused him so much embarrassment and inconvenience. He would probably find someone else with whom to contract a marriage of convenience, now that Bella was wed to John; that was what he had wanted, after all…

She felt a sudden constriction in her throat, and blinked her eyes, angrily.

Soft footfalls sounded suddenly on the grass. Someone was undoubtedly approaching her place of concealment. She peered anxiously through the leaves and russet fruit that masked the tree; she was not in the mood for conversation, that was why she had come here. It might possibly be one of the few remaining wedding guests; though most had now returned to their homes, except for the relatives, who would be sure to be indulging in a lengthy gossip with her parents. Whoever it was, he or she was unwelcome. Perhaps, if she remained very quiet, the interloper would presently go away again.

The footsteps did not recede, however, but came on, and presently Amanda could tell that the newcomer was a man. From her present position, it was difficult to say just exactly who he was. It seemed that he was making in this direction.

To her disgust, he eventually came and stood under the very tree where she was hiding. She opened her lips to cluck in annoyance, then quickly shut them again. The least sound must betray her presence. She held herself rigidly against the trunk of the tree, and gazed down at the intruder, scarcely daring to breathe. It was then that she made a disconcerting discovery.

The man was Charles Barsett.

She could not control a little start of surprise, and inadvertently knocked an apple from the branch. She held her breath in dismay as she watched it descend on his head. He let out a mild imprecation, and looked upwards.

His eyes alighted on a grubby white-stockinged ankle. He gave another exclamation, this time of surprise.

Startled, Amanda tried frantically to pull down her gown so that it covered the offending ankle. In doing so, she lost her balance. She made a wild grab for the nearest branch, missed it, and, her fingers clutching hopelessly at space, went hurtling through the air, a jumble of arms and legs.

He stepped forward, and put out his arms to break her fall. Together, they landed on the ground in an untidy heap. He disentangled himself, sat up, and laughed gently. She surveyed him ruefully, rubbing her arm.

"Are you hurt?" he asked at once, making as if to rise.

She shook her head, not knowing quite what to say. He relapsed easily on to the ground at her side again, a faint smile playing about his mouth. He scrutinised her carefully.

"There's a smut on your cheek," he said, at last, and handed her his handkerchief.

She took it with a murmured word of thanks, and scrubbed vigorously at her face in an embarrassed silence. Then she looked doubtfully at the now dirty handkerchief. After a moment, she hesitantly offered it back to him.

"No, pray keep it," he said, his smile widening. "I fear it's of no further use to me."

Amanda found her voice. "I — I suppose not."

Inspiration for further conversation completely failed her for the moment, so she began to rub some of the dirt off her hands. This was a strategic move in that it enabled her to avoid meeting his eyes, which remained fixed upon her face.

There was a moment's silence.

"What were you doing up there?" he asked, curiously.

She shrugged, still busy at her task. "Just — just sitting."

He raised a quizzical eyebrow.

"One might have supposed that the ground would afford more comfort — and less insecurity," he said, gently teasing.

"It happens that — I am very fond of this particular tree," answered Amanda, defensively. "John and I used often to climb it, in the old days."

He shot her a keen glance.

"You will miss John, will you not?" he asked, softly.

For some reason that she could not define, her eyes filled with tears at his tone. She lowered her head, and began to scrub once more at her hands with the handkerchief.

"Poor child," he said, compassionately. "If only there is anything I may do to help you!"

She looked up at that, surprised, and blinked away the foolish tears.

"Help me, sir? Why, how should you help me, and why?"

"That's the devil of it," he said, abruptly, starting to his feet. "There is nothing I can do to help, who would do anything in the world — but at least you do not need to pretend to me. If it can be any consolation to you, I know your secret. Would it help you at all to talk of it to me?"

She, too, came to her feet, and fixed him with a look of profound astonishment.

"I cannot understand you, Mr. Barsett. What secret do you know — of what should I speak to you?"

"You prefer that I should pretend to be ignorant of it?" he asked, sadly. "Very well, it must be as you wish."

Amanda's embarrassment was fast slipping away from her, and something very like irritation taking its place. Almost she stamped her foot.

"I wish you will understand, sir, that I have no secret. Be plain with me, I beg: to what do you refer?"

He studied her again. Even a partial observer could not have contended that she looked her best. The honey-coloured curls were tangled with stray leaves and blades of grass, there was a streak of dirt down one cheek, and scratches on both her arms. Her gown was in a sorry state, and she had now lost both shoes. To Charles Barsett, she looked, as always, adorable. His glance softened.

"I will say no more if you do not wish it. Forgive me."

This time she did stamp her foot upon the harsh, dry grass.

"Of course I want you to say more! Begin by telling me what exactly you mean!"

This time, it was evident to the man that she did not dissemble.

He hesitated, frowning.

"Can I be wrong?" he said, at last. "I had certainly supposed — you will pardon the assumption, I am sure — that you were — enamoured of John Webster."

Amanda stared, then suddenly burst out laughing.

He watched her in silence for a moment. Then a change came over his countenance; he threw back his head, and he, too, laughed.

"Do you mean to tell me that it is all a mistake?"

"Mistake?" Amanda gurgled in amusement. "However could you think such a thing? John and I — it is too ludicrous!"

"I don't quite see why," he said, a shade defensively. "You seemed always to turn to him in need."

"As I would have turned to a brother," replied Amanda, quietening a little. "But as for love — why, I don't love anybody!"

"Do you not?" he asked, quickly, involuntarily taking a step towards her.

"No," she answered, then hesitated. "At least —"

"At least —?"

There was a long pause.

"I don't know," said she, at last, frowning a little. "I am not perfectly sure what —what love is."

"What do you think it is, Amanda?" he asked, softly.

He had used her name, but she appeared not to notice. He stood motionless, watching her intently.

"Why, I should think —"

She stopped, a faraway expression in her eyes. He waited, saying nothing, but a muscle twitched in his cheek.

"I should think it is wanting to be with someone for the rest of your life — not being able to think of anything or anybody else I should think —"

"Yes?"

"I should think it happens before one knows. That suddenly one realises —"

Her voice faded away, consciousness came back to her face, and she blushed.

"Amanda!"

His voice forced her to look up, but she could not meet his eyes. What was it that Nurse had said to her? 'Look well into your heart.' She had done so for the first time, and knew that nothing could ever be the same again.

"You told me once, Mandy," he said quietly, "that you never wished to see or hear of me again — that you detested me. Is this still true? If so, you have only to say the word, and I will relieve you of my presence for ever."

She did not answer him at once. He drew nearer to her, but did not attempt to touch her, clenching his hands at his sides.

"You must answer me, Amanda!" he pleaded urgently. "It is only fair that you should."

She recognised the justice of this, and raised her head in the familiar, courageous gesture. Her blue eyes met his for a brief moment.

"I — I talked a deal of nonsense once, sir."

She heard his quick intake of breath. "You no longer detest me?" he asked, trying to read her expression.

"I don't think I ever did — not truly," she answered candidly. "You offended me, and crossed me, and so I was annoyed with you, and later, when I was determined to find you out in — in something discreditable it was more of an adventure to me than anything else, except that, of course, I did not wish you to marry Bella. But when I did go to — to that place — and discovered what — what went on there — I was not pleased at my discovery, but sad."

The last words came out in a rush.

He took a deep breath. "Do you know why you felt sad, child?"

She lowered her eyes. "I know now, though I did not at that time. It was because I didn't want to prove you evil, but — but honourable and noble."

He repeated these words with a depth of bitterness that seemed to arise from his very soul.

"That I can never be!" he finished, his lips twisting. "For that reason I may not say to you what is in my heart."

"But you are!" burst out Amanda indignantly. "All that the affair at Medmenham, your — your past indiscretions — all that is nothing. What I know of your relationship with your cousin proves the essential nobility of your nature."

She paused for breath, then added, with a touch of defiance, "And, anyway, even if it did not — which it most certainly *does* — still, I wouldn't care!"

He gazed at her, thunderstruck. "Not care?"

"No!" she answered emphatically. "Why should I? You see —" she paused, evidently mustering her courage for a supreme effort — "you see, the fact is — I — I love you. I have only just discovered it."

"My God!"

In a stride he was at her side, and had almost taken her into his arms. But he checked himself with a painful effort, and did not touch her.

"You can't realise," he said jerkily. "I — I cannot accept such a sacrifice. You are only a child, sweet, innocent, and I — I am not worthy."

The last words were wrung from his heart.

"Fiddle-dee-dee!" said Amanda, with misty eyes. "What is so saintly about me, after all? Everyone is agreed that I am a hoyden, and, moreover, I am immodest. I showed a total want of propriety in visiting the Abbey, and — and now I have just declared my affections in a manner that could only be called brazen!"

"You are the most wonderful woman in the world," he answered unsteadily, "and yet the most pure and innocent child. I — worship you, Amanda."

"I don't want worship, sir," she answered, a tremulous smile on her lips, "but only a warm, human love such as ordinary mortals know. Can you not — give me that?"

"I can, my love," he whispered.

"Then what on earth," asked Amanda impatiently, "are we waiting for? Do you not mean to — to — kiss me?"

He took her in his arms at that, gently and tenderly. But Amanda passed her strong young arms about his neck, drawing his face to hers; her warm lips met his with all the wholeheartedness of her impetuous nature.

Gradually his grip upon her tightened, and thankfulness filled his heart. The rake had found his true mate, and was at peace.

A NOTE TO THE READER

It's wonderful to see my mother's books available again and being enjoyed by what must surely be a new audience from that which read them when they were first published. My brother and I can well remember our mum, Alice, writing away on her novels in the room we called the library at home when we were teenagers. She generally laid aside her pen — there were no computers in those days, of course — when we returned from school but we knew she had used our absence during the day to polish off a few chapters.

One of the things I well remember from those days is the care that she took in ensuring the historical accuracy of the background of her books. I am sure many of you have read novels where you are drawn out of the story by inaccuracies in historical facts, details of costume or other anachronisms. I suppose it would be impossible to claim that there are no such errors in our mother's books; what is undoubted is that she took great care to check matters.

The result was, and is, that the books still have an appeal to a modern audience, for authenticity is appreciated by most readers, even if subconsciously. The periods in which they set vary: the earliest is *The Georgian Rake*, which must be around the middle of the 18th century; and some are true Regency romances. But Mum was not content with just a love story; there is always an element of mystery in her books. Indeed, this came to the fore in her later writings, which are historical detective novels.

There's a great deal more I could say about her writings but it would be merely repeating what you can read on her website at **www.alicechetwyndley.co.uk**. To outward appearances, our mother was an average housewife of the time — for it was usual enough for women to remain at home in those days — but she possessed a powerful imagination that enabled her to dream up stories that appealed to many readers at the time — and still do, thanks to their recent republication.

If you have enjoyed her novels, we would be very grateful if you could leave a review on **Amazon** or **Goodreads** so that others may also be tempted to lose themselves in their pages.

Richard Ley, 2018.

Sapere Books is an exciting new publisher of brilliant fiction and popular history.

To find out more about our latest releases and our monthly bargain books visit our website: **saperebooks.com**